LOCKED
IN
ICE

New York Times & *USA Today* Bestselling Author

CYNTHIA
EDEN

CHAPTER ONE

"Well, well, well...isn't this quite the predicament?"

Lane Lawson stopped jerking at the ropes that bound his wrists. His hands had been tied behind his back, the ropes twisted and knotted as they held him prisoner. His head stayed bowed for a moment as that warm, feminine voice washed over him.

And he didn't just *hear* that voice. He felt it sinking into every cell of his body.

Sonofabitch.

His head slowly lifted. Blood trickled down his forehead.

The door had opened, and light spilled into the little room. The light surrounded her, showing off Ophelia Raine in all of her glory. And, truth be told, she was a pretty glorious sight. Correction, a truly *gorgeous sight.* Long, thick hair that was raven black. Curves in all the right places. She wore black—Ophelia's favored color—and the pants hugged her hips and the top cradled her high, round breasts.

"I am so disappointed." Ophelia stepped into the room. Shut the door with a soft creak of sound. She kept her husky voice low as she told him, "You have this rep of being such an incredible escape artist." Her booted feet made no sound as she eased across the floor toward him. "I mean, you broke out of a maximum security facility. You were the infamous inmate who busted out when it should have been an impossible feat." A sigh. A rather forlorn one. "I had such high hopes for your skills. Yet here I find you, bound and gagged, in a three-bedroom ranch house in the suburbs. So sad. It's always unfortunate when someone doesn't live up to the hype."

If he could have talked, he would have fired a response back at her. Told her that the asshole had *tased* him and knocked him in the side of the head with the butt of a gun. The only reason that Lane believed he was still breathing?

I'm not the freak's preferred type. So the guy wouldn't get off on killing Lane.

No, the jerk's preferred type had managed to get away, thanks to Lane. He'd intervened before the killer could hurt another teenager. The cheerleader had rushed for safety while Lane had been getting hit with at least 50,000 volts from the bastard's taser.

The scent of roses teased Lane right before Ophelia brushed against him. "You are so lucky I spotted him dragging your sorry hide in this house."

How had she spotted him? They hadn't been working this case together. In fact, he'd been on a solo mission. Following up a hunch that had paid off in a rather brutal way.

Four teenage girls had been killed over the last two years. They'd vanished on their way home from school, only to be discovered days later. Mutilated. Murdered. The cops had reached dead end after dead end. So some of the family members had reached out to the Ice Breakers for help.

The Ice Breakers. Lane didn't know if the crime-solving group was his salvation or his damnation. Lane simply knew that working with them gave him a sense of purpose, more than just the fury that coursed through his blood so often. *I need more than fury and vengeance.*

"I swear, you're only like, a junior Ice Breaker." Her breath whispered over him just before her silken fingers skimmed over his cheek. "Why the hell are you even here?" She tugged the gag from his mouth.

He swallowed. Worked his tongue. Wet his lips. "Figured out who the killer was," he rasped.

"Um. Yes. I guessed as much when I saw him dragging your unconscious body inside his amazingly normal-looking home." Since she'd shut the door, total darkness reigned again, and Lane couldn't make out her features. Not that he needed to see her to know what she looked like. Ophelia's face was pretty much burned into his memory.

Fucking perfection. A delicate jaw. Slanting cheekbones. Small, straight nose. Curving brows that often arched over her incredibly pale, blue eyes. Eyes that seemed such a startling contrast to her dark, dark hair. She tended to wear bright red lipstick that just made her full lips appear even sexier. She often smiled. A wide, flirtatious grin that he was convinced she used just to disarm—and charm—those around her.

"Worried you might be dead at first," she added as her fingers skated over his jaw once more. "You were kind of just flopping like a fish while he tossed you around."

A growl built in his throat. "I was *unconscious.*"

"I thought you'd been getting Ice Breaker lessons. Lesson one clearly should have been...*don't get your ass knocked out by the bad guy.*"

Lane locked his jaw. "Untie me," he gritted out. Because the bad guy in question would be coming back. Actually, Lane wasn't sure that the creep had even left the house.

A gun *wasn't* the man's normal choice of weapon. But he had tased the other victims. Marks had been found on their bodies that proved that horrible truth. So when the sonofabitch had pulled out his taser that afternoon as he crept up behind the young girl in the blue and white cheerleading outfit...

I had to stop him.

Only Lane had wound up getting tased in her place.

Ophelia's hands slid away from his face. He felt a shift in the air and knew Ophelia had moved to stand behind him. She tugged on the ropes around his wrists. "What a clusterfuck," she muttered. "There is no *untying* this, by the way. I'll have to cut you out."

"Then get to cutting!" Why was the woman acting as if they had all the time in the world? A *serial killer* was in the house. Probably heading back toward them at any moment.

She tugged again. "Where is your gratitude? Where is your thanks? Because here I am, risking myself to save your amateur ass. I was worried you were being cut into pieces, dissected while you were still alive, so I rushed to the rescue, risking myself to save *you*. And all I'm getting for my trouble is grief."

"We are both going to be cut into pieces if you don't *hurry*." Lane kept his voice whisper soft. "Tell me that you have a knife on you."

Snick.

Yes. That sweet little sound had to be the sound of a pocketknife opening.

He felt another tug on the ropes. His heart slammed hard into his chest.

"I'm Ophelia Raine, PI extraordinaire," she murmured behind him as her knife sawed at the ropes. "Of course, I have a knife. I also stopped to call nine-one-one so that the cavalry would come rushing to the rescue. But like I said, I was worried he was cutting you open, so I headed inside instead of waiting for the cops to actually arrive—"

The door opened. Not just opened. The damn thing flew against the wall and hit with a thud as Lane's prey filled the doorway. Tall and wide. With a big belly that hung over his pleated khaki pants. Light spilled in behind him, and Lane could clearly see that the man had returned with his weapon of choice.

A big-ass butcher knife.

How fabulous.

Ophelia had stopped sawing at the ropes behind Lane.

"You should have stayed the hell away from me," Thomas Bass told him.

Thomas Bass, high school assistant principal, neighborhood watch organizer, and serial killer. The cops had never tied him to the murders of the four teenage girls who'd been found in Cobb County, Georgia. But the Ice Breakers had pegged him as a strong suspect. One of their top five. So Lane had been watching the guy...A gnawing in his gut had told him that the biology teacher turned assistant principal had secrets.

"You were going to take another victim," Lane snapped. "You were *stalking* her. A girl in your damn high school. No way was I gonna stay away while you hurt her!"

Thomas hit the light switch. Illumination flooded into the room. "I gagged your ass," he snarled.

Oh, shit. Yes, he had.

Thomas lumbered forward. "How the hell are you talking to me? How'd you get that gag free?"

Thomas hadn't seen Ophelia. Was she hiding behind the chair? Had to be. Ophelia was pretty small, so she'd stayed hidden. But while she was back there, why the hell wasn't she sawing the ropes? Why had she stopped?

Even as he had the question, Lane felt her slide the handle of her knife into his palm. He grasped it as best he could and started to saw the ropes himself.

Meanwhile, Thomas brought up the butcher knife and pointed it at Lane—

"Hi, there!" Ophelia said brightly as she popped to Lane's side.

For a moment, Lane squeezed his eyes closed. *For the love of God, Ophelia!*

"I am so sorry to interrupt what appears to be a kidnapping-slash-murder event," she continued as Thomas gaped at her. "But I feel like you should know that the cops are coming to this location. They are on the way as we speak. My advice to you? You need to run now and leave my ah, friend here, alone."

Thomas didn't run. His grip did tighten on the knife. And he angled his body—and the knife—toward Ophelia.

Oh, fuck. Lane sawed faster at the ropes. Had she just given him her only weapon? Thomas had at least a hundred pounds on her. Probably a whole lot more. And while Ophelia was older than Thomas's usual preferred prey, the man's beady eyes had lit up when he looked at her, and he was practically licking his lips. "Don't even think it," Lane snarled as he sawed with all his might. "You are not hurting her!"

Thomas laughed. "Who the hell is gonna stop me?" He motioned with the knife. "Lady, you picked the wrong—*ah!*" His words ended in a scream as his whole body jerked and vibrated. Electrodes flew at him, and the knife fell from Thomas's hand. It clattered onto the floor a second before Thomas hit the hardwood, too.

"*I'm* going to stop you," Ophelia told him. "Little old me, and the taser that I found in your bedroom when I snuck in through the unlocked window. I set it at maximum voltage and, judging by the fact that you just pissed yourself, I'm guessing max voltage feels like hell, am I right?"

Thomas couldn't answer. He was too busy jolting and shuddering and pissing himself.

The ropes gave way around Lane's wrists. Hell, yes. He immediately went to work on his ankles because Thomas had bound each ankle to a chair leg.

"I should tell you." Ophelia edged closer to Thomas. She kicked his butcher knife across the room. "Marjorie Mayweather sends her regards. Do you remember Mrs. Marjorie? She's in her late seventies now. A sweet grandmother. Or, she would have been, if you hadn't killed her only daughter. Patience, that was her name. She was stabbed one night at a local fair back when you and Patience were juniors at Oak Lawn High School. The cops never found her killer. Who would have guessed that it was football player Thomas Bass? The boy most likely to grow up to be a serial killer?"

One ankle was free. Lane kept his eyes on Thomas. The assistant principal had stopped shaking. And Ophelia was way too close to him. "Uh, Ophelia..."

"Everyone else forgot about Patience, but Marjorie didn't. A mother never forgets her child, no matter how much time passes. She hired me, and guess what?" Ophelia glared at Thomas. "You're going to rot in jail for Patience's murder because when I entered your bedroom, I found your treasure box. I saw Patience's class ring. I saw—"

"*Ophelia!*" Lane roared.

Too late. Thomas had grabbed her legs and tackled her to the floor. The bastard drew back his hand to hit her.

But Lane leapt from his chair. The last rope had given way. He grabbed Thomas's fist, stilling the blow.

"Shit," Ophelia whispered. "That tasing did not keep him down long enough." Then she yanked up her knee and rammed Thomas in the groin.

He howled in pain. With his right hand, Lane still held one of the assistant principal's beefy fists. Lane's left hand drove at Thomas's jaw. The powerful blow had Thomas's head whipping to the side. "Get away from her!" Lane blasted.

Then he hit again.

Thomas fell back onto the floor. Ophelia quickly scurried away.

Lane attacked. Right punch. Left. Powerful hits again and again. Thomas tried to bring up his hands and shield his face, but that effort was useless. A killing fury had seized Lane. This was one of the sonsofbitches who got off on pain. Who'd been torturing and killing for years while hiding beneath the guise of being one of the "good" guys out in the world.

"You thought you got away with it, didn't you?" Lane snarled. "Over and over...you thought you got away with it." Another punch.

Thomas wasn't fighting back. He sprawled on the floor. The cut ropes and the chair had fallen next to him.

Lane drew back his hand.

"Slugger, he is down for the count." Ophelia caught his fist.

His head whipped toward her.

"It's me," she said.

He blinked. "I know it's fucking you." His breath heaved in and out. In and out.

"Oh, good. For a moment there, I just thought you were lost in the ass-kicking zone and you were about to take a swing my way."

Hit her? *Her?* "Never."

A quick nod. "Excellent to know." Her hand tightened on him. "He's not fighting back now." Her gaze fell on the man who was, indeed, apparently unconscious on the floor.

Lane crouched near his opponent. Blood covered Thomas's face.

"The cops are here," Ophelia continued in what he realized was her "soothing" voice. Nice and musical. Easy. "I heard doors slamming outside. They'll be rushing in any moment, so I thought it would be best if you weren't actually in the act of beating a man to hell and back when they fly to the rescue."

Lane swallowed. "He was...going to hurt you."

"Well, we're going to make sure that he never hurts anyone again, aren't we?" Still her soothing voice.

He managed a jerky nod.

"I don't want the cops coming in here and seeing you attacking him. Let's look like the victims we are, shall we?" She used her grip on his hand to tug him upward. Slowly, he rose. The sound of Lane's heartbeat seemed incredibly loud in his ears. Drumming over and over. *Boom. Boom. Boom.*

Her gaze flickered downward. "Sonofabitch." Then she stomped her right foot. Hard.

His own stare flew to the floor. She'd just stomped her boot on Thomas's wrist. He'd been trying to stretch his hand for the knife that she'd kicked away earlier. The killer wasn't out. He'd been faking.

She stomped down harder.

Thomas screeched in pain.

And Lane heard the pounding of footsteps rushing toward them.

"Hands up," Ophelia warned him even as she let him go and lifted her own hands.

Uniformed cops spilled into the room. Their weapons were drawn. Their faces tense and hard.

"Thank goodness you're here!" Ophelia cried out. "That man...he attacked me and my friend!"

One of the cops squinted as he stared down at Thomas. "Principal Bass?"

Thomas clutched his right wrist. Blood poured from his busted lips. "They broke into my house!" Blood and spittle sprayed with each word. "Attacked me!"

Oh, the hell he was gonna play the victim.

"Check the bedroom," Ophelia retorted flatly. "Look at the box on top of his bed. Left it there for you, all helpful-like. This man is a killer—"

"Victim!" Thomas bellowed. More blood flew.

"Victims don't have souvenirs of multiple murders in their bedrooms," she threw right back even as she somehow managed to appear both vulnerable and tragically brave as she faced the cops. "And they also don't tie up people in their guest rooms." Her shoulder bumped into Lane. "My friend needs medical attention. He was knocked out by this monster."

Lane stiffened. He'd taken a blast from the taser and gotten slammed in the head with the butt of a gun. It wasn't like it had been *easy* to knock him out. And he didn't need medical attention. He was fine. Furious, but fine.

"He...attacked me!" Thomas spat out what appeared to be a tooth. He rolled and tried to get to his feet.

Lane tensed. This sonofabitch wasn't going to talk his way out of this mess.

"The box is here!" Someone yelled from down the hallway. "Jewelry...pictures of dead girls— *fuck!*"

And even though cops were in the guest room, Thomas suddenly tried to make a run for it. He lunged for the little window on the right. Like he could fit through that thing.

Lane casually extended his foot.

Thomas tripped over it and barreled into the wall even as the cops swarmed him. When he tried to swing at them, the cops took him down.

Hard.

Ophelia exhaled. Her hands finally lowered. So did Lane's. She stared at him. Waited. The cops were locking cuffs on Thomas. He was raging and screaming and making all kinds of threats.

Ophelia kept her gaze on Lane. "Well?"

His head ached like a bitch. He flexed his hands. "Well, what?"

A long-suffering sigh escaped her. "You clearly have no sense of gratitude."

His eyes narrowed.

"That should be Ice Breaker lesson number two. Always thank the people who save your ass."

Lane leaned toward her and ignored the chaos around them. "He had you on the floor," he said softly. "I saved *you*. Where's my thank you?"

She blinked her gorgeous eyes at him. Then her hand rose and patted his cheek. "That is precious. I had him right where I wanted him."

"The hell you did—" He stopped. Looked down. A gun pressed to his side.

His stare whipped back up to hers.

She winked. But then said, "Shhh. Let's not say the g-word and send all the cops into a panic, shall we? They're rather busy, and I'm sure they'll search us both soon enough." She tucked the gun back under her shirt before turning and strolling for the door. "Great job, officers," she called. "Protecting and defending. Love it. Five stars."

Lane curled his hand around her shoulder and spun her to face him. "Why didn't you use that weapon if you had it the whole time?"

She rose onto her tiptoes. Her hands curled around his shoulders as she tugged him close, then Ophelia whispered into his ear, "Because I was trying to keep him alive. Dead men can't give families closure. Ice Breaker, lesson number three. You should seriously be writing down the info I am giving you. It is gold. I get that you were given some guidance by Memphis Camden, and the guy *is* good, but I'm better."

"You—you—"

"Are better. Right." Her breath teased the shell of his ear. "That's what I said. Actually, for the record, I'm the best." She eased back down so her heels touched the floor. Stared up at him.

And winked once more. Why did he think that wink was the sexiest thing he'd seen in ages?

The cops shoved Thomas Bass toward the door—and toward them since they were standing in the hallway. Thomas's hands were cuffed behind his back. A female cop read the guy his rights. Fury twisted Thomas's face as he heaved against the officers pushing him forward.

"You're gonna pay for this!" Thomas raged at Lane. "You don't know who I am! You don't know what I can do—"

"Oh, we know," Ophelia informed him as she rolled her eyes. "Not like you're something special. You're a twisted freak who enjoyed hurting girls. And you are about to enter your own version of hell when you get locked away." She waved at him. "Give our regards to your cellmates. I am sure they will *love* meeting you."

He broke from the cops and lunged toward them.

Lane drove his fist into Thomas's stomach. As the killer doubled over in front of him, Lane grabbed Thomas and whispered into his ear. A private threat.

Thomas reared back. Fear covered his face. "Get me out of here!" he screamed.

The cops had clamped their hands on him once again. Hopefully, a much stronger grip this time.

"Out! Get me *away* from him!" Thomas's eyes were huge. "I did it! I started with Patience—she was the first. I-I hurt them! I did it! *Get me out!*"

The cops pushed him down the hallway.

"My, my," Ophelia murmured. She nibbled on her lower lip then cast a quick glance toward Lane. "Whatever did you say to him?"

"You don't want to know."

"Oh, but I assure you, I do." She pursed her lips. "I do hope you'll share later."

Don't count on it.

CHAPTER TWO

"I owe you, Ophelia," Memphis Camden said as he slid into the booth across from her. He'd been carrying two cold bottles of beer, and he pushed one toward her. "Drinks are on me."

She looked at the beer, then back at his handsome face. "Ah, Memphis, I'm afraid you owe me far more than just a cheap beer." But she was thirsty, so she picked it up. She saluted him with the bottle before taking a vaguely refreshing sip. "I hauled your new recruit from the grip of a serial killer today. Risked life and limb. Saved the day. Became the man's guardian angel, if you will." Another sip. "This is the kind of debt that doesn't vanish easily. Think large bills. Think designer shoes and luxury vacations."

She'd known Memphis for ages. The man *should* understand that she had expensive tastes. A cheap beer as thanks? Ha. Not even close.

Her gaze darted around the busy club and landed on Lane. Or rather, on Lane's back as he leaned over the bar and ordered his drink. "Why in the world was that man on his own?" The question was a censure directed at Memphis.

After all, Memphis was supposed to be training the guy in all things Ice Breaker.

"Lane was following a hunch."

She grunted and shifted her attention to Memphis. "That hunch almost had him sliced into little pieces. You didn't see the size of the butcher knife that Thomas was waving around."

"He saved a high school girl today. Stopped Thomas Bass before the man could grab her. She saw him and Lane in the alley. Lane jumped Thomas when the jerk was trying to tase her. Lane got hit with the volts, and the girl ran to safety. She tried to bring the cops back for Lane, but by the time they arrived, the alley was deserted."

Her index finger slid down the cold neck of the bottle. "I heard all of this already. During my fabulous four-hour stay at the police station. The girl has quite a case of hero worship for Lane." She did not look back his way. "Personally, I think the man needs some serious time with a shrink. We are talking some definite anger issues." She'd seen his face when he fought Thomas.

"Because he attacked Thomas? Thomas struck him first."

She knew that. She also knew a deep, dark fury when she saw one.

"You'll excuse me if I don't exactly regret the ass-kicking Lane gave him." Memphis thrust back his shoulders. "Not considering how many girls that bastard had killed."

She took a longer drink from the bottle. "I wanted to kick his ass, too."

"Lane?"

"No, that freak Thomas." She glowered. "He was *my* tag. I'm the one who hunted him down and linked him to the very first kill." *Patience Mayweather.* "Everyone else had forgotten about Patience. *I* took her mother's case." She didn't add that she'd done it free of charge because Marjorie's story had broken the heart Ophelia liked to pretend she didn't have. That info was need-to-know.

"Looks to me like you and Lane hunted the guy down at the same time. Lane saved the girl in the alley, and you saved him. Win, win." Memphis lifted his bottle.

Rolling her eyes, she clinked her beer against his. "If you say we make a good team, I'm out of here."

His lips parted.

"Don't you have like a million other cases to work?" She rushed to question. "I thought the Ice Breakers were supposed to be helping the Feds uncover the locations of all Henry Monroe's victims." Henry Monroe, a serial killer who'd been behind bars for years...only he'd just revealed the locations of more victims. *As in...a whole lot more victims.*

Talk about your twisted pricks. Henry was scary as hell, and there weren't a lot of things in this world that did scare her. *He's one of them.*

From the gossip she'd been able to pick up, the Ice Breakers were supposed to be working with the Feds to recover the newly disclosed victims. A long and slow process because she knew Henry wasn't exactly the forthcoming type.

Most killers of his caliber weren't.

The Ice Breakers had originally formed years ago. The group had started online. All from different backgrounds, the team had come together because they wanted to focus on the cases that had been forgotten by law enforcement. The man lounging so casually across from her, Memphis Camden—former bounty hunter—had been with the group from the beginning. And now that the team was being bankrolled by billionaire Archer Radcliffe, their reach was pretty much limitless.

Oh, but what I could do with a limitless bank account.

"We do like to stay busy," Memphis murmured. "And that's why I could sure use your help."

Her eyes immediately narrowed. "I worked a case with you not too long ago." A case that had involved a certain gold-medal-winning Olympic figure skater. And Henry Monroe. "I told you then, I am not interested in being a full-time Ice Breaker." Memphis often tried to pull her on board. Not going to happen. She had other plans. "I have a PI business." *And my own agenda.*

Her gaze dipped around the club. Lane wasn't at the bar any longer.

"He needs training," Memphis told her.

"No shit."

Memphis snorted out a laugh. "I'm not asking you to join us full-time. I get that you like to be the big, bad loner. I'm not looking for a lifetime commitment from you. I'm asking you to take him under your wing. Just for a little while."

Her mouth dropped as she gaped at him. "Under my wing? What in the hell is he? A baby bird?"

"No, he's a volcano that could explode."

That flat statement erased all traces of her humor.

"I know you've seen it." Memphis's gaze suddenly seemed very intense. "Lane is walking a very fine line. He lost part of himself when he was locked away."

Locked away—for murder. Because Lane Lawson had once been suspected of being a serial killer, too. The evidence had been strong, and he'd been tossed behind bars. And, if the stories she'd heard were true, he'd then had to fight for survival almost every single day because a bounty had been put on his head.

Lane had been set up for the crimes. Sent to die in jail. But he'd survived because he'd broken out of a maximum-security facility. And... "He locked you in a freezer," she said to Memphis. Ophelia had heard the story, and, honestly, it just amused her more and more each time it was retold.

A muscle flexed along his jaw. "Bygones."

"Bullshit."

The muscle flexed again.

She slouched back in the booth. "There is no part of you that believes in that bygones BS. Someone wrongs you, you wrong them back, harder." She got it. Truly. It was her way of life, too. And the reason she currently preferred to hunt solo.

"He was fighting for his life. I understood the motivation even if I didn't particularly like the result."

She crooked one eyebrow.

"He wants to be an Ice Breaker. He's been working with the team, and he's a fast learner. He just..." Memphis glanced around.

She waited.

"He needs to learn more control. He acts too much on impulse, and his victim interaction is shit."

"No, seriously, tell me how you really feel."

Instead of telling her how he felt, Memphis spouted out a large numerical figure. A very large one.

"Excuse me?" Her other eyebrow crooked to join the first.

"Train him for a month. Let him shadow you. See how you work as a PI. And that will be your payday when you're done with him."

Was it hot in that club? Or was she just sweating because Memphis had offered her a nearly obscene amount of money?

"Don't look at me that way. I won't be paying you. *He* will."

"Lane?" Why did his name come out as a squeak?

"He's loaded, but shouldn't you know that? You're always poking and prying in everyone's business. Kinda your specialty. Would have thought you did that on day one with him."

"I thought his assets were frozen with his arrest." And she'd been rather busy with other things.

"His assets were frozen. Then some jackass associates tried to steal from him while he was behind bars and his sister was fighting to prove his innocence. In the end, Lane got everything back. Sold a ton of his ventures. Made even more cash. Oh, and I think some Hollywood studio wants the rights to his life story or some crap like that, so he has money to burn." His nostrils flared. "If I had the time, I'd train him fully myself. But like you said, I have to work on the Henry Monroe case. And I can't just leave Lane on his own." A wince. "You saw what happened today. We came to town together, split up for some investigation work because we had multiple suspects to run down, and the next thing I know—"

"Lane is tied up and nearly cut open? Yes, I did see all of that. Very dramatic." She considered the day's events. "The way he took down Thomas was also very dramatic. Pretty sure Thomas lost one, maybe two teeth in the process."

"He's got a lot of rage." Memphis lowered his voice. "I understand that." His stare never left her face. "*You* understand that. You understand everyone, don't you?"

She swallowed and saw exactly where this was going. "When you bring up my past, it's hitting below the belt. Not the thing that friends do to friends."

"We all need someone at some point in our lives. Right now, Lane needs you. And I need you with him."

I need you with him. Dammit. Not like Memphis ever asked her for much. On the bright side, she could certainly use Lane's cash. "You want me to be his babysitter?"

"I want you to teach him everything you know about hunting criminals. The *right* way to do things. And..." A long exhale. If possible, his gaze became even more intense and focused. *"Don't let him go off the deep end.* He's got too much rage inside. I need someone to watch out for him. To make sure he doesn't do something he can't take back."

The pieces slid into place for her. This wasn't just about training Lane.

It was about leashing the monster that's been born inside of him. A monster that had taken its first breaths when Lane had needed to fight for survival as other inmates came after him again and again. And Memphis would know that monsters were her specialty.

"Do we have a deal?" Memphis pushed. His hand extended across the table.

She stared at him. "You are asking one hell of a lot."

"I—"

"Yeah, he is," Lane drawled.

Her head snapped to the left. Lane stood just a few feet away from their table. A mocking grin curved his lips but the smile never reached his green eyes. "And it's an entirely unnecessary ask," he added in his dark and dangerous voice. The one that tended to roll over her in all of the right—and wrong—ways. "Because I certainly don't need a *babysitter.*"

Ah, great. So he'd heard that part. Which meant he'd heard pretty much everything.

She put on her sunniest smile as her gaze drifted over him.

Lane Lawson. Mogul turned murderer. Or at least, that was what plenty of headlines had once claimed. That he'd gone off the deep-end and murdered women who reminded him of his twin sister. She'd read the profile on him, back at the time he'd first been arrested. She had contacts at the FBI, and, yes, his case had nagged at her from the beginning.

Something had felt off.

Lane Lawson had never experienced an easy life. Bloody and violent, not easy. She could respect bloody and violent, especially given her own backstory. One that she kept hidden from all but a select few.

Memphis would be one of those few.

Lane's father had murdered his mother. Tried to kill Lane and Lane's sister, Lark. Only Lane had wound up killing their dad, instead. And, when the man's autopsy had been completed, the survivors had learned the terrible truth.

Lane's father had become so violent and unhinged because of a brain tumor. If the tumor had been found before that terrible date when death hit Lane's family so hard...

Maybe things could have been different.

But no one got a do-over in this world. A lesson she'd learned long ago.

Lane stared back at her with green eyes that glittered. Lots of anger. A furious intensity. But the intensity only showed in his eyes. Everything else about him seemed ice cold. His expression was carefully blank. His body hard and tense.

Control.

She knew he had it wrapped tightly around him. But the thing about people who held *so tightly* to control...

Those are the people most likely to explode.

"You're staring," Lane finally told her.

"Sorry. Got swept away by your insane good looks."

No crack in his rock-hard expression.

Ophelia winced. "I can see that you are going to be a delight as a training partner. Nonstop laughs, am I right?"

"I'm not looking for laughs." He took a step closer to the table. His gaze swept over her. Damn if it wasn't *dismissive*.

Her spine stiffened. No one dismissed her. He would regret that mistake. She'd make sure of it.

His attention shifted to Memphis. "She's not the right person. I asked for someone with expertise on killers. I wanted to study with the best. This isn't some game for me—"

"No?" she cut in to ask. "You're not some bored rich boy looking to play vigilante and take down some bad guys?"

His head whipped back toward her.

He was very easy to play. And she rather enjoyed riling him up. It sent a thrill chasing through her veins. She waved at him. "Hi."

His stare hardened. Glittered so brightly.

"You shouldn't make judgments about people. You're way too early to the game in order to make any kind of good profile. Take me, for example."

He growled. A deep, oddly sexy sound.

She flashed her bright smile at him. "You have me pegged all wrong. Because I can assure you, I *am* the right person for the job. Probably the only one who can do it properly." Her head turned toward Memphis. "I'll do it. Consider me his trainer for the next month." And she extended her hand across the table to Memphis.

Memphis closed his hand around hers, being very careful with his strength. He was one of those guys, after all. The kind who always used care with someone he thought was weaker.

I am not weak.

"Great." Memphis let her go. "I've got places to be—places far from here—and a wife I need to see. So, I'll just leave you two, shall I? Let you get to know each other better while I get the hell out of town." He slid from the booth. Stood beside Lane.

Both men were tall, powerful. And a darkness clung to them. But Memphis appeared far more relaxed than Lane. She didn't have the feeling he was about to explode at any moment.

Memphis commanded his darkness. The darkness did not own him. As for Lane...

It's my job to find out just how dark he truly is. Because she knew Memphis had just hired her for *two* jobs. Training Lane? Sure, absolutely. That was the surface job, and she could certainly teach him all about the motivations of killers.

But the second job? The one that Memphis wasn't sharing and the whole reason she suspected he'd offered the gig to her in the first place?

Because I can see the monsters. I can see evil. And Memphis wanted to know if his new Ice Breaker recruit might one day go over the edge.

"That's it?" Lane glared at him. "You're dumping me on her and cutting town? Way to be part of a team, buddy."

"That's not quite it." Memphis slapped Lane on the shoulder. The gold wedding ring gleamed on Memphis's hand. "Good job getting Thomas Bass locked away and saving the cheerleader." The slap turned into a hard grip. "But next time, don't go in without backup. Would hate for you to become a victim when you're so dead set on being a hero." His stare lasered over at Ophelia. "Keep him alive."

"Will do." She saluted him with her beer.

Without another word, Memphis turned away and vanished into the crowd. Lane glowered after him. She took that moment to study him again. Or, to drink him in. Because she hadn't been lying before. Lane Lawson truly was a beast of beauty. Movie star handsome but in a rugged way. Hard jaw with a line of stubble. Thick, dark hair that framed the fierce angles and planes of his face. Killer cheekbones. She suspected people would pay crazy amounts of money for that bone structure. Firm lips. And those eyes...

His attention slid back to her.

What a wicked, wicked gaze you have. For just a moment, she knew exactly how Little Red Riding Hood must have felt when confronted by the wolf. *Gonna eat me up? Pretty please?* Her hand slid down the cold neck of the beer bottle. "I don't bite." *Do you?*

"Why the hell would Memphis think you were the best person for the job?"

So insulting. "Because I'm amazing? Because I saved the day for you? Because I've saved his ass multiple times, too?" Ophelia winked. "Does that make you feel better? That little old me also saved big, bad Memphis, too? Will that heal your pride?"

A furrow lifted his brows. "My pride has jack shit do to with this." And he eased into the booth. Not the spot Memphis had vacated. He sat right beside her.

Got all into her space.

So much for following social norms. "Please," she murmured, "do make yourself comfortable and tell me how you truly feel."

"That bastard today outweighed you by a hundred pounds. He slammed you onto the floor. If I hadn't gotten out of those ropes when I did, he would have *hurt* you." His eyes glittered. "You put yourself into situations like that often? Where *you* go in without backup and face off against freaks who get off on hurting women?"

Well, well. This was an interesting development. "You were worried about me."

His lips pressed into a thin line.

"That is so sweet," she added. Her left hand extended so she could pat his arm. "So very—" She stopped mid-pat because a charge of heat had just pulsed from the tips of her fingers all the way up her arm and was ricocheting throughout her body.

Dammit.

He blinked.

She snatched her hand back. "Sweet, but incredibly unnecessary." Her hand dropped to her lap. Fisted. Ophelia blew out a slow breath. "I had total control of the situation."

"Right." He angled his body toward her. His scent teased her. Sandalwood? Amber? A mix? Definitely masculine. Rich. Sensual.

Her nostrils flared as she drank him in. Then she caught herself.

"If I'm going to be paying an obscene amount of money for you," Lane snapped, "I'd like to know that I'm going to get my money's worth."

Her eyes widened at that blunt statement. "Want to rephrase that?" Ophelia asked him, voice silky. "Because it sounds like you're trying to pay me for sex."

What *could* have been a faint flush rose in his cheeks. She held his stare and didn't so much as blink even as Ophelia added, "Though, for the record, I am always worth it."

He swallowed. For just a moment, that mask of his seemed to crack. Ophelia leaned toward him and wondered if she'd see the real Lane. Finally. *Show me what's beneath the mask you wear.*

"Why," he gritted from between clenched teeth and Ophelia realized she was going to absolutely adore pushing every single one of Lane's buttons, "is Memphis so certain that you are the best trainer for me?"

"Because I know killers. Inside and out." She had the scars to prove it. "Before I hung out my PI shingle, I was one of the top recruits at Quantico. My superiors said I had a knack for seeing evil." But it had never been as simple as that. "You're a man on a mission, Lane Lawson." Did he think she didn't understand? That Memphis didn't? She'd witnessed Lane in action firsthand tonight. "You want to hunt."

A muscle jerked along his clenched jaw.

"You want to take down the worst of the worst. The killers that hide and escape their punishment while they destroy others." Her voice was low. For him alone. "That's why you went after Bass by yourself earlier. You wanted to make him pay."

"I wanted to stop him."

"Because you're tired of the innocent being punished while the guilty get away with their crimes?" She was making her own profile of him. Not that she'd tell Lane. Not yet.

His head moved in a jerk that could have been a nod.

"If you want to know how to find the baddest of the bad, then you've come to the right place. Or rather, to the right woman." She rolled her shoulders in a careless shrug. "You see, twisted killers are my specialty." Every woman needed a hobby, right? "If you stick with me, I can teach you everything that most people *don't* want to know about them. By the time I'm done, you'll know monsters inside and out." Her hand lifted. This time, she schooled herself before she touched him. Ophelia's hand skimmed down his cheek. The surge of heat hit her, but she didn't let it show. "I can assure you, my lessons will be worth every dime you pay."

His pupils flared as she touched him. A hungry need flashed in his eyes. Was that a physical need? Did he feel the same, unsettling desire that was knifing through her?

Or was that need because he wanted to know more about the monsters out there?

Because you fear that you are one, don't you, Lane?

"So, shall we be partners?" Ophelia asked him as she kept her tone light. "Or do you want to do the smart thing...and cut and run now? You have a nice, safe life that you can live. Walk away. Stop playing with the dark. Go back to—"

"There is no going back." Rough. "*Partners.*"

Your funeral, my friend. "Then the first training session will start now. Hope you're ready." Her hand fell away.

Or, tried to fall away.

He caught her hand. The faint calluses on the tips of his fingers skated over her skin and goose bumps chased over her body. Staring straight into her eyes, Lane told her, "Don't worry about me. I'm a very fast learner."

"Great to know."

CHAPTER THREE

The arousal was inconvenient. The dick that shoved stubbornly against the front of his jeans was a problem that he would keep ignoring. Lane could pretend it was a side effect of the adrenaline rush that still rode him, even after all the long hours at the police station.

The crash from the events of the day hadn't hit yet. It would hit, sooner or later.

Not yet.

No, the hard-on that he had wasn't because of the adrenaline or the whole nearly dying BS. It was because of her.

Ophelia Raine.

The woman he'd first met months ago, via Memphis. The PI who lived on the edge, who had the sexiest smile he'd ever seen in his life, and who was now...

His partner.

Trainer?

He held her wrist, and his thumb traced over her drumming pulse. Ophelia appeared completely at ease, but her racing pulse belied the pose. A good point to note—Ophelia was very, very good at disguising her real feelings.

Then again, so was he.

Otherwise, Ophelia would have known that he'd been lusting after her since day one and that she'd starred in more than a few of his late-night fantasies.

After he'd been cleared of the murder charges and officially released, there had been a line of women eager to warm his bed. Those women had wanted to fuck him for a variety of reasons. Some had wanted the thrill of being with a celebrity—because he'd gotten celebrity status with his face being splashed all across the news. Others had been drawn to him for a darker reason.

Because they wanted to say they fucked someone dangerous.

They'd all wanted to use him. No one had given two shits about who he really was. Probably a good thing. These days, Lane wasn't exactly sure *who* he was, deep down.

Good or evil? What the fuck am I? What had he become in those cells?

"Okay, fast learner. Are you going to gaze soulfully into my eyes all night or do you want the lessons to begin?"

His thumb stopped mid-stroke. He was not gazing soulfully into her eyes...was he? Hell. Maybe. He let her go. Dropped his hand to rest on the table.

"I'll take that as a 'Yes, please, Ophelia, let's start our lessons.'" Her hair slid over her shoulder as she made herself comfortable against the back of the booth.

"Are you ever serious about anything?"

"I was serious about saving your gorgeous ass earlier. Which, you know, you still haven't thanked me for doing. But I'll help you out with a thank you idea. I like chocolates. Not dark chocolate—too bitter for me. Milk chocolate, please. And flowers work wonderfully."

"I'm not buying you chocolates."

"Yeah, you are. And I'm always serious. But it's easier to catch people off guard if they don't think you're a threat. They see me as harmless, flighty, whatever—it puts them at a disadvantage. People won't be as careful with what they say or do around me if they think I'm not dangerous. Take you, for instance. You've seen me in action, yet you still doubt me. And you let yourself slip when you shouldn't."

Do not change expressions. "How did I slip?"

Her bow-shaped lips tipped up in a faint smile. "The caress along my wrist. The flash when your pupils expanded. You forgot to act like I was a general annoyance to you, and you let the desire you feel for me peek through."

Fucking hell.

"And there is also the fact that you lost your shit—not literally, of course, but you get where I am going—when Thomas Bass knocked me down. A necessary test I had to perform in order to see your reaction. I wondered...would you care if someone you viewed as physically weak was in danger?"

Anger stirred inside him. "You were testing me?"

"*You* cared about whether or not I got hurt. So while you might pretend to be some unfeeling robot slowly walking around the vast void that is life, you're not. In fact, your reaction to me being in danger was quite primitive. Primal. It's the primal responses that I think are the most important. You can't fake instinct."

Primitive? Okay, sure. "If by primitive you mean...did I want to rip the bastard limb from limb? Then, yes, guilty as charged." He wasn't sure it could get more primal than that.

Her long lashes flickered. "I suspected that Memphis wanted me to work with you. He hinted as much to me previously, so when our paths crossed in the, uh, rather unusual way they did earlier, I took the opportunity to—"

"Run an experiment on me? Because I'm what—your science project? You're Frankenstein, and I'm the monster?" He did not like this. Not at all. *I don't want her poking beneath the skin to see what hides inside.*

"Is that how you see yourself?" Husky. "You think you're a monster?"

Fuck this. His nostrils flared and that just had him pulling in more of her heady scent. The woman smelled too good and his dick did not get the message that she was off-limits. "I noticed some things about you, too."

"Do tell." Her right hand stroked over the neck of the beer bottle.

He really wished she'd stop doing that. Those long, slow strokes... His gaze flew from her hand to her face, and he found her watching him far too closely.

A former Fed who'd trained at Quantico? Yeah, he could see that. Now. He could also see that she loved for people to underestimate her. "You look like a wet dream."

Her eyes widened. "Pardon? It's loud in here. Why don't you say that again?"

You look like my wet dream. "You use the fact that you're attractive—sexy—to disarm those around you."

Now her head cocked. That long, dark hair shifted over her shoulder once more. "Are you feeling disarmed by me?" The prospect seemed to delight her.

"You like to play games."

"Well, I don't want to walk around and be bored all the time so…"

"You want me."

No mocking comeback. Just another flutter of those long lashes. Lashes that framed her pale blue eyes so perfectly.

When she remained silent, he pushed, "Your pulse raced beneath my touch."

"I could be afraid of you. Trembling in my boots."

Hell. She could be. Maybe he'd just read her all wrong. Maybe—

She leaned toward him. "But I'm not scared of you. Because when the chips were down, you were focused on protecting me. That's something I won't forget. It's something that matters. It's the whole reason I decided to give in and help you on whatever path it is that you seem hell-bent on taking."

It was his turn to fall silent.

"And you are absolutely right. I do want you."

What. The. Hell? Shock surged through him. She'd just admitted it? So casually? Like it was nothing?

"But it's been a really long day," Ophelia continued. "What with tracking down a serial killer and us about to stop a would-be predator in the next five minutes so...how about we bench the attraction discussion until later, yes? Good plan?"

He didn't— "What?" What predator? And within five minutes? What was she talking about?

"Why do you think I chose this booth when I came in the club?"

His brain just wasn't following the conversational turn. His dick had taken charge again, dammit. *She wants me.* Her confession had derailed him.

"I'll help you out. I picked this booth because of its location. We're sitting at the back of the club. From this vantage point, I can see every single individual who enters the place. We have the optimum position."

"It sounds like you're hunting."

"I am. Correction, *we* are. Now that we're a team, *we* are hunting together." She inclined her head toward him. "Why don't you look at the crowd and see if you can spot our prey?"

He hauled his gaze off her and glanced toward the crowd. When they'd first arrived, he'd wondered why in the hell they'd gone to this place. Too many people. Too much booze. People were dancing and drinking, and he'd blocked out most of the noise as he focused on Ophelia. Luckily, she'd picked the far booth, so they'd had a bit of privacy.

Luck had nothing to do with it. She's hunting. And his admiration for her notched up more.

"I'm not just working one case while I'm in town. Thought I'd take on two. I'm a big multitasker. Something you should know about me. Always working more than one job."

He grunted.

She slid closer. The scent of roses teased him even more. "See, a young woman came to my Savannah office not too long ago," Ophelia confided to him in her husky, make-a-man-beg voice. "She was quite shaken. She'd been out clubbing with some friends, and the next thing she knew, she was in an alley, the world was spinning, and some bastard was trying to jerk off her shirt."

His gaze roved slowly over the dance floor, then moved to the bar even as angry tension knifed through him.

"A bouncer had been getting off his shift. He came out the back and saw what was happening. He shoved her attacker away, and the guy fled into the night." A pause. "The woman didn't go to the hospital. She ran back to her hotel as fast as she could. Since she didn't get checked out, I have no proof that she was given a spiked drink, though, based on her description of losing time and having the world spin around her, I think that's a pretty safe guess."

Sonofabitch. "You suspect he's hunting here."

"This *is* the club in question for her. She wants answers, you see. Closure. Wanted to know if it was real or if...well, let's just say that our minds can trick us. She wants to make sure her mind isn't doing that. A few days after the incident, she discovered that some pics of her had been uploaded to social media. The group she was with? Some of the girls were taking pictures at this bar. One of those pics was a shot of my client dancing with a dark-haired male, looked like he was in his early twenties. Piercings glinted in his left ear, and a closer study of the photo showed that he had a black rose tattoo on the side of his neck."

Lane zeroed in on their prey. Hard to miss with that tattoo. The guy casually leaned over the bar counter.

"In the picture," her voice hardened, "it seemed to me like the guy was holding her up as they danced. Her body had already started to go slack. Not that any of her friends noticed. They were all too busy partying."

He didn't take his eyes off the target. The man's fingers were tapping against the bar in tune to the beat. "What's the plan?"

"Well, my client certainly doesn't want some predator roaming around out there looking for other victims. If he's drugging women and attacking them, he belongs in jail, don't you agree?"

His hands had fisted.

"The plan is simple. We catch him in the act. We get proof to nail his ass to the wall."

His stare swung toward her in surprise. "We're gonna let him drug some woman while we just watch?"

"Oh, that is freaking adorable. You think I'm going to risk someone else's life?" A roll of her eyes. "No, fast learner, that is not the plan."

"Then what *is* the plan?" Lane bit out from between clenched teeth. Because he thought a great plan might be to just walk across the bar and start kicking the guy's ass.

She leaned conspiratorially close. "We're going to let him drug me."

"Like hell."

"I knew you'd be on board. Now, let's move."

He wasn't moving any place—

"Do you want him to drug another woman or do you want to stop him?"

Lane didn't want anyone drugging *her*. He didn't want Ophelia in danger at all. Not in any way. "Ophelia—"

"Move it, sexy. Time is ticking."

***

"I am so glad I met you." Ophelia trailed her index finger down her target's arm. *Royce Nicholson.* And she was glad. Very glad. The odds had been against her finding him on the first night of her hunt, but fate had shined on her.

Royce preened. It had been so easy to sidle up next to him at the bar. To mutter about her "asshole ex showing up," as she jerked her thumb over her shoulder to indicate a glowering Lane. Royce had been all about jumping in to heal her wounded heart.

Royce was big, with muscles that strained his leather jacket. And that dark tattoo on his neck just screamed badass. Or, at least, she thought that was what he wanted it to scream.

"Let me buy you a drink," Royce offered with a wide smile. "Then how about we dance the night away?"

"Sounds wonderful." She stared into his eyes. Dark eyes that glinted with charm. He even had a dimple in his left cheek that winked with his smile. She was sure he worked that dimple at every opportunity. "But I can't have too much alcohol. I am such a lightweight."

He motioned to the bartender. Gave a quick order, then leaned in close to tell Ophelia, "You don't have to worry. I'm one of the good guys. You get too drunk, and I'll take care of you."

The way you took care of Sylvia? But she just nodded. His fingers were on her thigh. His touch sent chills coursing over her. It took all of her self-control not to grab his hand and break a finger. Say, his pinky finger. It was the easiest to break, after all. One quick snap, and she bet Royce would be howling in pain.

But she wouldn't have any proof. She'd have his pain, yes, but Ophelia needed more.

"Why don't you go find us a booth?" Royce asked. "I'll bring the drinks to the table for us. That way, you don't have to stay here at the too-crowded bar."

Tricky bastard. Acting so kind and considerate. But, really, she knew Royce wanted her away from the drinks. The better for him to add a little something special to hers.

But she just smiled and bobbed her head. She made her way to a booth, far too conscious of

Lane's glower. The man seriously needed to dial things back. Granted, this was their first case together and she *had* sprung it on him suddenly, but you didn't learn to swim by staying on the beach. You had to get in the water.

So come get in the water, Lane. Dip those toes in.

She sat at the booth. Rocked in tune with the blasting beat of music.

Royce joined her. He had a whiskey for himself and some bright green drink for her. "Something sweet and sexy." He winked as he sat across from her. "Just like you."

Oh, but the man could not have been more wrong. Sweet was not a word that had ever been used to describe her.

"Cheers," he said as he lifted his whiskey.

She toasted him and brought her drink to her mouth as—

"Ophelia, what the fuck are you doing with him?" Lane snarled.

Ah, so he'd decided to interrupt at the perfect time. She could have clapped. Definite points for him. Instead, as Royce's head whipped toward a seemingly furious Lane, she lowered her drink beneath the table and poured a healthy portion of it onto the floor. She kept the other half. They'd need that as evidence.

"She's having a drink, asshole," Royce snapped back. "What does it look like?"

She clutched her glass. "Lane, we're over." Flat.

"Yeah, Lane." Royce jumped out of his seat. "Over." He made a shooing motion with his hand. "So why don't you get your ass lost?"

Lane didn't get his ass lost. Instead, he stepped closer to Royce. "You don't want to fuck with me."

"No, I want to fuck with her." Royce smiled at him.

What a dick.

"So run along," Royce advised him. "Before someone gets hurt."

Lane stared at him…and laughed.

Royce's face flushed dark red.

"I'd really, really like to see you *try* hurting me," Lane said.

Dammit. Maybe the blow to the head that Thomas had given him earlier was impacting Lane's brain functions. *See, this is why he should have gone to the hospital for observation, but, oh, no, Mr. Tough Guy just had to refuse treatment.* Now he was screwing things up for her. She put down her drink and shoved out of the booth. Ophelia positioned herself between the two men. "Stop this." And to Lane, her gaze said…*Seriously, stop this. You can't screw this up.* She wasn't going to get another chance. Royce knew her face now. "We aren't together any longer. Go find some bimbo to screw. I'm busy with Royce." She put her hand on Royce's chest. "Royce, let's dance." Her head turned toward Royce just in time to catch him looking down at the table.

At her half-empty drink.

And she caught the flash of his wide, satisfied smile.

Oh, Royce, I will be wiping that smile off your face very soon.

But first, she led him onto the dance floor.

***

The bastard needed to take his hands *off* Ophelia. They were sliding down her back, dipping toward her pert ass, and Lane was about to teach the prick that you did *not* touch what did not belong to you. Not ever.

"You're with Ophelia?"

He turned his head to the left. A big, hulking guy in a white t-shirt and jeans shuffled toward him.

"Derek," the stranger said, like Lane was supposed to know him.

Lane stared back at the fellow.

"She texted me. Said to get her drink and bag it." Derek wet his lips. "Is this shit going to work? We really taking him down? Because I'm sick of that creep preying on women here. After what he tried to do with Sylvia..."

Okay, pieces connected. Fast. "You're the bouncer."

Derek nodded his head in agreement.

"And you're working with Ophelia?"

"No one fucks with Sylvia." Derek's dark eyes blazed with fury. "I want him *stopped*."

So, that would be a yes. And from what Lane was gathering, Ophelia had already texted the bouncer and told him that she was springing her trap. His gaze returned to Ophelia only to see her body sagging against Royce's much bigger frame. For a moment, he tensed.

That looks too real.

"She said he'd take her out back. We're supposed to be there." Low, from Derek. "She wants me filming with my phone. But I can do one better than that. I convinced the boss to put a security camera out there. If she gets the dick to confess or if he tries to hurt her—we'll have perfect footage."

Good to know because Royce was already starting to pull Ophelia from the dance floor. Her head bobbed and she stumbled.

Lane stepped toward her.

Derek's hand flew out and pressed to Lane's chest. "You can't interrupt now!"

Interrupt? He wasn't interrupting, he was about to rip—

"We need evidence! Sylvia wakes up crying at night. That shit is stopping. She's my girl now, and I am not gonna let her be scared. That is not happening. Ophelia is helping her. So we do what Ophelia says."

Ophelia was currently being held too tightly by Royce as the guy half-carried her toward a door marked STAFF. "Your new girlfriend went to Ophelia for help." He was trying to follow along. The fact that Ophelia had told him practically nothing did not help. This was not the way partnerships were supposed to work.

"*I* sent her to Ophelia. No good PIs in this town. Cops need hard evidence, so we're getting hard evidence." His big hands clenched. "Ophelia helped a cousin of mine out before. Knew we could count on her. She never takes a case she doesn't close."

Interesting. He filed that tidbit away. Ophelia and Royce had just disappeared behind the STAFF door. "That door leads to the alley behind the club?" The club—a too busy pit called Pyro.

"Yeah, it takes you out back."

"You go through that door, make sure the bastard doesn't try to leave with her, and I'll circle the building. We'll close him in." He surged for the main door.

But, once more, Derek's hand hit his chest. "We get the evidence first. Got to bag it."

"Fine, you get the fucking evidence. I'm getting her. She's my—" *Dammit.* "She's my partner, and I have to watch her back. Now move the hand or I break it."

CHAPTER FOUR

"I...don't feel so good." Her voice slurred. Cold air hit her as they exited the club. Her eyes fluttered and her head bobbed up and down. "Why is everything...spinning?"

"You had too much to drink," Royce told her. "Don't worry. I said that I'd take care of you, and I will."

She tripped. Almost slammed into the ground, but his strong hold around her waist held her up. "I...only had half a drink." She faked the slurring of her words. Just as she faked her tripping.

"That was all it took. Half a drink. You're a lightweight, remember?" He pulled her tighter against him. Walked toward the shadows.

Shadows wouldn't work so well. She wanted to stay as close as possible to the bright light near the back door. That would make for better image quality when Derek filmed, and the bouncer had *better* be filming. She'd texted him the order right before Royce had arrived with his green drink.

Ophelia dug in her booted heels. "No...sick...stop." She threw out a hand and touched the brick wall near her head.

"Fine. Guess this is good enough." He shoved her back, and her head banged into the bricks because she hadn't been expecting him to get so rough, so fast.

Really, Ophelia? You thought a guy who drugged women was gonna hold back? "Ow!" she called out, letting her voice slur even more as it rose. "Wh-what are you doing?"

"Having some fun. Like I told that ex of yours, I plan to fuck you." His hands went down to the hem of her shirt.

She swatted at him. "You...the world is spinning..."

"Sure it is, baby girl. You're flying high and you won't remember a damn thing soon."

Her eyes opened wide. "You drugged me!"

"You and plenty of others. Had lots of fun in this alley, in the one down the street, and in the one—"

She dropped low and punched him in the dick. As hard as she could. Pain and shock had him stumbling back from her as he grabbed his injured cock.

"You bitch!"

"That is no way to talk to a lady," Lane's low voice came from the shadows. The same shadows Royce had wanted to enter. If he'd taken her there, he would have found a dangerous surprise waiting for him.

As Ophelia rose to her full height, Lane stalked from the darkness. His hands were fisted at his sides. His eyes went straight to Ophelia. "Did he hurt you? In any way?"

She had the feeling that if she said yes, he'd rip Royce apart right then and there. "I'm good."

Royce straightened. "What the fuck is this? Why is your ex here? *Fuck, fuck, fuck—*" He lunged for Ophelia.

She didn't even need to tense. Lane had already moved to stand in Royce's path. A perfect shield. When Royce swung with his wild fist, Lane took the blow. Didn't even stagger back as it hit him in the gut.

Ophelia winced for him. "Uh, Lane?" *You got this?* Her head craned. Where the hell was Derek? He'd better be getting this all on camera.

"You hit me first," Lane said quietly to Royce. "So I'm totally within my rights to do this." And then he swung. First his right fist. A hit that caught Royce under the jaw and sent his head tipping up sharply. Ophelia could actually hear the sound of his teeth snapping together. Lane's second fist hit Royce in the mid-section.

"Oof!" All of the air left Royce's lungs. He hunched over, hugging himself.

Ophelia's fingers skated across Lane's tense back. "Have you seen a bouncer?" she asked quietly. "About six-foot-one, white t-shirt, goes by Derek and should be filming right about now?"

At that one word—*filming*—Royce's whole body jolted. He whirled around and fled. But he didn't get too far.

Derek stepped into his path.

Derek who was *not* holding a phone to record this scene. Seriously? *Seriously?*

Royce tried to shove Derek to the side. Derek shoved back, and Royce lost his footing. Down,

down he went with a scream. Or maybe he screamed because when he landed in the dirty alley, Derek immediately kicked Royce in the side. When Royce rolled to try and avoid another kick, Derek just plowed his sneaker into Royce's dick.

"All of this effort and he's not filming?" She stomped away from Lane. "Derek, what the hell?"

Derek froze. He looked up at her. Then pointed. Behind her. To the right.

She spun around and saw the small security camera perched just beyond the back door. A wide smile flew across her face. "Derek, I love you right now."

"Convinced the owner we needed new security," Derek rumbled.

She could have kissed him. Instead, she grabbed him and hauled him away from a now crying and moaning Royce. Not like she wanted video footage that could be used against Derek. Ophelia hauled out her phone and called one of the detectives she'd met earlier that day.

"Detective O'Brien?" Shay O'Brien. A female detective who'd seemed pretty no-nonsense and down to earth. "This is Ophelia Raine. No, I'm not actually calling about Thomas Bass."

Royce let out a long moan.

"Got another guy for you to lock up. How fast do you think you can get to Pyro? Yep. The club. Wonderful. I'll be in the back alley waiting for you. Oh? What's this about? You need more details?" She rolled her eyes. "Fine. Royce Nicholson. A man who has been drugging and attacking women in the area. Got a glass with his fingerprints on it, a drug still *in* the glass." At least, she had it if

Derek had bagged the drink as she'd instructed. "And oh, yes, I have a full confession that was just caught on a security camera. Plus, of course, I can give you my wonderful witness testimony. Basically, I've got everything tied up in a big, red bow for you."

Lane closed in on her.

"See you soon," Ophelia promised the detective before ending the call. She kept her eyes on Lane as he stared down at Royce. Ophelia could feel the tension pouring from him. "We need to make sure Royce is subdued."

"I can knock his ass out," Derek offered.

Lane nodded. "I can, too."

"Or..." Since a camera was watching, and they were *not* the bad guys. "We can cuff him." She dug into her purse. She'd had it on her the whole time. A black cross-body that held a few necessities inside. Like...

A taser.

Her phone.

She put the phone back in the bag.

A gun.

And...

Ophelia took out a pair of handcuffs.

Lane's brows rose.

"I never leave home without a pair," she told him.

"I'll remember that."

Ophelia beamed at him. "See? I'm teaching you fabulous things already. You're going to love training with me."

His shoulders squared. They'd already been pretty square, but he thrust them back and squared them up even more. "I'm sure the experience is going to be unforgettable."

That was certainly one way to look at things. She caught his hand and slapped the cuffs in his palm. Ophelia ignored the heat that surged between them. There would be a time and place to address that heat. In the back of a dirty alley, with a twisted freak of a perp on the ground? *Not* the place. "Cuff him, partner."

***

"You're in the room beside mine," Lane growled.

Ophelia sent him a sunny smile.

It was nearing two a.m. The woman had helped apprehend not one but two asshole perps that day. She'd nearly been assaulted in an alley.

She'd had to endure countless hours of questions with the cops, both with the Bass case and with that Royce prick.

She should be dead on her feet. Instead, she seemed to shine with energy. He'd heard about people who lit up a room when they entered it. Ophelia seemed to light up the whole damn world.

At nearly two a.m.

"You *are* observant. Getting you all hunter ready is gonna be a breeze." She turned and propped her shoulder against her hotel room door. They were alone in the hallway. He'd stopped next to room four-oh-eight. She was beside four-ten. "When did you make this wonderful conclusion? Were you suspicious when you arrived at the hotel and saw me waiting in the lobby for you?"

They'd separated at the police station. She'd driven away in a sporty Jeep. He'd returned to his hotel, figuring he'd meet up with her the next day. But then he'd pulled up short when he found her standing in the hotel's lobby admiring the chandelier that glittered overhead.

"Or perhaps you figured things out when we rode up the elevator together? You *were* very silent on the elevator ride."

Because he hadn't known where the hell to start with her. How about...*Don't ever be bait for some creep like that again. Seeing his hands on you made me want to rip the fucker apart.* Or maybe something like...*If any sonofabitch ever tries to hurt you like that again, I will make him scream for mercy.*

No, both of those had seemed wrong.

Wrong. That word seemed to echo in his mind. So much seemed wrong these days. He seemed wrong. His emotions were wrong. The darkness within him—*wrong.*

And that night, when Ophelia had been on the dance floor and that bastard Royce had put his hands on her...

Wrong.

Lane had wanted to break every finger that touched her. He knew that wasn't normal. He'd slid so far away from normal that he didn't know how to ever get back. He felt like a predator all the time. The darkness inside wasn't easing. It was just getting stronger. Thicker.

"Or was it when the elevator stopped on the fourth floor and I got off with you? Did you get suspicious then?" Her warm and sensual voice seemed to cover him. Lightly teasing. Completely captivating.

He gripped the keycard too tightly in his hand. "Don't play with me." This was not the time. Too late. Too much adrenaline. Too much hell. He needed to go inside his room. Shut the door.

Get his control back.

"Okay, fine. I'll confess. You've got me. I wasn't originally staying in this hotel. But I learned from Memphis that you were, so when I left the police station, I decided a move was in order. I convinced the sweet guy at the check-in desk that we were lovers, so I needed a connecting room in order to properly surprise you."

Lovers. He blinked.

Her smile stretched a little wider. "Surprised?"

Not the right word.

"I travel pretty lightly so switching hotels was easy for me." She patted the overnight bag that was currently slung over one delicate shoulder. After waiting a beat, her pink tongue slid over her lower lip. "Generally, conversations work best when two people exchange words. Otherwise, you'll just have one person—me—talking to herself."

Yes, he should say something. But when he tried, a growl came out.

She nodded. "That's progress." Then her left hand reached out and squeezed his arm. "Thanks for having my back tonight. Not too bad for our first at bat."

He looked down at her hand. A cold rage had engulfed him ever since he'd first learned about Royce and what the other man had done. But when Ophelia touched him, Lane could feel heat spreading through his body. Something finally combatting the cold.

"If we're going to work together, I have to know I can count on you." She didn't let him go. "I threw you into the deep end, and you didn't sink. You were exactly where I needed you to be. That's important."

She should stop touching him. He didn't tell her that, though. Instead, his eyes lifted to meet hers. "What would sinking have looked like?"

"Oh, you know, you blowing things. Storming across the dance floor. Punching the jerk and breaking his jaw because we both hate the predator that he is." A pause. "Blowing things would have looked like you not waiting for the cops to arrive and taking justice into your own hands. Or us not stopping Derek when he wanted to keep kicking Royce until the man was nothing more than a bloody pulp." All said in her breezy voice like she was just talking about the weather.

She wasn't talking about the weather. She was talking about pain and punishment and the slippery slope of darkness that could engulf a person. "Who the hell are you?" he breathed. Because she talked about darkness like it was an old, trusted friend even as she smiled the sunniest smile he'd ever seen.

"I'm Ophelia Raine, your new partner. You must be really exhausted if you've forgotten that." Her hand fell away. "Get some rest. We'll chat tomorrow.'

"Ophelia." In a flash, he'd caught her wrist. Mostly because he needed to see—

Her pulse raced beneath his fingers. Too fast. *Yes.* Some of the tension eased from him. She was not nearly as controlled as she pretended to be.

"Don't throw me into the deep end again," he warned her. "I could sink. Or drag you under with me."

Her head tilted. That thick, dark hair drifted over her shoulder as she pursed her lips.

"Don't leave me in the dark," Lane added.

"I won't. That's the whole reason I'm here."

Her words seemed to wrap around him.

He swallowed. "I meant, don't spring cases on me."

"Sure, that's what I meant, too."

Her words felt like a lie. "I need..." Lane floundered.

She just watched him with her pale blue eyes. Ghostly eyes. He had a feeling those eyes could see every sin he'd ever committed. Every sin he'd thought of committing. Lane let her wrist go. He saw her fingers stretch and flex, but he knew he hadn't hurt her.

I wouldn't. Not her.

"What do you need?" Ophelia asked softly.

You. The response that wanted to spring instantly to his lips. But this wasn't some partners-with-benefits situation. Ophelia wasn't looking to fuck him, even if she had told the guy at the front desk that they were lovers.

Except...

Except back at the club, before she'd set her trap for a predator, she'd stared straight into Lane's eyes and told him...*You are absolutely right. I do want you.*

Her words had blasted through him. Then she'd casually said they were benching the discussion. Like they were chatting about a movie and would pick up the talk later.

"I can practically see your thoughts spinning." A soft sigh escaped her. "Too much for one day, hmm? Go inside, Lane. Sleep off the adrenaline crash. Have good dreams. And we'll pick up in the morning." She turned away from him and pulled her own key card from her pocket.

"My dreams are never good." Rough. Rumbling.

A nod. She didn't look his way. "Neither are mine." No flashing smile. No casual tone. Just soft. A little sad. "Maybe one day, we can compare nightmares."

Was he seeing the real Ophelia? The light flashed green near her lock, and she pushed the door open. But she stopped before going fully inside. "We're going to need to trust each other completely in order for this to work. You understand that, don't you?"

He didn't really trust anyone completely. His twin sister, yes. He'd live and die for Lark. Anyone else? *No.* "Trust isn't easy."

"Tell me about it. But it has to start somewhere. I started trusting you tonight. I knew if anything went wrong, you'd have my back in the alley. I was scared out there. I get scared, just like everyone else. I *hated* for him to touch me, but I knew he had to be stopped. My fear was the price I paid to stop him." Now she turned her head. "You had my back. *Thank you.*"

Sincere words. He could feel it. See her sincerity in her eyes.

There is so much more to Ophelia than I realized.

Her head tilted to the right as she studied him. "You need to understand that I'll have your back, too. You can count on me."

"You're...just doing this for the money." This—working with him. Guiding him. He was paying her for the training. This wasn't some goodness-of-her-heart BS or bonding experience.

"Sure. The big bucks. Doesn't mean you can't trust me, though. Good night, Lane." She crossed the threshold of her room. "Oh, wait. One quick question. It's been nagging at me for hours and hours." She dropped her overnight bag inside and turned to stand in the open doorway. One hand pushed against the door, to keep it open, and the other hand gripped the wooden doorframe. "What was it that you said to Thomas Bass? Right at the end? Before he went into panic-and-confess mode, you whispered something to him. What was it?"

He edged closer to her. Her scent drew him in. How could she still smell so good after the day—and night—they'd had? But she did. And he wanted to drink her in. Every bit of her. "I'll tell you, but you have to answer a question for me in return."

"That seems completely fair. In the interest of showing that I *trust* you, I'll even go first," Ophelia offered with a roll of one shoulder. "That way, you can get my answer, and I'll just trust that you'll hold up your end of the deal."

He could not look away from her eyes. He was in front of her now, towering over Ophelia. "You trained at Quantico."

"Um. That's not a question. To be a question, you'd need to change it up so that it was something like, 'Did you train at—'"

"Why did you leave the FBI?"

Pain flashed. A brilliant, glittering crack in the beauty of her face. There one moment, and gone the next. She sucked in a breath and let it go, and he wondered if she was going to refuse to answer. But her chin lifted. "I could say it's because I didn't like all the red tape. The rules. The regulations or even the constant travel. I could say it's because I wanted to be my own boss. Choose my own cases." A swipe of her tongue over her lower lip. "But I think it's best if I don't lie to you and you don't lie to me. Helps with the trust situation, you know?"

A lock of hair had fallen across her cheek. He caught that lock and tucked it behind her ear. His hand lingered, for a moment.

"There's that," she muttered as a little shiver skated over her body. "Have to deal with that sooner or later. But probably not the best plan to tackle it when we're running on fumes."

His gaze sharpened on her.

"So, back to your question. Why did I leave the FBI? I lost someone important to me." A nod. "Sudden death. Violent. It ripped my world apart, and I couldn't be the same person any longer. I couldn't wear the badge, so I became someone new." Her lips tipped down. "I think you know all about becoming someone new, don't you?"

He started to respond—

Her hand flew out and pressed to his chest. Right over his heart. "Don't answer that. One question for me. One for you. We agreed to that. Answer my original question. What did you say that got Thomas to start confessing?"

Her hand seemed to burn through his shirt. Brand his skin. She did feel the attraction between them. Not a normal arousal. A dangerous, blistering intensity. A match that had been lit, one that might blaze into an inferno under the right— or wrong—circumstances.

"I told him that I had already broken out of one prison. I could easily break *into* another one. He would never be safe from me unless he confessed. I would find him, and what he'd done to his victims would pale in comparison to what I'd do to him."

He waited for her to flinch. To back away and say that he'd gone too far. That he'd crossed lines. That he was dangerous. A freak.

Wasn't that how he felt?

But she nodded. "Good bluff."

It had been no bluff.

"You scared the monster. Takes a lot to do that."

It had just taken the truth.

Her gaze darted down to her hand. She didn't immediately stop touching him. He wondered if she could feel his heartbeat because as she kept touching him, the beat seemed to get stronger. Harder. Almost like his heart was beating faster just for her.

Her hand slowly returned to her side. "Good night, Lane."

He should move away. "Good night, Ophelia." Her name was beautiful. Haunting. A million years ago, in a different life, he'd studied a bit of Shakespeare. Back when he'd been in college and had thought maybe his life could be different.

Once upon a time, I even thought I could be a doctor. Save lives.

But...

Maybe he'd been meant to take them instead. "She went mad."

Ophelia backed up a step. "Excuse me?"

"Your namesake? In *Hamlet,* Ophelia went mad."

Soft laughter trickled from her. Musical. Sensual. "Don't worry about my madness."

And he could have sworn that—hanging between them—were the words...*Worry about your own.* He retreated a step. *We both just backed away from each other.*

But she didn't close the door, not yet. "'God has given you one face, and you make yourself another,'" she said.

"You just quoted Hamlet."

Another soft laugh. One that seemed to dip beneath his skin. "With my name, how could I not read it? But I believe the quote applies, don't you?"

"Depends on what you think the quote means."

"Touché. Could just mean Hamlet thought his girl was cheating and called her two-faced. You know, because he was pissed and what not." A roll of one shoulder. "I like to think it means we are all two people. We have our real faces, and then we have the faces that we show to the rest of the world. The person we actually are. Then the person who we like to pretend to be. Saw that a lot when I would profile with the FBI. There are the people who wear the faces of heroes. Who claim to be so good." She leaned forward as if imparting a secret. "But the devil hides behind every smile they share."

He did not change expression.

"Hope your dreams aren't too dark tonight. If they are, just remember, I'm right next door. Knock if you need me." She backed up and closed the door.

Fuck.

Lane was very afraid that…he did need her.

CHAPTER FIVE

Ophelia released the breath she'd been holding. She turned around and pressed her back to the door.

Too intense. The day—and night—had been too much. She'd skirted the edge and gone over it, and it had taken all of her self-control not to fall apart right in front of Lane. She didn't usually get afraid. No, fear was a luxury that she did not allow herself.

But when she'd been in that alley, when her head had banged against the brick and darkness had been lurking so close by, and when she'd felt the hot stir of Royce's breath against her, another time had flashed into her mind.

Another night.

Another alley.

A killer who'd wrecked her world.

I was sixteen. I didn't know how to fight back. She hadn't known how to do anything but scream as the blood seeped through her fingers.

It wasn't just adrenaline that fueled her. Fear and fury had churned within her. Holding onto her control during the police interrogation and just *talking* like a semi-normal person had been so hard.

Then going to the hotel...seeing Lane when they were alone. The tension had mounted to a fever pitch.

She'd wanted to let the control rip away. She'd wanted to grab Lane. To kiss him and see if the fire would burn just as brightly when their mouths met. Where would the wild attraction go? What would happen between them? It had been so long since she'd wanted someone so badly.

Relationships weren't for her. She didn't want someone swearing love to her. Promising forever. Forever ended in blood and pain. Or at least, it had for her.

I'll love you forever, Ophelia.

Forget forever. She wanted pleasure. Release. Forgetfulness and the oblivion that could come from an amazing orgasm.

Her phone vibrated. Ophelia had figured the call would come. Sooner or later. She sagged onto the floor. Stretched out her legs and drew out the phone. "Yo, Memphis. Are you still driving? You sure were hell-bent on getting out of town."

"Not driving. I'm settled for now." A pause. "Did you have an eventful night?"

The slightly censuring tone of his voice told her that he already knew all about her night. Ophelia bristled. "What was I supposed to do? *Ignore* the predator right there in front of me? I had already taken the job before I shook hands with you. At the time I planned my trap for Nicholson, I certainly didn't expect I'd have a new partner."

"That shit could have gone badly tonight."

"Well, clearly, it didn't." But, yes, it could have. "Who told you? Was it Lane? Did he call you while I was still talking to the cops or something?" *Way to rat me out, Lane.* That would have to be another rule they discussed.

"I checked in with him. He might have mentioned you were both at the police station."

Okay, so Memphis had called Lane. Not the other way around. But...still. "Two bad guys are off the streets. I think you should be giving me gold stars instead of grumbling at me."

Another pause. His pauses could say way too much. After a beat, Memphis noted, "Your voice sounds...different."

Crap. Sometimes she forgot how observant the former bounty hunter could be. "I'm tired. Running on the cinnamon roll I had for breakfast. Sorry I'm not my normal bright and perky self for you. Try calling me at a decent hour in the morning and I will be better."

"I need to know what you think."

"I think it's late. I think I should be in bed, but I'll probably be getting a shower first and then crawling between those crisp, hotel room sheets—"

"About Lane. You know why I want you with him."

Well, of course, she knew. "You want me to profile your new protégé."

"You'll be training him, too."

"Um, of course. That's why he is paying me, after all." She'd known the moment that Memphis asked her to work with Lane that a profile had been his objective. "You're worried about him."

"His sister is worried. Oliver Foxx is worried."

Oliver. She knew him well. Once upon a time, they'd even worked together at the FBI. Oliver liked to think he was incredible when it came to killers.

If she'd stayed with the Bureau, she would have given him a run for his money. Or...*I would have been better*. Actually, she was better. "Did Oliver work up a profile on Lane?"

"He did that ages ago, *before* Lane went to jail. He's different now."

"They say prison changes you," she murmured.

"*Ophelia*. This shit is serious."

"Like I don't know that?" She was serious. Being locked in a cell *did* change a person. One hundred percent. Her left hand lifted to press against the back of her head. It was vaguely tender thanks to that hit into the bricks.

And if her head was tender, what about Lane? He'd been hit by Thomas Bass. How was his head feeling? Should she go check? It would be nice and partner-like to check on him and any injuries he had.

"Lane wants to hunt the bad guys. Great. More power to him. But I need to know—" Memphis stopped.

So she graciously finished for him, "If he's gonna go all Dexter on you and be the killer who hunts killers? You worried he lost himself in that cell and came out as someone brand new, aren't you?" It took all of her power to make her voice seem flippant. *Your past is yours. Buried deep. Keep it buried.*

"I didn't know Lane before the cell, so I can't say what the hell he was like then. I just know he's a hunter now. Before I pull him deep into the Ice Breaker fold, I want to be sure of him."

Because Lane had obviously done something to set off Memphis's alarms. "He has control." Complete control.

"He also has rage."

Don't we all? But Ophelia just said, "Understandable, given his past."

"But he has so much freaking potential."

"Um. Potential. In spades."

"And if he's focused, if I know I can count on him, he'd be invaluable on the team."

"Laser-like focus. Check. He's got it. Don't think you need to worry about that."

"Ophelia."

"Memphis."

"I know I'm asking a lot of you."

"Oh, just the usual. You're cutting me open. Poking at my darkest spots and expecting me to feel no pain." Her eyes widened. *Crap.* She had not meant to say those words. She was far closer to crashing than she realized.

"Ophelia?" Now worry laced her name. "I don't know what you're—" Memphis broke off before continuing in a far more careful voice, "If this is too hard for you—"

"It's not too hard. I'm just tired. We're heading back to Savannah tomorrow. I'll profile him. I'll train him. If I see any giant, waving red flags, you will know. Now, uh, the bed is calling and I must answer. Night, Memphis."

She hung up before he could say anything else.

And it was only when she ended the call that Ophelia realized a tear had leaked down her cheek.

***

Thirty minutes later, she walked out of the bathroom as steam drifted in the air. She wore a pair of black jogging shorts and a white cami top. Her wet hair trailed down her back, and she probably should think about drying it, but that was just gonna have to wait.

Ophelia was too dead tired.

She crawled into the bed. Stretched out her legs and sank blissfully into the mattress. The bathroom light shone as the steam drifted out— she always kept one light on when she slept. An old habit.

She hated waking to darkness.

Her eyes closed and—

A knock sounded on the connecting door. The door that *connected to Lane's room*. Her eyes flew open.

The knock came again.

Keeping her eyes on the door, she slid from the bed. Her bare feet made no sound as she tip-toed across the room.

The knock rapped once more. And this time, she even heard... "Ophelia." Soft. His voice.

She flipped the lock on the connecting door and hauled it open. "What's the problem?" Ophelia began with false brightness. "Can't you sleep—"

The last word died in her throat. Lane filled the doorway. Big. Powerful. With muscles that flexed and stretched and were easy to see because the man wasn't wearing a shirt. Just jeans that clung loosely to his lean hips.

It would have probably been polite not to ogle him. But it was the middle of the night and he'd come knocking on her door, so ogle away, she did.

Until her gaze hit on his scar.

A long, twisting scar that ran up his side.

"Shanked," he said. "Had to let the bastard cut me so I could get taken to the infirmary. I aimed the slice, though, and made sure he didn't hit anything vital. Still, the wound bled like a bitch."

Her gaze lifted to meet his.

"Two years of med school," he explained. "Changed my mind about the career last minute. When I planned for my escape, I knew just where the wound had to go so that the guards would be convinced I was in mortal jeopardy."

She'd heard this story before. Actually, she'd read about the attack. The newspapers had been full of details. Even pics of the makeshift weapon that had been used on him.

"Either I made it look like I was dying or I would have *been* dead in that hell within a few days. I knew my time was running out." His gaze fell. Swept over her body. Paused on her breasts.

Because, right, white top. See-through since it was so thin and her nipples were at tight attention. Her arms immediately crossed over her chest.

"Sorry," he muttered.

"I ogled you first." It seemed only fair to point that out.

"Sorry," he said again. Rougher this time.

Her head tilted as she studied him.

"I...shouldn't have woken you."

"I wasn't asleep. Besides, I told you that if you needed me, all you had to do was knock." And he had.

His nostrils flared. "You smell so good."

Her bodywash. *Never leave home without it.* But this didn't seem the moment to point out that bit of Ophelia lore.

His hands clenched and released at his sides. Clenched and released. "Reporters still chase me. That's why I'm not in Nevada anymore. Had to get as far away from there as I could."

His face had been everywhere, for a while. But as with everything, a new story had come along to steal the spotlight. A new drama.

"I was cleared, but when people I meet find out who I am, half of them still look at me like I'm guilty as hell."

Her toes curled against the carpet. Once some people heard that you were a killer, they would never believe anything else. Their minds would be made up, especially if they saw a news story that was sensational enough. A story deliberately designed to terrorize or anger the audience.

"You don't look at me like that," he said.

"Well, I do have the benefit of having read your file." Many times. Another bit of Ophelia lore that she would not be sharing with him in that particular moment. What she could tell him? "I know you didn't kill those women." One hundred percent, Ophelia knew she was staring at an innocent man.

Or, at least a man who wasn't guilty of murder. *Innocent* might be a stretch. Because other than children, who were the innocents of the world? Everyone had their sins.

Some just hid those sins better than others.

"Didn't kill them," he rumbled. "But you know...what I did when I was locked up."

"I know you fought the people who came after you. What were you supposed to do? Stand there and let them attack you like a good boy? Your choice was to either be an easy victim or to give them a reason to fear you."

His brow furrowed. "You're supposed to keep me in check."

"Is that what I'm supposed to do?" Her hands had balled into fists when she'd crossed her arms over her chest.

"I heard you tell Memphis—"

"Oh, yeah, right. I'll stop you from crossing lines. Done. If I see you going over the deep end and trying to hurt someone, I will immediately launch to intervene and stop you from shedding blood. Done. You can count on me, partner."

He looked down at the floor. No, at the threshold that separated his room from hers. "Stop me now."

Her heart thundered in her ears. "Excuse me?"

Silence.

"I don't see an enemy here," Ophelia spoke slowly. Maybe she was just too tired and not following along properly. "You don't look like you're in danger of killing anyone so..."

He swallowed. "Not that line."

"Is there another one I should be aware of?" She rocked forward onto the balls of her feet. The adrenaline made her a little shaky. Correction, a lot shaky. The high had worn off and emotions battered at her. Anger. Fear. Sorrow. *The past needs to get out of my head.*

"Yeah, you need to be aware." A long exhale from Lane. "We both do."

Then please continue. Warn me.

"You said you wanted me. I've been in this room, and maybe I should be thinking about the killer who fucking tied me up and threatened to gut me today..."

"Yes, that would be something to keep you awake at night." That would be something to give most people nightmares forever.

He wasn't most people. Neither was she.

His green gaze lifted and locked on her once more. "I only thought about you."

Oh. Her breath whispered out.

"A cold shower didn't help."

"I took a hot one. It didn't help, either."

His bare feet crept a bit closer to the threshold. "Shouldn't you be telling me that you have rules? That you're not going to fuck a partner?"

Now she pushed back on her heels. "I'm not the FBI. I'm also not an official Ice Breaker. I don't work for any group that has a long list of rules and regulations about fraternization when it comes to partners."

Lane blinked. "What are you saying?"

"I'm saying…I don't have a rule about not fucking a partner at my PI agency. Mostly because I've never had a partner there, so this is the first time the issue has come up. And since I'm the boss and make my own rules…" She shrugged and let her hands fall back to her sides. "That's not a line for me. We can cross it if we want."

He stepped over the threshold.

Should I consider the line crossed?

"So we're going to fuck and still work together?" Lane asked in the dark and dangerous tone that had her toes curling and so many parts of her *yearning*.

"You are so blunt," she told him.

His eyes seemed to burn hotter. An emerald fire.

"I like that," Ophelia added immediately. "Say what you mean. Don't bullshit with me. It makes life a million times simpler."

"Will you do the same?" His hand lifted toward her, but he caught himself before he actually touched her.

"Avoid BS? Absolutely." Tension practically had her vibrating.

She'd worked with Lane before. A different case. A flash of violence and fury and danger that had brought their worlds colliding ever so briefly. And after that case, maybe she'd delved deeper into his life. Maybe she'd been curious about the man who seemed to keep himself wound so tightly.

You get too tightly wound and you just might explode.

"You didn't answer me." Rough. So dark.

Her fingertips skimmed over the tops of her thighs as she tried to wipe her suddenly sweaty palms on her jogging shorts. "I did. I told you I would absolutely—"

"Are we going to fuck and still work together?"

She wet her lips.

His gaze burned ever brighter at the movement of her tongue. His hand wasn't in the air any longer. He wasn't reaching out for her, but she could have sworn she felt the heat of his body rubbing against her skin. "They are two distinct things. Ah, fucking and working together," Ophelia elaborated, aware that her voice had gone way breathless.

He stalked a bit closer. They were practically toe to toe.

She tilted back her head, the better to stay focused on his face and not let her gaze wander down to check out his abs again. "You're paying me for training. That's it. And when the training clock stops, whatever we do on our own time is our business."

"Never thought you were a whore, Ophelia."

A flash of fury tore through her. "Good to know. Never claimed to be one."

And his hand did rise. It skimmed under her jaw, and that touch electrified her. "You think you're the only one who has done research?"

Her heart slammed into her chest.

"I got curious about you. The woman who showed no fear. No matter what went down. Memphis respects the hell out of you and so does Oliver Foxx. But when I tried to ask questions about you, they shut me down. That made me curious."

Now *she* was curious. And he was still touching her. Lightly caressing the line of her jaw with his callused fingertips. "What did you discover?" Not much. She'd carefully cultivated the information that others could access about her. Her true secrets were buried so deeply that no one would find them.

"You're not involved with anyone. No boyfriend. No long-term ties. No bastard who will get pissed at me for all the things I want to do with you."

"If there was a boyfriend, I would have slammed the door shut on you the minute you started talking about fucking." She wasn't a cheater.

"You don't sleep around."

"Do tell."

"Gonna say I'm a liar?"

"No, I don't sleep around. I know exactly how dangerous it can be to hook up with strangers." She'd seen the nightmares firsthand.

"You don't think it's dangerous to hook up with me?"

"You're a different kind of danger."

"So are you."

Damn him. He'd almost made her send him a real smile. "So you researched me. Discovered I don't have a lot of relationships." *Correction— any.* "Anything else I should know about myself?"

"Why didn't I discover that you were a former Fed?"

"A civilian wouldn't easily access that info."

"I feel like that is just the start of the secrets you keep."

True. "My secrets are *mine*. People have to earn them. We're not there yet. You don't get to know every deep, dark detail about me."

His hand slid down her throat. His fingers were so careful. A delicate skim, but he had to feel the fast racing of her pulse beneath his touch. "Fair enough."

Her hands lifted and pressed to his chest. "Do you feel it when we touch?"

"The fucking surge of heat that shoves through my blood like a missile? Yes, I do."

"Good." His hand was still on her throat, and the touch felt like a brand. "I really would hate to be alone in this."

His head lowered. His mouth came temptingly close. "Just sex? That the deal for us?"

"What else would it be?" They were adults. They could do this. "Not like you're looking for love."

"And you're not?"

"I gave up on love long ago." In an alley when she'd watched the sweetest boy she'd ever known bleed out in front of her.

No, Ophelia. Do not go back there. Don't.

Lane's brow furrowed. He was—

"Are you always this chatty before sex?" she asked him, truly curious.

"No."

"Then I'm special."

"Yes."

Huh. "Good to know," Ophelia murmured. "But the way I figure it, we can keep talking all night or ...we can do this." She shoved onto her tiptoes. Pressed her mouth to his.

Detonation.

CHAPTER SIX

She'd wondered what kissing Lane would be like. When she felt electricity with just a touch from him, a kiss had certainly held great promise. That promise was more than fulfilled as her mouth met his. Lust flooded through her body. A storm of need that swamped everything else.

Sure, she could blame it on the adrenaline.

On being too late at night. On exhaustion. Anger. Fear.

She *could* blame the riot of desire on a ton of things, but she didn't feel like lying to herself. She wanted Lane. They were adults. Unattached. And—

And I make my own rules. She hadn't wanted anyone this way in so long—*I've never wanted someone quite this way*—so she wasn't going to hold back.

A life lesson she'd learned long ago.

Holding back got you nothing but regret.

Her lips had parted beneath his, and his tongue thrust into her mouth. His taste was a wicked delight that tore a moan from her. Her hands flew up over his chest—such a powerful, strong chest—to curl around his shoulders.

His hands were on her waist. Locking tightly to her. Bringing her flush against him and there was no missing the hard length of his cock as it shoved against the front of his jeans.

She rubbed against him. Ached.

Sanity would tell them to stop. Sanity would say they were going far too fast.

Good thing she was in the mood to forget some sanity that night.

With his grip on her waist, he lifted her up.

She wrapped her legs around his waist and pushed her sex against the thick ridge of his cock. Ophelia rode him, rocking back and forth, and the friction amped up her desire for him even more.

She wasn't going to last long. She knew it. Her body was too primed. Too tight and ready. Maybe she'd gone too long without a partner. Maybe that was why she was practically about to come just from kissing Lane and dry humping through their clothes.

Or maybe...it's him.

He took her back into his room. It was dark in there. No light spilling from the bathroom like she'd had in her room. Lane moved unerringly to the bed even as his mouth trailed over her neck.

Oh, yes. Right there. A soft lick. A light bite.

Her body shuddered.

He lowered her onto the bed. She'd thought they might be fast and dirty. Stripping in a fury as they pounded together. Truth be told, she could have used some fast and dirty action.

But his hands caught the edge of her shorts as she sprawled on the side of the bed. He dragged them down her thighs and tossed them onto the floor.

"No panties?"

She thought that answer was obvious. And since he was being so accommodating as to strip her, she'd go ahead and take off her cami top for him.

Except...

Ophelia didn't get the chance.

"Been dying to see how you taste." He shoved her thighs apart and put his mouth on her. His tongue slid between her folds, scraped over her clit, and thrust into her.

A sharp cry broke from her when his tongue withdrew, only to immediately lash at her clit. Again and again and again—

His fingers pushed into her as he licked and she came on an orgasm so powerful that her whole body quaked and she was pretty sure those quakes shook the entire bed. She'd cried out his name. At least, Ophelia thought she had. Her body was still in bliss mode and the orgasm had her inner muscles contracting greedily around his fingers.

"Fucking beautiful." His breath blew over her sensitive core. "I want you to come again."

So did she. Coming again sounded great. Fabulous, genius idea. Maybe she'd do that after she caught her breath and her heart stopped racing so fast.

He shoved away from her and stripped. The jeans hit the floor. His dick surged toward her.

She should do something other than just lay there. Absolutely. She should. But her eyes were on him. She wanted her mouth to be on him, too.

"Do you always come that fast?"

Her gaze jumped from his dick to his face.

"You're the fucking sexiest thing I've ever seen. You went off like a rocket, and I just want to make you do that again and again and again."

Yes, please. Like that sounded like a bad idea in what universe? But she'd promised him no BS, so... "It's been a long time for me." When he'd said that he looked into her life and found no boyfriends, he hadn't been wrong.

"How long." A demand.

She scooted back on the bed. Made room for him. And tossed her cami to join the other discarded clothes. "A year." At least.

"Why. Me." Again, a demand. Not a question.

"I have no idea. I just know that when we touch, I've never felt hotter." Her thighs trembled and her sex quivered. "And no, I don't usually come that fast. Guess you're special, too." Hadn't he told her that earlier? When she'd asked why he was so dang chatty? And, since she was sharing, "That was the best orgasm of my life."

"Fuck."

"I thought that would be next on our agenda, yes—"

Lane jumped on the bed with her. His mouth took her nipple and he licked and sucked ravenously. Her head tipped back, her fingers dug into his shoulders, and she arched against him. Heat shot from her nipple to her groin, and she rubbed eagerly against him.

His dick pushed at her core, demanding entry.

She wanted him in. Plunging hard and fast and sending her crashing straight into that headlong rush to orgasmic bliss.

If sex had been this good before for her, she wouldn't have gone a year without it.

He kissed a path to her other breast. Licked and scored her nipple with his teeth. Had moans and gasps ringing from her. One hand let go of him so she could work it between their bodies. Down, down she went. Her fingers circled the base of his cock. She squeezed, then pumped. Squeezed.

"Fuck, your hand feels good."

His mouth had felt like heaven.

"Need a condom, *now*."

Oh, but she really, really hoped he had a supply in that room.

"Don't *move*."

And he was gone. He'd jerked off her and went toward a bag at the end of the bed. The panting of her breath seemed way too loud. Her stiff nipples thrust toward him. Her legs shifted restlessly on the bed.

As she watched, he took out a condom and ripped open the packet. He rolled on the condom as his dick kept standing at full attention. His eyes seemed to drink her in.

And since he was looking for a view, Ophelia deliberately spread her legs.

"Beautiful." He stalked back to her. Slid one hand right between her spread thighs. "You are so wet." One finger sank into her. Stretched her as she lay on the bed, sprawled open for him. A second finger worked inside her. "You're going to feel fantastic."

"So are you." Actually, he already did feel great. Her hips were rocking against his hand. His thumb rubbed over her clit in a maddening rhythm even as his fingers worked in and out of her. In and out. Her orgasm hung just out of reach.

Her body tensed as he stroked her. She needed more. She needed his cock inside of her. Driving them both into madness.

His hand slid from her.

Dammit. "Lane!"

"Roll over. Get on your knees."

She rolled. Got to her knees.

"Hands on the headboard."

She'd already grabbed it to help balance her body.

"Hold on tight." He came up behind her.

Her hips arched back and up, and the head of his cock pushed lightly inside of her. It wedged right there, and she froze. Or maybe time froze. Everything seemed to become so still. She could feel her body aching, a quiver deep in her sex. Her muscles wanted to clamp down on him and squeeze as tightly as she could.

His hands rose and curled around hers. His body covered hers. He was all around her. She could smell him. Taste him.

He slammed deep into her.

Feel him.

Her mouth opened on a hard scream but she choked the sound back. Not pain. Not that at all.

She was too ready and eager for any pain. He was withdrawing and thrusting and all she felt was pleasure. In and out. Over and over. His hips pounded against her, and she drove her hips back up against him.

One of his hands freed hers. His fingers curled around her breast. Worked her nipple.

He kept driving into her.

His hand dropped down. Skimmed over her stomach and dipped lower. Lower. His fingers strummed her clit. Faster and faster.

He thrust into her. In and out.

Her hips rammed back against him.

His fingers squeezed her clit—

She came. Her grip whitened around the headboard as she held onto the thing for dear life as the orgasm ravaged through her. One of his hands still stroked her clit, driving the pleasure to a heightened, *I-can't-handle-this* degree while the other had clamped tightly around her waist. He ground her hips back against him with that grip. Without that hard hold, she might have shoved right off him because the pleasure had made her wild.

When it ended, when she could breathe and see again, her body bowed forward.

"Felt fucking *insane*." He withdrew. "My turn."

Lane plunged deep.

In and out. In and out. Her sensitive nerve endings screamed in bliss, and he roared her name when he pounded into her and came. His hold was so tight that he might be bruising her, and she didn't even care.

She was too wrung out with absolute pleasure.

Gradually, the thundering of her heartbeat eased. Or had that mad pounding been his heart? Theirs? His hand stopped gripping her waist and turned into a caress.

"Ophelia?"

"About to fall." Her knees were gonna give way. "Warning you..."

But she didn't have to worry. He eased out of her. Pulled her down. Tucked her under covers they'd pretty much wrecked.

No need for tucking her in. She should get out of his bed and go back to her room.

His footsteps padded away from the bed. She heard water running in the sink. "Leave the light on," she called out drowsily.

Silence. She didn't open her eyes. She would. She'd open her eyes, and she'd go back to her room in just a few moments.

"Why?" he asked softly. "Are you afraid of the dark?"

"No. Love the dark." The words came out all sleep slurred. Every muscle in her body was limp and the last of her adrenaline crash had hit extra hard after the second orgasm ripped through her. "But if bad guys are sneaking into the room, I like to be able to see them as soon as I open my eyes."

The mattress dipped a little beneath his weight. "What if a bad guy is in bed next to you?"

"I don't fuck bad guys."

"No? You sure about that?"

She was. One hundred percent.

She should get out of the bed. Now. She started to roll to the side.

But his arm curled around her. "Stay," he rasped.

Her head turned back toward him. Her eyes opened. Staying felt like a bad decision. Staying felt intimate.

"Why did you trust me enough for that?" Lane asked her.

"For sex?"

He watched her too carefully. Watched and waited.

Fine. The man would get one answer, and then she was sleeping. "You always this chatty *after* sex, too?"

His lips quirked for just a moment. A hint of a beautiful smile. "No. Just with you."

She stretched. Oh, but she would be sore tomorrow. "Because I'm special."

"Yes."

She sent him a small smile in return. "You let Thomas Bass get the drop on you."

He blinked. His thick hair seemed even darker against the white pillow. "And that...what? Made you want to have sweaty sex with me as soon as we were alone?"

If she hadn't been so sleepy, she would have laughed. Instead, she snuggled close to him. He was just so wonderfully warm. "You could have waited. Picked a different time so that you weren't the one who got knocked out."

"If I'd *waited,* Thomas would have tased the girl in the cheerleader outfit."

"Right. He would have. But he would have been distracted by carrying her and dumping her in the trunk of his car. You could have gotten him, no problem."

He kept watching her.

"You didn't want her to be hurt. Not even for a few minutes. So you let yourself be hurt." Her hand rose and pressed to his cheek. "I get that you aren't the same man you were before cell doors swung shut on you. But you are also not some horrible villain, either. No matter what dark thoughts you might have rolling around in that gorgeous head of yours. Villains don't take pain meant for other people. They don't sacrifice for victims."

"You're saying…" Slow. Thoughtful. "You just had sex with me because I let my ass get tased and tied up?"

Soft laughter. Sleepy laughter. "I had sex with you because I've never wanted anyone as much as I want you. When you touch me, heat seems to pour through my veins. I had to see if the sex would be all that I thought it could be with you."

"And…was it?"

She'd already told him, hadn't she? "Best orgasm."

Now, time to get out of his bed. Go back to her room.

But his grip tightened when she started to roll away once more.

"Stay," he whispered.

And she was too tired to argue. Too comfortable, too. Her breath sighed out.

"You were the best for me, too," he rasped. "It was all I thought it would be...and a hell of a lot more." His fingers curled around her hip. "Now what the fuck am I supposed to do about that? What the fuck am I supposed to do with you?"

Luckily, she was too tired to voice the thought that flew through her head.

Anything you want.

***

Her eyes flew open. Ophelia didn't know what sound had just pulled her from sleep. She just knew that her heart was suddenly trying to gallop out of her chest, and her wild gaze searched her surroundings for a threat.

Her hand flung toward the nightstand so she could grab her gun.

No weapon. Not my room.

The light spilled from the bathroom so that she could see the interior of the hotel room. Lane's room. Because she'd fallen asleep in Lane's bed.

Her head turned. The pillow beside hers was empty.

For a moment, she just listened. But there were no sounds from the bathroom. No creaks that would indicate footsteps. No running water. Nothing.

Naked, she slipped from the bed. Ophelia padded to the open bathroom door just to be certain that she wasn't wrong. Nope. Empty.

Her clothes had been picked up. Carefully folded over the lone chair that sat next to the small desk in the hotel room. She grabbed the cami and tugged it over her head.

Then she glanced toward the main door and pulled up her shorts. Ophelia walked toward the door. Opened it. Let it close.

Snick.

She knew what had woken her.

The bedside clock told her it was 3:23 a.m.

Where had Lane gone?

***

Getting into the rear holding area wasn't hard. At this time of the night—or the morning, depending on how you looked at it—only a skeleton crew would be on staff. And that crew would be tired. Distracted.

As long as you looked as if you belonged, people didn't tend to give you a second glance. He had the needed accessories. A badge. A uniform.

He avoided all the security cams. Took his time and made it back to the cells.

And his prey.

No one else was in the cell with Thomas Bass. The guy had the area all to himself. The other cells in the back were also empty. All the other prisoners were in the main holding area in the front of the building.

You're alone, and that makes things so much easier. Maybe the cops had thought they were protecting Thomas when they put him in isolation.

They were just helping me.

The bastard was spread out on a cot. Snoring. Sleeping like he didn't have a care in the world.

That man had murdered so many women. No, girls. They hadn't reached their eighteenth birthday. Thomas had seen to that. Now the prick thought he'd make a deal with the DA. Tell him all about his vics in exchange for less time locked away.

Hell, no.

There weren't going to be any deals.

Unlocking the cell was as easy as entering the holding area had been. He made no sound as he headed toward his prey. For a moment, he stood over the sleeping assistant principal.

The bastard's chest rose up and down. Up and down.

Thomas was on the lower bunk in the cell. No one rested on the top bunk. But a mattress was up there. Threadbare. Old. A stained pillow.

He grabbed the pillow. Bent over his prey.

You won't hurt anyone else.

He crouched over the sleeping man. Then slammed the pillow down against his face. Covering Thomas's eyes. His nose. His mouth.

Thomas jolted. His hands flew out to try and pry away that pillow so he could pull in a breath.

But Thomas wasn't dealing with a weakened and scared teenage girl. *I'm not your usual prey.*

The pillow stopped Thomas from making any sound. No cries for help. Help wouldn't come.

Soon enough, the pillow stopped Thomas from living.

And it sent him straight to hell.

CHAPTER SEVEN

Lane slowly opened the hotel room door. His eyes went straight to the bed in the middle of the room.

Ophelia's body was turned away from him. Her dark hair flowed over her pillow. She didn't stir when he entered, and he held his breath as he pressed the door shut.

Snick.

He ditched his shoes and tugged his shirt over his head. His focus remained on Ophelia as he advanced toward the bed. She didn't make a sound as he lifted up the covers and slid back into place beside her.

Mental note, Ophelia is a sound sleeper.

He reached out to touch her, but stopped himself. He stared at his hand as it hovered over her.

Don't touch her. Not now.

His hand fisted and fell back down. He stretched out on his back and stared up at the ceiling.

It was a long time before he fell asleep.

***

Ophelia's eyes opened. She eyed the bedside clock.

4:48 a.m.

She didn't go back to sleep. At 6 a.m., she pushed the covers away and slipped from the bed. Tiptoed back to her room. Shut the connecting door behind her.

She'd just exited the shower when a fierce pounding had her whole body tensing. The pounding wasn't coming from the connecting door.

Frowning, she headed for the main door. Ophelia put her eye to the keyhole. Surprise had her drawing back and flipping the locks. She opened the door and said, "Detective."

Because Detective Shay O'Brien waited on the other side of that door. A way too early visit.

Ophelia tightened the belt of the lush, white bathrobe she wore. "Is there a problem?" Had to be. Why else would a cop be at her hotel room door so early?

Shay nodded once, and the small hoop earrings in her ears swayed. "Big problem."

Crap. "It's not Royce. I *gave* you evidence on him—"

"Royce is fine. He was in a different holding area. We'd secured Thomas Bass separately. Due to the nature of his crimes, we thought it best to keep him isolated." Her lips thinned. "That certainly worked against us."

Oh, bad feeling. Like she hadn't gotten a bad feeling as soon as she'd seen the detective. "What's happening?"

Before Shay could reply, the door to room four-oh-eight flew open. Lane surged outside. Lane, wearing just his jeans.

Shay's gaze dropped. Raked over him.

"What the hell is happening?" Lane demanded.

Shay's gaze rose. Swept back to Ophelia. "You two had separate rooms."

"Certainly looks that way." Both she and Lane had asked what was happening—why hadn't Shay told them yet? *Oh, I have such a bad feeling. One that is getting worse by the second.*

"So you don't know where he was last night?" Shay motioned to Lane. "And he doesn't know where you were?"

Oh, yes, this was bad.

"We were in bed," Lane said, his voice flat and hard.

Ophelia didn't blush. She'd never been the blushing type. Besides, he hadn't said they were in bed *together*. Just in bed. "It's awful early for an interrogation. Usually, I prefer to save all of my interrogations until *after* I've had at least two cups of coffee." A flippant response when she felt anything but flippant. Alarm bells were raging in Ophelia's mind. *She's trying to get our alibis.*

Shay's head bobbed. "I needed to stop you from leaving town. I came straight over."

"How—exactly—did you even know we were here?" Ophelia hadn't given the detective that info.

Shay pointed to Lane. "He gave the front desk officer this location at the station. In case there were follow-up questions." A hard pause. "I have follow-up questions."

"Fine." Ophelia moved to stand in front of Lane. She had the weirdest feeling that she needed to protect him.

Weird? Nope. Maybe it was just serious foreshadowing. She knew suspicion when she saw it, and suspicion was all over Shay's face. And the detective had said she wanted to stop them before they left town. Oh, so bad. Because you stopped *guilty* people from leaving. You didn't care what innocent people did. "Lane and I should get dressed. Then we can talk. Why don't you go wait in the lobby, detective?"

"Neither of you have alibis, do you? After you left the police station and came here, you each went in your rooms. You have no alibis."

Ophelia drove her hands into the deep pockets of her robe. "Why would we need an alibi?"

"Because..." Shay watched her carefully. No doubt, looking for a tell or a slip up as the detective dramatically announced, "Thomas Bass was murdered in his cell. Right around four a.m. this morning."

Ophelia glanced back over her shoulder at Lane. And in that instant, she could hear his words running through her mind. As clear as day.

I told him that I had already broken out of one prison. I could easily break into another one. He would never be safe from me unless he confessed. I would find him, and what he'd done to his victims would pale in comparison to what I'd do to him.

Lane's eyes widened. His face—his mask locked down even harder than normal. He opened his mouth—

Her right hand flew out and pressed to his chest. "Isn't that just horrible?" Ophelia injected shock in her voice. *Murder is always horrible, so I'm not really faking anything.*

A little furrow appeared between Lane's dark brows.

She looked back at Shay but kept her hand on Lane's chest. "I'm sure the holding cells were equipped with video cameras."

Shay blinked. "Not in the rear section. Not where we had Thomas. That was an older part of the facility. Cameras are up front. No one can get back there without clearance."

"So you're saying a cop killed Thomas?"

"No, dammit, that's not what I'm saying! I'm—*no one should have gotten back there without clearance.* But someone did. The cameras up front caught sight of a male, tall, dark hair, wearing a cop's uniform and flashing a badge. He entered the facility shortly after 4 a.m. Left fifteen minutes later. And during those fifteen minutes, this individual killed Thomas Bass." As she'd described the person on camera, Shay's gaze had jumped to Lane.

Male.

Tall.

Dark hair.

"Not this shit again," Lane growled.

Not this shit. Not the accusation of being a killer.

"I'm assuming you couldn't clearly see this person's face?" Ophelia queried carefully. She needed to know what evidence they were facing.

"He hid from the rest of the cameras. Turned away. Smart sonofabitch." Shay's attention was still on Lane. "He knew exactly where they were. As if...he'd been there before."

Fuck. Lane had gone back into holding. She remembered him walking away with one of the younger cops.

"An officer reported his uniform missing shortly after we wrapped up questioning at the station—after Bass's booking. Didn't think anything of it at the time," Shay admitted. "Figured he'd misplaced it or that someone had grabbed it out of his locker by mistake. Now, of course, I see the situation in a whole new light."

What the detective meant...*She sees Lane in a guilty-as-sin light.* Shay thought he'd swiped the uniform while he'd been at the station. That he'd taken note of all the cameras so that he could avoid detection. While Ophelia had been answering the last of the seemingly endless questions that Shay had for her, Lane had disappeared for a while.

And he'd disappeared the night before. Leaving right at 3:23 a.m.

Now the detective was looking at Lane like he was her chief suspect. Because he was. Time to nip this nonsense in the bud. "Lane was with me last night," Ophelia said. "We have separate rooms, but we shared the same bed."

Shay smiled at her. "Nice try, Ophelia."

It hadn't been a try. It had been the truth.

"But I spoke to the man at the front desk when I came inside. When you flash a badge, you'd be surprised at how talkative some people get."

Considering that Ophelia had once possessed a badge, no, she would not be surprised.

"The friendly fellow gave me your room numbers, and he also mentioned how puzzled he was when Lane strode through the lobby at 3:30 this morning."

Her hand remained pressed to Lane's heart.

"Lane...alone, at 3:30," Shay added with a shrug. "He went out the lobby doors and into the night. And he didn't return—again, alone—until nearly 5 a.m." Her brows rose as Shay focused on Lane. "Gonna need you to come down to the station so you can tell me *exactly* where you were during that time."

A low curse broke from him. "I'm going to need a lawyer."

Shay smiled. "The guilty always do."

Ophelia felt Lane tense even more beneath her hand. So she gave him a reassuring pat. "No worries, Lane. Your lawyer is right in front of you." She beamed at Shay. "My client and I will get dressed then head down to the station with you. But you will *not* ask him any questions without me being present, you understand?"

"You're a PI," Shay snapped.

"Um, absolutely. I am. But *before* I got my PI license, I was—once upon a time—a law student. And I am currently licensed to practice law in the state of Georgia. My *client* and I will be happy to cooperate, and when we're done, I am sure that you will be apologizing for the inconvenience you've caused us."

Shay's gaze hardened. "Or I'll be throwing your client in a cell."

"Yes, I suppose that could be another option." *But one I will not let happen.*

***

"Since when are you a lawyer?"

He'd just entered Ophelia's room through the connecting door. She finished tugging down her blouse before turning toward Lane. He'd kept his voice low, no doubt due to the fact that the detective was waiting in the hallway. "You and Shay," Ophelia sighed. "Why do you both seem surprised by my skills? Shouldn't you just be grateful right now instead of firing questions at me?"

He took a step toward her, but seemed to catch himself. Lane's eyes glittered with intensity. "You haven't asked me where I went."

No, she hadn't. "Plenty of FBI agents have law degrees. Not like me having one is anything out of the ordinary." The law degree had given her a more competitive edge, yes, and when she'd first entered the Bureau, competition had been her game. She'd wanted to prove herself so desperately.

She'd wanted to take the killers off the streets. To find the darkest monsters out there and stop the predators who lived to torture and terrify.

But I didn't find them. They found me.

Or, one in particular had. He'd found her in her home. Where she should have been safe. But she hadn't been safe since the day she'd joined the Bureau.

Ophelia swallowed and lifted her chin. "Trust me, would you?"

He opened his mouth—

A fist pounded into Ophelia's hotel room door. "Hey!" Shay called out. "You two talking in there? What the hell?"

Ophelia grabbed her cross-body bag and marched for the door. She whipped it open and frowned at the detective. "What the hell, indeed. Yes, we are talking."

"Getting your stories straight?" Shay glowered.

"Conferring with my *client*," Ophelia corrected ever-so-smoothly. "And I am telling you, Detective O'Brien, you are wrong. Lane should not be a suspect."

Shay just grunted.

"But we'll play by your rules. For now."

A somewhat dazed shake of Shay's head. "Playing? Is that what you think we're doing? Lady, I never play when it comes to murder."

"What a coincidence. Neither do I."

***

Fucking fuck. This could *not* be happening. Lane sat at the small interrogation room table, a cold and extremely stale tasting cup of coffee in front of him. He'd been in so many rooms just like this one.

He *hated* interrogations. Cops tried to use their mind games. Tried to push and push. Cop after cop had attempted to break him when he'd been suspected of murder before.

Multiple murders.

Three women who all looked far too much like his twin sister.

And the reason he'd been suspected so hard? *Because I was near one of the crime scenes.* A late-night walk that had led to the fires of hell opening up and swallowing him whole.

Now it was happening again. Another cop trying to link him to a murder. And he had no one to back him up.

Fucking fuck.

"You came to town because you were hunting Thomas Bass, isn't that correct?" Detective Shay O'Brien asked him. Another female detective—she'd identified herself as Jules Carter—stood a few feet away, silently watching.

"I came to town because I was looking for a killer," Lane replied.

Ophelia sat beside him. She reached for the coffee cup in front of her. Took her first sip and—"OhmyGod," Ophelia exclaimed as she made choking noises. "Are you poisoning us? Do you *hate* me?"

Shay sent her a quick glare before focusing right back on Lane. "You were hunting him. Because you fancy yourself one of the Ice Breakers now, isn't that so? Because being all vigilante is so much better than letting the actual authorities do their jobs."

"Well," Ophelia said as she pushed her cup very far away from her person, "if the actual authorities had done their jobs, no one else would have needed to hunt the *serial killer* you had working at a local high school. And, frankly, I can't speak for my client, but I was absolutely here to hunt him. You are welcome for my services."

Shay's jaw locked. "I don't need your alibi," she gritted.

"Good. Because I haven't given you one yet."

Shay pointed at Lane. "You were hunting him."

That was a statement, not a question, so he just stared back at her. He'd learned that the less you said in interrogations, the better.

Before, I tried to make the cops understand that I wasn't guilty. I had nothing to hide, so I cooperated—at first. Only every word he'd spoken had been twisted and used against him. The next thing Lane knew, the cell door had been clanging shut on him.

"You deliberately let yourself get caught by him, didn't you?"

"Oh, this is new," Ophelia interjected with a hint of interest. *A hint.* "Please continue, Detective. I'd love to see where this walk will take us."

With her nostrils flaring, Shay did continue as she charged, "You acted as if Thomas got the drop on you, but you wanted him to take you. All part of your master plan. If you gave the appearance of a victim, then you could kill him and claim self-defense."

He didn't move. Lane was highly conscious of his surroundings. The hard chair beneath him. The old clock on the wall with its faint tick, tick, tick. Ophelia's lush rose scent teasing his nose.

The suspicion on both of the detectives' faces.

"You were going to kill him and act like it was self-defense, weren't you? But she..." Now Shay's index finger stabbed toward Ophelia. "She arrived and messed up your plans. So you had to reevaluate everything."

Ophelia's head turned toward Lane. She studied him in silence, then just nodded.

Uh, as his lawyer, shouldn't she be doing...*more?*

"You realized you'd have to attack Thomas Bass later. So while everyone else was busy at the station, you stole a cop's uniform. You headed over to holding. Got your eyes on all the security cameras in the building. You figured out exactly how to get to the prisoner. And you made your plan. You'd come back in the dead of night—"

"Technically, the killer arrived in the early morning," Ophelia cut in to say.

Shay's eyes narrowed. "*In the early morning,*" she corrected, "and you snuck into Thomas's cell."

"Oh, wait!" Ophelia held up one hand. "Snuck in? Can you elaborate? Was the lock forced open? Did the killer use a key?"

"Stole a key," Jules announced. Her voice was cold and flat as she finally broke her silence. "Bold as you please."

Ophelia's head turned toward her. "Thank you. Very helpful. So the killer stole a key and entered the cell—then, how exactly, was Thomas murdered? I missed that part. Or, actually, I just don't think it was mentioned yet." Her head swung back to Lane. "Am I wrong? Was it mentioned?"

He shook his head. *No.*

"Maybe Lane would like to tell you how he killed the man," Shay snapped.

Ophelia released a long sigh. "Lane can't tell me something he didn't do." Utter confidence.

And the fist that had been squeezing his heart so tightly began to ease its fierce grip.

Lane blinked at Ophelia. How was she so certain?

"Hey, there," Ophelia said softly to him. "You look like you're only now realizing you're not here alone. Haven't you seen me? I've been at your side the whole time."

His head tilted.

A faint smile lifted her lips. "What kind of partner would I be, if I turned on you at the first sign of trouble?"

"I thought you were his *lawyer,*" Shay rushed to say.

"I am. Lawyer. Partner. You keep getting stuck on me only being one thing. I like to wear all kinds of hats. I find them stylish." Ophelia slowly focused once more on the detective. "I am still not hearing how Thomas died."

"Suffocation," Jules supplied.

Shay whipped around. "*Detective.*"

Jules rolled one shoulder. "He was smothered with a pillow from the cell."

"Interesting." Ophelia eased back in her chair. She reached out for the coffee, but caught herself. "Not making that mistake again," she muttered. Her shoulders rolled back. Louder, she added, "I'll assume Thomas woke up once a pillow was shoved over his face, and he couldn't breathe. He was a big guy, so his assailant had to be strong."

"We already saw in the video that the attacker was tall and well-built." Shay spun to glare at Ophelia, then at Lane. "Fits your description, doesn't it, Lane?"

"I agree, Lane is ripped. But fitting a description isn't enough to lock a man away for murder." Ophelia still carried her air of utter unconcern. "Let's get back to Thomas—"

"How about the fact that Lane snuck out of his hotel room right before the murder was committed and didn't return until after Thomas was dead? Based on what the desk clerk told me, Lane would have been gone *exactly* long enough to walk to the station, slip inside, and then walk back."

"Oh, so you're sure he didn't drive there?" Ophelia asked.

"Checked with the hotel. His vehicle never left. They have cameras in the lot." A nod from Shay. "You knew that, though, didn't you, Lane? So you left the car. You took off on foot, and you came to finish what you started." Now she leaned forward. "You hate them, don't you?"

"Who?" Lane asked.

"The killers who get away with their crimes. You were locked up, but they're the ones out there hurting innocents. Slicing. Torturing. Hiding bodies. You *hate* that you were punished while they get away scot-free."

He would not take the bait she was throwing at him.

Ophelia sniffed. "Well, I certainly can't say I *love* to have killers running around in the world and not being apprehended by the law. Not on my favorite-things list."

"This isn't a joke." Shay's cheeks splotched with pink color.

"Good. Because Lane's not laughing. Neither am I. By the way, you're making an awful lot of statements. Not asking questions. I don't mean to tell you how to run an interrogation..." Ophelia winced. "But this is not it. And to think, I was impressed enough with you yesterday that I called you about the Royce Nicholson collar." Her eyes widened. "That perp is still alive and breathing, right?"

Shay tapped her short nails on the top of the table. "Lane Lawson."

He inclined his head toward her.

"Did you come to this town intending to hunt Thomas Bass?"

"I came to this town intending to find evidence of his guilt or innocence." A careful answer.

"And when you realized he was guilty as sin, did you decide to punish him?"

He needed to be punished. The innocent shouldn't suffer while the guilty get away so easily.

"Oh, for goodness' sake!" Ophelia exclaimed. "Is this a profile that you're trying to build?

Because Lane was innocent and put in a cell, he now goes after the guilty and administers his own brand of justice?"

"Works for me," Shay said. Her nails tapped again.

"It doesn't work for me," Ophelia fired back. "I'd like to see the cell."

Lane blinked. Where had that come from?

"And crime scene pics." Ophelia looked at her watch. "Wish you had left the body in there for me to view, but I figure he's been taken to the morgue by now. Though, I would like to formally request a view of the deceased." She peered expectantly at Shay.

Shay stared back at Ophelia as if she believed the other woman had lost her mind.

Meanwhile, Lane wasn't sure what the hell to think.

No alibi. Again. Just like before. The past kept rearing its head and trying to drag him back under. He *had* left the hotel. Ophelia had been sleeping. Looking like the sexiest fallen angel ever in his bed.

The devil tempted you to sin.

He'd wanted to sin with her over and over again. The way she'd ignited beneath his touch had blown him away. He'd been desperate for her. So far beyond rational thought and control. He hadn't been able to stop.

He'd wanted to take and take and take...

But she'd been sleeping.

And he'd needed to put some space between them. He couldn't have Ophelia thinking he was too—

"Lane?" Ophelia prompted.

Shit. He'd missed something.

"Just tell them where you were," she said when he remained silent. Ophelia reached beneath the table and took his hand. Her fingers squeezed his. "I have your back."

No, she didn't. No one did. *No alibi.* Another interrogation room. Another murder. And cops looking at him as their chief suspect. He tried to pull his hand from Ophelia, but she just tightened her grip.

"Yes, do tell us," Shay encouraged him. "Tell us how you left the hotel—alone. How you...oh, wait, let me guess..." A wide smile covered her face. "How you just 'walked aimlessly into the darkness without a real destination in mind.' You just 'walked as the silence surrounded you.'"

Lane stiffened at those words. His words. Words he'd given when he'd been arrested before, and the cops wanted to know where he'd been going. What he'd been doing.

Lane hadn't been able to provide an alibi for the murders he'd been charged with committing. He'd been out, walking late at night. He did that all the time. Just walked into the dark. As he tried to get away from demons that just would never leave him in peace.

He'd had no alibi before, and the cops had locked him up. Only his sister had believed his protests of innocence.

But he'd still lost months. So much time. Caged up. And the man he'd been before the nightmare? He'd changed.

Now it was happening all over again. He had no alibi. *I can't go back in a cell again. I won't.*

"Here." Ophelia let his hand go, but then immediately pulled out her phone and slapped it down on the table. "This will speed things along." She swiped across the screen. "There's Lane leaving the hotel. See, he's right under the streetlamp so you can clearly see that's him." Another swipe. "And here he is turning east on Bright Way. East, not west. West would have taken him toward the police station and your holding cells. But he didn't go that way." Another swipe. "Walking in the park here. Really shouldn't be doing that. I've heard there have been some muggings in that area." She clicked the pic. Details appeared. A time stamp. A location. "Oh, look at that," Ophelia noted in mock surprise. "Unless Lane has some magical powers that I don't know about, I just don't see how he could be in two places at one time."

His heart seemed to jerk in his chest.

"I think that's called an alibi, but, seriously, it's been a while since I have actually done my lawyer routine." Ophelia pushed the phone closer to Shay. "Tell me if I'm wrong, would you?"

Ophelia followed me? She took pics of me?

"Why the hell..." Shay spoke slowly, with quiet fury in each word, "did you not just tell me from the beginning that you had photos of him? That you could alibi him?"

"Because I wanted to know more about the murder. Cops always get chatty when they are trying to trip up suspects. Figured you'd talk more to me this way. If I gave you the pics first, well, we wouldn't all be in the station together right now, would we?"

He sucked in a breath. Beneath the table, his hands fisted.

"And since we are here," Ophelia continued in her silky voice, "how about you let us see that cell? And you make that appointment for us to view the body?"

Shay shot to her feet. "Why in the world would I do that? You are *wasting* my time—"

"I would do it because I think *you* were set up, Detective O'Brien. I think someone might have just tried to frame my partner. Someone was watching, someone saw Lane today and realized he'd make a great fall guy. The man you viewed briefly in the video? Tall, muscled, with dark hair? He could have even been wearing a wig so that he would look more like Lane."

"You followed me?" Lane asked, aware that his voice came out as a growl.

"I prefer to think of it more as I was looking out for my partner, but, sure, following works, too." Her gaze never left Shay. "And I didn't waste your time. I just cleared your prime suspect for you. Now I'm offering you my services. I know you dug into my background after you met me yesterday. How could you not when I served up two perps for you with big, beautiful bows tied around them? I think you already knew I had a law degree. I think you know I spent time at the Bureau. Probably pulled some strings to get that info." A pause. "And I think you know—deep down—that I could help you on this case. So let me see the cell. Let me view the body. If I can't help, I'll get out of your way."

"Get out of my town," Shay snapped. "Both of you."

"Right. Sure. We'll do that," Ophelia agreed. "But really, viewing the cell will take like—what? Five minutes? And it's already been cleared by your crime scene team. Consider it payback for me gift wrapping Royce for you."

Shay stormed for the door. Jules followed right behind her.

The door slammed shut.

"I think that's a yes," Ophelia told him. "Let's just sit here for a moment and see, shall we?"

He didn't reply.

Another soft sigh slipped from her. "On a scale from one to ten, how pissed are you?" Ophelia asked as her head slowly turned and her blue eyes landed on him.

Again, he didn't reply.

"It'll take that as a nine? Maybe a ten?"

"Why in the hell did you follow me?"

"Eleven it is," she declared with a wince.

CHAPTER EIGHT

"That's the first question you have when we're finally alone?" She jerked her thumb toward the mirror behind her. "And I'm sure you've been in enough interrogation rooms to know that someone is probably behind that glass watching us. Maybe the loves-to-be-silent Detective Carter hustled in there. Just a friendly reminder in case you feel the urge to say something that should really just be kept between us." Her blue eyes blinked innocently.

He was realizing there was nothing innocent about her. "Why." A demand.

"I was worried about you."

Just that. Nothing more. He waited. She simply stared back at him. So he leaned out, caught the arms of her chair, and hauled the chair around to face him. The chair legs screeched over the floor. "Why."

"Why was I worried? Because you're my partner. I'm training you, remember? If something bad had happened to you, how would I have been able to keep up my end of the deal?"

I am something bad. "You don't trust me."

She leaned forward. Put her hands on his shoulders. "*You* don't trust me."

I don't trust anyone.

"When we were in my hotel room, I told you to trust me. You didn't need to be all stressed in here. I would have told you about the photos sooner, but Shay didn't give us a moment of privacy."

No, the detective hadn't. She'd driven them to the station. Stayed with them every moment.

"I'm sorry you had to go through all of..." Her gaze darted around the interrogation room. "*This.*"

He grunted.

"I'm sure it brought back all kinds of bad memories."

"Not exactly like I had the best moments of my life in interrogations." No, instead, he'd seen his life being snatched away from him.

Her blue eyes came right back to him. "I wouldn't let someone send you away, Lane. I have your back. Even if I hadn't gotten those pics..." But she stopped. Her shoulders tensed right before she surged forward and put her mouth at his ear. "*I wouldn't have let them send you away,*" she whispered. Her breath feathered over his ear.

Arousal surged through his whole body.

"*We're a team. I'll protect my partner. Promise.*" She eased back in front of him.

Her hands were still on his shoulders. His were still locked around the arms of her chair, caging her in.

"You're probably wondering why I took the pictures."

One of the many things he wondered, yes.

"Honestly? Impulse. Or maybe just habit. As a PI, I'm always trailing people and I snap pics as I go. They help me to visualize scenes later. Sometimes, the most random thing in a pic can turn out to be a major key in a case for me. Plus, pics give me time stamps and locations. Very needed info in my line of work." Her lips pressed together. "Right now, I think we should just both be glad I'm a nosey PI."

The door flew open. "Five minutes," Shay snapped.

Lane shook his head. No, she had not just agreed to Ophelia's terms.

But the broad smile on Ophelia's face said otherwise. Sonofabitch. How did the woman keep convincing people to do so much for her?

"Five minutes," Shay repeated. "Then you are out of my town. Out of my life."

His hands dropped from the arms of the chair.

Gracefully, Ophelia rose. "You are going to miss me when I'm gone. My absence will leave a hole in your life."

Why did those words seem to sink right through him?

"I highly doubt that," Shay replied.

***

"You don't have to come back there with me." Ophelia turned to block the corridor that led to the rear holding area. Or, more specifically, to the holding area that had been used for Thomas Bass. She tucked a lock of hair behind her left ear. "I know this is hardly your favorite place." *Jail cells must be hell for you.*

The faint lines around Lane's mouth had deepened. She'd hated having to sit in interrogation with him. She'd tried to get the man to understand that he was safe. That she had his back.

But she'd felt him withdrawing. His body had gotten stiffer and stiffer beside her. And his eyes?

Desolate.

"No need for you to walk back into a nightmare," she added.

His gaze had been focused over her shoulder, on the cells that she knew he could already see, but at her words, his green stare shifted to her.

"Can we move this along?" Shay called. She was already inside the narrow corridor. "Your five minutes are already winding down."

"I'm coming," Lane said.

"*We* are coming," she corrected. She reached for his hand and laced her fingers through Lane's. "You're not alone any longer. Get that in your head, would you? Partners don't abandon partners." She rose onto her tiptoes. "They also don't leave them alone in bed while they go for a casual four a.m. stroll, but we'll talk about that later." She eased back and turned around to go inside the corridor.

"*They also don't follow their partners and take clandestine pictures.*"

Fine. He had a point. But... "Those pics saved your ass, so let's just let that one pass, shall we?" The clock truly was ticking, so they'd have to revisit that issue later. And, yes, definitely, Ophelia got that Lane was pissed. But she *had* provided the man with an alibi, so maybe he could forgive and forget?

Oh, who was she kidding? She wasn't the type to forgive and forget, so she doubted if he was, either.

She marched down the corridor, moving quickly past the empty cells. One empty cell. Two. Her fingers remained intertwined with Lane's, and she didn't care what Shay thought about that situation. Lane was walking into a personal nightmare, and she wanted him to know he was not alone.

Three cells. And finally...

Unlucky number four.

The cell door was open. Shay gripped the bars with one hand. "Don't understand the purpose of this. The techs went over this place. What do you think you'll see that they didn't? That *I* didn't?"

"I won't know until I find it." She crossed the threshold and entered the cell, but as she crossed over, Ophelia finally let Lane go. If he didn't want to come in after her, she wasn't making him.

But he walked into the cell. His haunted gaze swept the scene. Went to the bars. The bed. The toilet.

How long were you locked up? He hadn't been granted bail. He'd been deemed a flight risk by the judge. His assets had been frozen. She'd read so much of his file, but she couldn't remember how many days and nights he'd spent in a cell, one far too much like the one they were in right then.

"Do you have any idea how many fingerprints are in this place?" Shay wanted to know. "They dusted but, hell, we all realize the results will be shit."

Ophelia headed for the bed. The mattress had been removed. No pillows. She looked at the top bunk. Nothing up there, either. Her gaze swept the walls. Dirty. Dark. Ophelia bent to look under the bottom bunk.

Nothing there at all.

"The place was searched," Shay said, sounding more than a little annoyed. "Don't think your super PI self is going to turn up something that everyone missed. Hate to break it to you, but you're not some special shining star."

"That hurts," Ophelia told her. "My mom always said I was a shining star. Now you're calling her a liar." She remained crouched beneath the bed. "Did Thomas have anything beneath his nails? He must have fought back."

"Fibers." A grudging response. "But I'm betting they'll be a match for the fibers in our cop uniforms. That *is* what the perp was wearing. Or maybe they were just from the pillow."

From her crouched position, Ophelia looked back at the detective. "Why are you so sure it *wasn't* a cop?" Slowly, she rose. Lane wasn't speaking, but she knew he was taking in every detail of the scene. "The local news covered Thomas's arrest on the evening show. If it wasn't a cop who hated what Thomas had done, then it could have been someone related to his victims. Someone who wanted justice."

"Thanks so much for telling me how to create a suspect list. Not like I can't do that on my own," Shay returned with a hard narrowing of her eyes.

Right. Dammit. Ophelia's stomach had been knotting ever since she heard about Thomas's death. And the fact that it felt like someone was definitely trying to pin this thing on Lane...

I need as much intel as I can get. But there is nothing here. Just an empty cell. "I want to see the body."

Shay laughed. "Playtime is over."

"I thought we already covered that we weren't playing."

"*I'm* not playing," Shay replied. "Not really sure what the hell you're doing. But I do know one thing." She looked at her watch. "Your five minutes are up." She swung the cell door, and the hinges groaned.

Lane jerked.

"Time to get out of my town," Shay finished.

***

"It worries me when you go silent," Ophelia told Lane. They were out on the street. The sun burned down on them even as cars whizzed past. Shay had offered to have a uniform drop them off at their hotel, but that would not have fit Ophelia's plans. At all.

So she'd opted for a walk. A very silent walk with Lane. She could feel the tension pouring off him. Did the man know that long, heavy silences were her arch nemesis? "I didn't think you were leaving to commit a crime," she blurted.

He stopped walking. Turned slowly toward her.

Ophelia lifted one hand to shield her face from the sun. "I don't think you're the bad guy, Lane."

"Then what am I?"

"My partner. I followed you because I was concerned. You'd had one vicious day. You were nearly sliced open by a serial killer. I wanted to make sure you were all right." She wet her lips. "And in the interest of full disclosure, yes, of course, I know you always take night walks. That's the whole reason the cops were able to pin those charges on you before. You had no alibi. I was curious about the walks. I wanted to see..." How to explain? "*You.*"

A bitter laugh spilled from him. "What was there to see? Me, wandering in the dark?"

"You were looking for something." He'd walked with purpose every step of the way.

His jaw hardened.

"Don't tell me what it was. Fine. But do remember that my stalking self saved the day, okay?"

He didn't speak.

She stopped shielding her face and rubbed the back of her neck. Tension knotted there. "I'm about to make a pitstop," she informed him. Because partners *should* tell partners their plans. That should be one of their rules. "Lesson four. Always tell your partner where you're going."

Otherwise, you could find yourself needing an alibi or backup that just isn't there.

"Lesson four?" A rumble, as if the question had been pulled from Lane against his will. "How did we get to four?"

Her mouth dropped open. "Seriously?" A huff. "You need to remember the pearls of wisdom I give to you." Maybe she'd type them up and send them to him later, but for now... "To recap, lesson one was *don't get your ass knocked out by the bad guy.*"

His nostrils flared.

"Lesson two was to *always thank the people who save your ass.*" Ophelia sniffed. "I believe that means a thank you is in order since I provided you with an alibi and thus saved that gorgeous ass of yours."

A muscle flexed along his jaw.

"Moving on..." *We'll come back to my thank you.* "Lesson three was that dead men can't give families closure." The wind caught her hair and tossed it around. "But that isn't on us since we didn't kill Thomas."

"No, I didn't." Gravelly. Rough. Deep.

She probably shouldn't have found him sexy in that moment. Some things could not be helped. The man's voice was hot. And he wasn't a killer.

So, since her new partner hadn't murdered their serial killer, it was her job to figure out who had. Unsolved mysteries nagged at her too much. "I think that brings us up to lesson four. Always tell your partner where you are going."

"Where *are* you going?"

"You can come with me," she hurtled onward, "or, if you prefer to keep your hands clean and *not* potentially get on the bad side of local cops, then you might want to return to the hotel."

"We were told to leave town."

Her hand stopped rubbing her neck. It fell to her side. Pressed to her thigh. "I don't always do what I'm told." A grimace. "To be honest, I usually do the exact opposite of what I'm told to do. I'm wired wrong like that."

"I do not understand you."

"I get that a lot. Truly, I do. So, I'm trying to explain." Ophelia blew out a breath. "I can't leave town yet. I need to see the body. That is where I'm going. To view Thomas's body."

"Why?"

"Because...I don't like it. I don't like that the guy *we* bagged was killed his first night in lockup. I don't like that the cops went straight to you. I don't like that I've got a lump in my throat because my instincts are telling me that I might have missed something."

His brow furrowed. "You didn't find anything in the cell. What on earth makes you think you'll find anything on the body?"

An excellent question. "Maybe I won't find anything. Then I'll leave town. Follow the detective's orders."

"And if you do find something?"

"I'll point it out to the cops, of course."

"*They* can find things on their own."

She stared back at him. "I'm sure they can. But I want to see the body. You don't have to go with me—"

He stepped closer to her. Seemed to block out some of that bright sunlight. "I'm your partner."

"Good of you to remember." He was big. Heat seemed to pour from his body. And damn but his mouth was kissable.

Focus. You have a dead body to see. They hadn't talked about the, uh, extracurricular activities of the night before. They'd been too busy dealing with the cops and a murder suspicion. Maybe they wouldn't talk about it. Just move forward.

Be businesslike.

Professional.

His hand rose and curled under her chin. Immediately, her whole body tightened with eager need. *Just from a touch.*

Clearly, she had a problem with professionalism. Her bad.

"Partners stick together," he murmured. "Lesson five."

"I'll add that to our list," she breathed. His voice had been deep and rumbling, and pretty much what she believed sin sounded like. "So...that means you're coming with me to see the body?"

"That means I'll come with you wherever the hell you go. You lead the way, and I'll walk through the fire with you."

She swallowed. "No fire necessary. Just some cold storage freezers and a murder vic." She should back away from him now. Get to business. But...

Something felt different.

No, there *was* something different about the way he looked at her. Only Ophelia couldn't quite figure out that difference. In her mind, a faint alarm bell began to ring.

He started to pull away, but her hand flew up to curl around his wrist. "What is it?" Ophelia asked him.

A faint line appeared between his brows.

"Something changed." She could *feel* it.

"You're my alibi."

"Well, yes, I was. *Still waiting on that thank you.* Though, considering she'd stalked him, she got where he would be hesitant to show gratitude.

"Never had one of those before," he said in a bemused tone. "If I had, I would never have gone to hell."

Were her fingers sliding lightly along his wrist? They were. She should stop. "You can count on me." He needed to understand this. "You're my partner. I don't plan to throw you to the wolves."

"Good to know."

She made herself back up a step. Free him. "The dead only wait so long."

His eyes narrowed. "How the hell are you even going to get access to his body?"

"Don't worry. I'll figure something out." She usually did. "Besides, I know a guy…" Ophelia turned away from him. Her fingers curled. *I can still feel Lane.*

***

It should have been harder to get access to a dead body.

Lane certainly didn't expect Ophelia to just march up to the medical examiner on duty, flash a hundred-dollar bill at him, and then get instant access. But, turned out...

Ophelia truly knew the guy.

No wonder she seemed so certain that she'd figure something out.

"You can't touch him," the ME—Dr. Benedict Pearson—said as he pulled on his gloves and made his way to the body. Benedict was in his late twenties, with thick, brown hair and dark eyes. When Ophelia had knocked on his office door, the man had greeted her with a fierce hug.

A far too tight hug.

Lane didn't think he'd growled but the temptation had certainly been there. He hadn't liked the sight of the man's hands on her. Not one bit.

Why the hell was he getting so territorial when it came to her?

She's my alibi. The first one he'd ever had. Fuck.

"I know the drill." Ophelia craned her head to peer around Benedict and look at the covered body.

"Wasn't talking to you. Was talking to the glaring guy *with* you." Benedict pointed at Lane. "You can't touch the body. You can't contaminate evidence at all. Basically, you look and go, and you were *never here.* Understand me?"

"Don't worry. My partner is good," Ophelia assured him without missing a beat. "So, you haven't started your exam yet?"

"Ophelia, I got the body less than an hour ago. I'm fast, but not that fast." He waved toward the lockers. "Besides, I've got others in front of him. Some bastard who got off on torturing and killing girls isn't exactly high on my priority list." He headed toward the nearby body bag. He pulled down the zipper, revealing Thomas's face.

"Seriously, Benny? I'm going to need more." Ophelia walked right up to the body and leaned over the dead man. Like it was something she did all the time. Her nose didn't even twitch at the odor that filled that lab room.

"The man was suffocated," Benedict told her. "The pillow was found over his face. There's not going to be a whole lot *more*."

"Such a lie. You and I both know that there will be fibers in his lungs. Fibers you'll need to match to the pillow that I am assuming was bagged and tagged." She pointed to Thomas's closed eyes. "I'm also assuming you at least checked them?"

Benedict huffed. "Of course, I did." Then he pried open one of Thomas's eyes with his gloved finger.

The brown eye stared sightlessly forward.

"Bloodshot," Ophelia murmured.

Lane leaned forward to stare at that one eye. He did see a lot of red around the eye. Vessels appeared a lot darker than normal.

"It's a sign of suffocation," Benedict told him as Ophelia's head turned toward the ME. "You look at the eyes. You check the lungs. When you first come across a suffocation victim, you could just think the person had suffered a heart attack or stroke."

Lane actually already knew this. He'd known about the red splotches that would be present in the eyes with the bursting of blood vessels and he knew that when the lungs were checked, there should be signs of petechial hemorrhages.

He'd *chosen* not to become a doctor, but he'd fucking aced his med school classes.

"Those are the ways you can tell your vic was suffocated. Unless..." Benedict cleared his throat. "Unless the killer is ever so helpful—like the guy who offed Thomas—and just *leaves* the murder weapon in place. Hard to take Thomas's death for anything else with the pillow still on his face."

"The killer wanted us to know exactly what he'd done," Ophelia said.

Sure looked that way to Lane. "What about defensive wounds?" he asked.

Benedict peered at him. "You a former Fed, too?"

This guy knew about Ophelia's past? They were clearly closer than Lane realized.

"No," Ophelia answered before he could. "Lane's background is in medicine, so while we both appreciated your talk about the blood vessels, Lane already knew all of that."

Lane slanted her a quick, surprised glance.

"You're a doctor?" Benedict questioned. "I don't think I caught your name when you came in."

"You didn't catch it." Lane hadn't given it. Neither had Ophelia. "You were too busy hugging her and taking the cash."

Benedict released Thomas's eyelid. He straightened quickly. "I was being *friendly*—"

"Save it, guys," Ophelia still peered at the body. "I want to see his arms."

Benedict huffed but pulled down more of the zipper to reveal Bass's upper body and arms. "Bruising can take some time to occur, as I'm sure your *doctor* partner is well aware."

"I'm well aware of it, too," Ophelia tossed back. "Don't be so grumpy, Benny. We appreciate you letting us in. And you can totally consider your debt to me as paid in full now."

Debt? But *she'd* given the guy a hundred—

"Someone took some compromising pics of Benny once," Ophelia explained to Lane. "He didn't want anyone in town knowing about them, so he paid a visit to me in Savannah."

"*Client confidentiality.*" Benedict's face turned blood red.

"Partner." Ophelia tapped Lane's chest. "The PI office is keeping your confidentiality. Relax. Besides, not like I told him what was in the photos, though if you don't hurry and show me what I need, I just might—"

He yanked the zipper all the way down.

"Was that so hard?" Ophelia wanted to know. "It didn't look hard. In fact, it looked as if it required minimal effort to me."

Lane thought it looked as if Benny—Benedict—might pass out at any moment.

"Let me see his hands," Ophelia said.

"*Do not touch*—" Benedict began.

"You lift them up. You're the one wearing the gloves. Come on, Benny. Be a team player."

"I have to scrape his nails for fibers. Dig out any potential evidence that could be there. You are not going to mess up my exam, Ophelia." But he lifted Bass's right hand. "This is what you get. Look at it from where you are. Don't you even think about—"

Ophelia surged backward. A fast, hard step in retreat. She stumbled and would have fallen, but Lane grabbed her. His hands locked around her waist as he steadied her. "You okay?"

Her head swung toward him.

Benedict's face had been too red.

Ophelia's had gone sheet white. Her eyes were wide and stark and...scared?

He'd been quite convinced that nothing scared her. Until this moment. "Ophelia?" His grip tightened on her waist.

"Ring finger," she said, the two words barely more than a breath.

Both Lane and Benedict turned to look at Bass's ring finger.

"It's a string." Benedict poked the one finger up in the air. "Probably came off the pillow during the struggle and got lodged there. See, this is why you shouldn't be looking at the body. You're going to mess with my evidence. This little scene is *over*—"

"It's *tied* around his finger. Not lodged." She pulled from Lane. Stepped back toward the body even as her body tensed. "The killer tied that string around his finger."

"Maybe the vic tied it around his own finger." Benedict was clearly not convinced. "Guy might have wanted to remember something."

"*Forget-Me-Not,*" she whispered. A shudder shook her whole body. "He is *dead.*"

"Uh, yeah." Benedict tucked Thomas's hand back in the bag and hauled up the zipper. "Clearly, he is dead. That's why he's here with me. Now you saw the body and you need to leave. Great to see you again. Now, bye."

She didn't budge. "You have to call Detective O'Brien. You have to tell her that I'm here."

Benedict's eyes bulged. "That is a horrible idea! Why would I do that?"

"Forget-Me-Not," Ophelia repeated but her voice was stronger. More adamant. "You have to call her. And the Feds."

Lane caught her shoulders and swung her around to face him. "You're gonna need to bring me up to speed here, *partner.*"

Her eyes gleamed with what *could* have been tears. Tears? From Ophelia? He'd pretty much been convinced the woman was invincible, but in that moment, he wanted to pull her into his arms, hold her tight, and protect her from whatever the hell it was that had just sent a shudder racing over her body.

"Why are you so upset over a string?" Benedict asked in confusion.

The same confusion Lane felt.

"Because it's not a string." She didn't look at the ME. Her stare remained on Lane. "It's a signature. One that was never made public. *He is dead.*"

"Uh, once more, yes," Benedict told her. "The man is clearly dead—"

"Not Thomas Bass." A long exhale. "The string is a killer's signature. A serial killer." She released a slow breath and never broke eye contact with Lane. "We called him the Forget-Me-Not killer because he left a string curled around a finger of every victim he murdered. He can't still be hunting. *This can't be happening again.*"

Lane leaned in closer to her. It took all of his control not to pull her against him. He did not like it when Ophelia was afraid. "How are you so sure?"

"Because I killed him." Ophelia's words were so low they only carried to him. "And ghosts can't murder anyone."

CHAPTER NINE

"So, is it normal for you to receive a police escort out of town? That the way things typically tend to work for you?" Lane asked in what he thought was a very civil tone as he joined Ophelia as she stood beside her Jeep. He'd tailed her to Savannah, always keeping her vehicle within sight during the drive. She'd finally stopped on the side street in the historic district, and, after parking his own ride, he ambled toward her.

Ophelia whirled to face him. "No. Not typical." Anger vibrated in her voice. Apparently, the drive hadn't cooled down her temper in any way. "The detective ignored everything I had to say."

"When you told her a *serial killer* was hunting in her town."

Ophelia's hands went to her hips.

"A *dead* serial killer," Lane corrected because he did think that was a relevant point. "Though you didn't mention the dead part to her. Just me, so I'm wondering—"

"Let's get inside the house and not discuss this on the street, okay?" She slung her overnight bag over her shoulder and, muttering beneath her breath, she headed to the sidewalk that ambled to the front of the home.

He started to follow.

"You're gonna need your luggage, Lane," she called without looking back.

He hesitated. "Figured you'd want me staying in a hotel."

"Why? There are plenty of unused rooms in the house. I get you have money to burn, but save yourself the cash and the fire, would you?"

But will I be in one of those unused rooms...or will I be sharing a bed with you? Definitely not the time to ask that question. Maybe she thought they were one and done. Meanwhile, fuck, he couldn't get her out of his head.

So he grabbed his bag and hurried to follow her. When he caught sight of the house's exterior, he froze. Studied. Nodded. "You live in the Addams' Family house."

"The former owner painted it black, okay?" She'd already climbed the steps that led to the porch. "I haven't gotten around to changing colors." She drove her key into the lock and pushed open one of the double doors at the entrance. But Ophelia didn't cross over the threshold. Her head turned toward him. "I like the color, if you must know. I could have changed it. I just didn't want to."

He had not said a word.

"Suits my dark soul. There. Happy? And it's a Victorian, like so many of the houses in this district. It's got character. And, yes, it's kinda creepy, but I wanted it the minute I saw it."

The way I wanted you? Not that he'd ever told her that. Lane nodded. "I like the house. And I'm not a bit surprised you live here." In fact, he thought the place suited her perfectly. Dark and mysterious. With an air of danger.

Perfect Ophelia.

She hurried inside. Her bag hit the wooden floor in the foyer. A crystal chandelier hung overhead, and his gaze traveled up the worn banister and wooden stairs that led to the upper level. Her stairs were black, too.

"Two guest rooms are upstairs. Take your pick of either one."

So she wasn't planning to share a room with him. Message received. Now his dick could just settle down. He pushed the door closed. Flipped the lock.

She paced into the den as nervous energy seemed to hum in the air around her. "I can't believe the cops didn't listen to me."

Not that he was defending them, but... "The detective *was* pissed that you'd ignored her orders and gone to see the body."

"Yes, fine, granted."

Granted? He almost smiled. He hadn't truly smiled in ages. After being in the cell for so long, being hunted, Lane hadn't thought he would ever smile easily again. But Ophelia kept throwing him off his guard.

Her hands flew into the air. "I had useful intel." Her hands dropped as she kept pacing. "And Benny just shut me down completely. He wouldn't talk to me at all after the detectives arrived."

"Because Benny was trying to cover his own ass." Too late for that. Benny had been busted allowing civilians to view the body.

"If I hadn't seen the body, he wouldn't have known how valuable that string was. You heard him. He thought it was a fiber from the pillow. A random thread that had gotten stuck on Thomas's finger during the struggle. Benny, Detective O'Brien, her partner—they all would have overlooked an important piece of the case."

He wasn't so sure the string was important. "You don't think there's a chance the string got there the way Benedict thought? During the struggle, it *could* have just become tangled on his finger." It wasn't impossible. "The detective believed that—"

"She's wrong. Benny is wrong. There is a difference between a tangle and a tie, and I've *seen* that exact knot before." Her hand raked through her hair. "It's not a coincidence that he took out Thomas. I collar the killer, and he executes him. No coincidence." She stopped in front of a gray couch. One with big, fluffy, black pillows. "They didn't even call the FBI. I *told* them to bring in the Feds."

He propped one shoulder against the wall of the den. "Because you think a serial killer is at play. One you murdered."

Ophelia whirled toward him. "Could be a copycat. Has to be a copycat, doesn't it? But only a few people knew about the perp's signature. And those few people are all Feds. The string was never public knowledge."

Yes, okay, he was bone tired. Hell of a night. Hell of a day. And he was pretty much running on fumes. Lane ambled to her couch. Slid down. *Damn comfortable.* He rolled back his shoulders and settled in. "Partner, I think you're gonna need to bring me way more up to speed."

She did a double take at the word *partner.* Why did she look surprised? She'd been telling the world they were partners. Now he got on board, and Ophelia looked at him as if he had two heads.

And she was also not bringing him up to speed as he'd directed. That had to change. He was missing things about this case. And *not* just because he was tired. Because Ophelia wasn't sharing properly. "Lesson six. Don't keep secrets from your partner."

"I'm the one training you! You don't get to add lessons! That's what I do." A huff. "That will not be lesson six."

Fine. For now. "How may vics?" Lane asked. "How long did your killer hunt?"

"He was *not* my killer."

"How did you catch him? And when did you kill him?" His gaze swept over her. Delicate. *Fragile.* That was how she looked, at least to him. Sure, determination and intensity cloaked her, but Ophelia was physically so much smaller than he was.

How had she taken out a killer? And had his death been the reason she left the Bureau?

Her arms wrapped around her body.

She didn't answer any of his questions.

"I'm at a major disadvantage here," Lane noted. Was he supposed to operate in the dark? "You know pretty much everything about me, but I know zero about you."

"Not true." She wet her lips. "You know what it feels like when I come around your dick."

He jolted and nearly leapt off the couch. But he caught himself. His hand gripped the arm cushion beside him. Hard. "Trying to distract me?" *Because, baby, nice technique. Bravo.* One that was definitely working. He'd just gotten a fast and furious memory of being balls deep in her and feeling her inner muscles squeeze him as if they'd never let go.

"No, I'm just saying—you actually know me a hell of a lot better than most people do. Maybe that's good. Maybe it's bad. I don't know." Her hands fell. Fisted. She started to pace once more. "How can he be back?"

The most obvious solution had to be voiced. "Maybe he was never dead."

Her pacing stopped. She slanted a glance his way. "I put a bullet in his heart. Pretty sure that hit sent him to hell. And I was standing right over him—with his blood spatter *on* me—as he took his last breath."

Okay, so that would cover the *how* part of the equation. "You shot him when you were a Fed."

"Junior Fed. Fresh-faced and looking to prove myself." Her eyes squeezed closed. "I warned them. They should have listened to me. Instead, they told me I was wrong."

He leaned forward. His hands dropped to dangle between his spread knees. "Who did you warn?"

Her eyes opened. The pale blue echoed with pain.

"Ophelia?"

"I do know a lot about you. I wouldn't have agreed to take you on if I hadn't done my research. And it was done long before I sat down in Pyro with Memphis."

He'd already suspected that. "You started researching me when we met on the ice-skating case, didn't you?" The case that had first brought her crashing into his life.

"You interested me. The innocent man thrown into the cell. The prisoner who escaped because he wanted to protect his sister. The tarnished hero."

He shifted on the couch. "Don't believe all the hype."

"You don't see yourself as a hero?"

More as a villain. "My sister was in danger, yes, but so was I. If I'd stayed in that cell another night, I would have been dead."

"Judging by the scar on your side, you were pretty close to death."

"I know how to take a hit without dying."

She crept closer to him. Not tense pacing. Careful, slow movements. And her stare never left his face. "You made your injury seem worse than it was so that you could get to the infirmary. From there, your escape was much easier."

"You don't expect someone at death's door to suddenly mount an escape." She was right in front of him now. If he lifted his arms, he could wrap them around her waist. *Do not touch her.* He knew better than to lift his arms. He'd learned his lesson in the hotel room. When he touched Ophelia, he lost control.

"You think it's possible I didn't kill him, don't you? That my shot missed and the killer somehow escaped. That he faked his death."

"I don't know what to think. You've barely told me anything." No, actually, he did know one thing for certain. "The dead don't come back and kill. So either your perp isn't in the ground—and you made a mistake when you thought you'd killed him—or someone else is hunting in his place." His head tilted back as he stared up at her. "Or, option three, the string didn't mean a damn thing."

"It's the small details that are important. Most serials have signatures. Consider that part of your training. And the signature has meaning. Always. That can be lesson six." She licked her lips. "Signatures mean something. They can often mean everything."

Do not touch her. "And the meaning of the string? Care to enlighten me?"

"He doesn't forget what they've done."

Lane's brows lowered. "What who has done?"

"The victims. He's judge, jury, and executioner." Her hand rose and curled over his shoulder. "The guilty must be punished."

The heat from her touch seemed to burn right through him. But...more. Her words sent unease slithering through his veins.

"In TV shows and movies, we root for the protagonist when he goes after bad guys. It's okay for the bad guys to get tortured and murdered in horror films, because they deserve it, right? So when he started his crimes, I think some people looked away. Until they couldn't."

Lane was trying to follow along. And not liking where this was going. "He took out killers."

"Not just killers. Some were guilty of assault. Rape. Arson. If he found your crime, he'd go after you." Her hand lifted. She took a step back.

His hand flew up and curled around hers.

Mistake. I knew better than to touch her. But he'd done it anyway. Her gaze darted to their hands. Then back to him.

"How many people did he kill?" Lane asked.

"I first noticed the signature because I'd been hunting one of the people he killed. A guy tied to robberies that resulted in deaths. That string shouldn't have been there. But it was. And it nagged at me. Two weeks later, I happened to be close when the body of a drug dealer was recovered. Same damn string. Tied the exact same way. No one had noticed the string before. Such a small detail. And like I said...I think some people looked away."

He realized her *looked away* was Ophelia-speak for...*They weren't trying hard to solve the crimes.*

"Different vics. Different ages. Different sexes. Different parts of the country. So easy to miss the connection. *A tiny piece of string.* But I started digging. Trying to find any reports where someone else might have actually noticed the strings. I knew most hadn't seen them, but some crime scene techs, some MEs, some detectives *must* have commented on them. There had to be notations of them in some files, somewhere."

A weight settled in his gut. "How many did you find?"

"Fifteen."

Fuck.

"I know there were more. There had to be more. So many missed strings." A weary shake of her head. "Now he's back. No, now *someone* is finishing his work, and they want me to know." Her hand tugged free of his grip. "Had to be watching me." Her voice had lowered, and it was more like Ophelia was talking to herself than to Lane. "Could have followed me all the way to Thomas Bass. Could have seen us both." Her gaze flickered to Lane. "When we turned away, he went after Thomas. Sending us a message...Sending me a message."

Lane rose.

She backed up another step. Tipped back her head.

"Or..." He kept his voice flat. An easy task because he was always keeping himself in check. *Except last night. With her. I let go of my control. Finally.* And it had felt good. Better than good.

Hot enough to burn him alive.

What a hell of a way to go.

"Or..." Lane repeated. "The string means nothing."

She shook her head.

"One of Thomas's victims went after him. Or a cop who couldn't stand what the man had done.

Someone right in the station would've had perfect access to his cell. Would have known how to avoid the cameras and get to the prisoner. You don't *know* that this is the same killer. Especially since you just told me that you put a bullet in his chest."

"What else was I supposed to do, when he came after me?"

Lane felt every muscle in his body tense. "The bastard came after you?" A hot splash of red filled his vision for one moment. *Rage.*

"I knew what he was. I was building the profile. Everything was falling into place. I had to stop him. *He'd been wrong* about his last victim. He took out a woman who had never committed any crime. He thought she'd set her house on fire and injured one of her kids. But it wasn't her." Her words came faster and hardened with intensity. "Her ex had been the one to ignite the place. Then her ex lied and put the blame on her. All she did was run into the fire and pull her son out. They both had burns." A fast blink of her eyes. "They were recovering. But the media picked up the story about her being a suspect. *Forget-Me-Not.* He went after her and she was innocent. He *killed* her. A mom who burned to save her son. *How many others were innocent?*"

His chest ached. "Ophelia..."

"He came after me because I was stopping him. I survived. He didn't." Her gaze fell to the floor. "He didn't survive," she said again, as if convincing herself. "I was there at the funeral. I watched him get lowered into the ground."

He wanted to take her into his arms. Hell. When was the last time he'd actually wanted to comfort anyone? But he wanted to hold her. Wanted to take Ophelia's pain away. "Who was he?" She hadn't given him a name.

Her lower lip trembled. She caught it between her teeth. "I trusted him."

Fuck. He realized that this had been very, very personal for her.

"He was my supervisor at the FBI. He taught me almost everything I know about hunting predators." A wan smile tilted the corners of her lips. "And in the end, he came to kill me. But I was faster on the trigger than he was."

"Ophelia—"

She backed up. "I told you there were two guest rooms upstairs." Ophelia turned away from him. "I should have mentioned that the one to the right of the staircase has a balcony that overlooks my back garden. Since you can't stand being locked up, I think that is probably a better choice for you. When the walls start closing in, you can handle your claustrophobia by stepping outside into the night. That way, you don't have to go on your stroll."

"Who told you I have claustrophobia?" Lane didn't confirm or deny it.

"You were locked up for months, Lane. In a six-by-eight-foot cell. You barely saw sunlight, and when you did, you were monitored all the time. When you weren't in your usual cell, they put you in isolation because you fought so much."

"Protecting myself," he corrected. "Not fighting."

"Anyone would be claustrophobic after that. It's a normal response."

I'm not normal, baby.

"You don't have to take that room. Just thought you might like it better." She headed into the foyer and scooped up her bag.

He followed. "Where will you be?"

She pointed down the hallway. "Ground floor bedroom." Ophelia took three steps forward while he watched her. Then she stopped. "We should talk about it, shouldn't we?"

"It?" Lane sawed a hand over his jaw. "A whole lot has gone down since I signed on to be a partner with you. Got to say, sure feels like a crash course. You'll need to be a whole lot more specific about the 'it' in question."

Ophelia glanced over her shoulder. "I was referring to the sex. You. Me. And the bed we tried to break last night."

His hand froze mid-saw.

"We should talk about it, shouldn't we? That's what mature people do. Not act like it didn't happen."

"Acting like it didn't happen isn't a possibility for me." He took his time closing in on her.

She eased around to fully face him. "Why is that?"

"Because I want it to happen again." Didn't get more blunt than that.

Her eyes widened.

"Were you thinking it was a one-time thing?" Laned asked, for clarity's sake.

Her tongue slid along her lower lip. "I had no idea what it was. Thought it might have been a bad idea."

Fuck, no, it wasn't—

"Or thought it might have been the best idea I'd had in ages." One shoulder rolled. "Still trying to figure out for certain."

"Hmm." *Definitely the best idea I've had.* "When you figure it out, how about you let me know?"

She sucked in a breath.

And when she released that breath, he took it. Lane leaned forward and his mouth pressed lightly to hers as he stole her breath. A faint, tender kiss.

One that surprised the hell out of him because he hadn't thought he had any tenderness left inside of him. "And when you do figure it out," he rasped, "remember I'm upstairs." Then, keeping his control in place, Lane climbed the stairs.

One slow step at a time.

And he felt her eyes on him every inch of the way.

***

Ophelia waited until she heard the bedroom door close upstairs. Such a faint creak, then she bolted for her study. Her hands were shaking as she threw open the door and hurried across the small space to the bookshelf. She reached for the second shelf from the bottom, and Ophelia locked her fingers tightly around it as she hauled the entire bookshelf—*actually a secret door, not just a bookshelf*—open.

She'd been a big fan of Scooby Doo growing up. Sue her. She freaking loved secret passages and scary houses, and she'd fallen in love with this place at first sight. The study had actually been *two* rooms when she first purchased the place. A sitting area and then a much bigger "visiting" room. Or, at least, that was what the real estate agent called it. Ophelia had just known it would be perfect for her.

She'd put up a wall of shelves, installed the bookshelf door to blend perfectly with them, and ta-da, she'd had her secret sanctuary. She rushed into her sanctuary right then.

Her files waited for her. Ophelia ignored the big board with her victim profiles—all left over from her hunt for Thomas Bass—and she went straight to the cabinet in the back of the room. When she pulled out the manila file, it was so thick that it took both hands to hold.

Forget-Me-Not.

As if she'd ever been able to forget him.

She slapped the file down on her desk. It hit with a thud. Her fingers were still shaking when she opened the file.

And the grisly crime scene photos stared back at her.

FBI Special Agent in Charge Samuel "Sam" Hitchcock. Decorated agent. Hero. Impeccable case closure rate. Her training officer.

And the man she'd killed.

The only time that she'd had to pull a trigger and take a life.

She stared down at his face. And remembered the last words he'd spoken to her.

Right before his fingers had begun to squeeze the trigger, Samuel had said...

Always knew you had killer instincts, Ophelia.

"You sonofabitch," she whispered.

CHAPTER TEN

The bedroom door creaked open.

Lane had been sprawled on the bed and staring at the ceiling. The balcony doors were wide open, letting in a faint breeze. A lucky thing to feel in Savannah.

He glanced at the door and saw the outline of her body.

He'd wondered if she'd come to him. More like fucking *hoped* she would.

He knew it was close to one a.m. The clock on his bedside had told him that truth just a few moments before. Her silhouette remained in the doorway, but she didn't enter his room. Not yet. Patience was a virtue, and he sure as shit didn't have many of those left, but he remained still.

Come to me, Ophelia. Come inside. Come to me.

His eyes had long been adjusted to the dark. So he just stared straight at her. And she—

Began to pull the door closed. Ophelia was leaving.

Running away?

Not like he could allow that. "Trying to make sure I haven't snuck out for another walk?" His voice came out as a low and deep growl.

She jerked in surprise.

"I'm still here," he assured her. "There something you need?" *Say me, sweet Ophelia. Say you need me.*

"I need..."

Tell me, baby.

"I need to tell you the truth."

Well, hell. That was hardly as interesting as her needing to use him for hot, dirty sex. He sat up and let the covers fall to his waist. "What deep, dark truth might that be?" He wanted her closer. *Step into my parlor.* He felt like a spider just waiting to pounce. "Gonna confess another killing to me?"

"Sam—Samuel was the only person I've ever killed." She still remained just outside of his room.

He waited.

Ophelia lingered. Her rose scent drifted in the air to him.

Come to me, Ophelia. He'd been in that bed, and his mind hadn't been plagued by the usual torments. The nightmares that wouldn't stop. Memories of his mother. His father. Their brutal end.

The nights locked away in a stinking cell. The attacks that kept coming.

For once—finally—his mind had been on something that wasn't about pain. Not his own version of hell. Instead, he'd had a slice of heaven filling his head.

Ophelia.

He'd thought of her. Thought of going down the stairs. Finding her. Taking her into his arms and taking *her*. Driving straight into oblivion with her until there was nothing left for either of them.

"The Feds covered everything up. No one—no one outside of the agency knew about the murders Sam committed. All the lives he'd claimed. I gave them the evidence I had, but they said there wasn't conclusive proof. The story that circulated was that he had an obsession with me. He broke into my home. Tried to attack me. I just defended myself and shot him before he could kill me."

He climbed from the bed. Suddenly, he couldn't wait for her to come to him. Lane crossed the room and went to her. He stood over her. He reached out and flipped the light switch on the wall.

Illumination flooded the guest room.

Ophelia wore black cotton shorts. A black t-shirt. Her hair tumbled around her shoulders, and her eyes seemed so big. So deep.

So sad.

"I left the Bureau. I couldn't trust the people around me." She looked down at her hands. "I couldn't trust myself."

"You *stopped* him." How the hell could she not trust herself?

She bit her lower lip.

Hard.

Too hard.

His hand rose and his fingers stroked along her lower lip. "Don't, baby."

She stiffened.

Shit. Shouldn't have used an endearment. It had just slid out. A slip of the tongue.

His hand fell away.

"I stopped him, but I didn't see what he was. Not until too late."

His heartbeat seemed way too fast. "You worried you're gonna do the same thing with me? Not see me for what I am until it's too late?"

She shook her head. "I know exactly what you are."

Was that good? Or bad?

"But you don't know what I am," Ophelia added quietly.

Bullshit. "I have a pretty good idea."

Her brows lifted. "Really." Not a question.

But he nodded.

"Then do share," she invited.

She still wasn't in his bedroom. Her gaze had dropped to his chest. Skated over him like a touch. What would it take to get her to cross the threshold and come to him?

"I'm waiting," Ophelia told him. Tension whispered beneath her words.

Fine. He'd play her game. He'd learned a fucking lot tailing Memphis for the last few months. "You like stopping the bad guys. You see it as a mission."

Her face lost all expression.

"You hunt, and I'm betting it's because…something bad happened in your past, didn't it, Ophelia?" *Tell me. I want to know every dark part of your life. I want to know every part of you.*

"I think it's too late for us to talk. I should have stayed downstairs." She turned away.

But his hand curled around her arm, and he stopped her before she could leave him. He wanted to know all of Ophelia's dark parts, so it was only fair that she know his. "You know the bloody details of my past. My dad killed my mom right in front of me and Lark." He'd never be able to forget that moment. "He started screaming at her, attacking her, and wouldn't stop. I *tried* to stop him."

Now she shook her head. "You did stop him, Lane. I read the police reports on your father. Your mother was fighting to live. You ran up the stairs. You got a gun. You rushed back downstairs and ordered him to stop. But he grabbed your sister. He put a hand around Lark's throat, and he raised his knife. Lark fought to get away. He was swinging his knife—*you had to save her.*" A fierce nod. "You save victims. That is what I know about you. You had to shoot to protect your sister. Just like you had to stop Thomas before he could take the cheerleader, and you helped me in the alley. You're not some bad guy. I don't care what others have said."

"Police reports can be wrong. Especially when people lie." His thumb slid over her skin.

"I-I don't understand."

But he could see in her eyes... "Yes, you do."

She swallowed. "It's really late."

"You wouldn't let lesson six be that there were no secrets between partners. So I'll call it lesson seven. Trust has to start somewhere, doesn't it?" This was important. He could feel it. This tense moment in the dead of the night. This woman. "I wasn't the one who pulled the trigger and killed my father."

Her eyes widened.

"I didn't want my sister getting in trouble. We were just fucking kids. Our mother was dead. Our father had been shot. I didn't know what would happen. Couldn't have Lark going to jail." A scared-ass kid, that was what he'd been. "Lark was sent to a hospital after the attack. I...stayed there. Watched them bag up my mother. My father. And I said it was me. I told the cops that I'd done it." Over and over again, he'd claimed responsibility for the shot that had killed his father. Hell, he'd even fired the gun *after* Lark had because he'd watched enough cop shows back then that he'd known he needed gunshot residue on his hands to look guilty. "Lark wasn't going to suffer. Her life wasn't going to be thrown away. I took the blame."

"OhmyGod." She blinked. "The original profile on you—the one that Oliver created—" She broke off.

"The one that helped get me locked up?" His lips pulled down. "Yeah, it was wrong. Built on a lie that I created. Oliver knows that, now. Lark told him the truth. I wasn't going to do it. I would never put my sister at risk." He would have carried the truth to his grave if Lark hadn't told Oliver.

Ophelia searched his eyes. "You're telling me right now. Why?"

"Because you think I don't know what you're doing? What Memphis wants you to do?" He had to give her credit, the woman had zero tells. Ophelia didn't flinch. Didn't change her breathing. Didn't do anything but keep staring at him with her wide, pale blue gaze.

"I figured it out when you told me about the Forget-Me-Not killer." And he'd called Oliver while he'd been in the guest room. Screw it being late. He'd needed answers. "Spoke to my brother-in-law after we came back home." *Home.* That word had just rolled out. He hadn't lived in a real home in longer than he could remember. *Since my family was destroyed.* Lane swallowed. Why the hell would he think of Ophelia's creepy house as home? Shaking his head, he told her, "Oliver gave me some details about you."

"Prying into my life, were you? No wonder you think you know me." She tugged free of his hold.

He did know her. "Oliver said you were incredible at profiling. That you noticed things he didn't. That you could have been better than he was—"

"First, I am better. Let's just get that straight right now." Her chin notched up. "Or at least, I'm certainly just as good as the infamous Oliver Foxx. But I don't like being in a killer's head twenty-four, seven. Messes with my own mind. So I can't live the way Oliver does. I knew that, and I made the decision to get out of the Bureau." Her lips twisted. "Pair up my dislike of being in a killer's head every minute with my Bureau *issues,* and I think it's clear that I wasn't meant to be an FBI agent for long."

She might not have been meant to stay in the FBI. But she definitely had a skill set. "You see killers when others don't. That's what Oliver kept saying."

She didn't speak.

So Lane kept going. Why not get right to the bloody heart of the matter? "Memphis wants you to find out if I'm going to slide off the deep end."

Again, no tells. "Memphis wants me to train you."

"Like you can't do both at the same time? Profile me and train me? And here I thought you were a multitasker." A furrow appeared between her delicate brows, so he said, "You told me that yourself, when you said you went off to hunt two predators at once in Atlanta." He wanted to reach out to her so badly, but he also wanted truth between them. He needed it. "That brings me back to lesson seven. *No secrets between partners.*"

"Yes."

Lane waited and realized as the silence ticked past that she wasn't going to say more. "Yes— what? Gonna need you to expound on things there, Ophelia." Why the hell did he like her name so much? He liked the way it sounded when it rolled off his tongue.

I like the way she tastes on my tongue more.

"Yes," she repeated but added, "I can do both at the same time. I *am* doing both."

Suspicion confirmed. He'd basically known as much from the beginning, but anger still simmered inside of Lane. And there was one thing that he absolutely had to know. "Does fucking me help with the profile?"

"Why was your sister the one who pulled the trigger and not you?"

It was his turn to blink. Why had she—the question was—

"Your question was rude, by the way. I think you should apologize."

Lane gaped at her. He felt like he'd lost control of the conversation. If he'd ever had it in the first place. With Ophelia, you just didn't know.

"I fucked you because I wanted you." Crisp. A bit cool. But her eyes didn't seem cool. "Just like you wanted me. I get that you're angry because you think I'm somehow misleading you, but I'm not. This is the first time you asked me if I was profiling you. And I've answered you directly. No secrets. No lies. I am."

Hell. Confirmation pissed him off and made him feel...nervous. Uncertain. Something he hated. The last thing he wanted was for Ophelia to see him as some dangerous predator.

"But..." Not so cool. Soft. Gentle. "I can already say I don't think you're going to turn into some dark villain who goes out and attacks every person he sees."

"Good to know." Then he realized her wording had been very, very specific. Ophelia-speak. "Not every person." He let that sink in. "What do you believe, that I might have a specific victim type in mind?"

Her head tilted and her hair slid over her shoulder. "Do *you* think you have a specific victim type in mind?"

Talking with her this way was dangerous.

"Why did your sister pull the trigger and not you?" Ophelia went right back to that question.

His hands fisted.

"You and Lark went into foster care after the deaths of your parents. The autopsy showed that your father had a brain tumor. The tumor led to his violent outbursts and uncontrollable anger. Suddenly, he was pitied, and you—because you'd taken the blame for the shooting—you were the one people were whispering about. They talked about you, Lane. Teachers at school didn't trust you. Foster families didn't want to keep you. Yes, I read it all." She swiped a hand over her cheek.

Hold the hell up. Was Ophelia *crying?* He gaped at her. "What is happening right now?" He'd been on the bed, fantasizing about her, she'd come to his door and somehow—*she was crying.* Her crying had been in zero of his fantasies.

Ophelia flipped her hair back and sniffed. "You want us to share secrets. In the middle of the night. When we are both dead on our feet. You also just accused me of fucking you to create a profile. Which, yep, I get that you don't have official FBI training, but I can assure you, that is *not* the way one creates a profile. They don't teach you to do that at Quantico."

His mouth opened. "I..." Had he hurt her feelings? Was she crying about his past? He needed to stop those tears, but Lane had no clue how to do that. He hadn't comforted anyone in years. When he'd been locked away, hell, he'd even told his sister to give up on him. To protect herself.

Lark hadn't exactly been comforted by those words. She also hadn't listened to him. Instead, she'd fought until he'd been cleared.

I think Lark and Ophelia would probably like each other.

His eyes widened at the thought. What. The. Hell? Lane rubbed a hand over his chest because it suddenly seemed tight and the whole night was just out of his control.

Ophelia cleared her throat. "You know what? I don't think we should talk about this anymore tonight. It's too...raw." Another swipe of her fingers over her cheek. "Or maybe I'm too raw. I have a profile on you, one that I've been working on, yes, but I can tell you right now, if I thought you were morphing into someone evil, I would never have climbed into bed with you. It had been a *year* since I had sex with someone. You really think I'd hop back into the saddle with someone I thought might be a demented killer in the making?"

Shit. Yes. This would be the moment he realized he'd just well and truly fucked things up. *I did hurt her.* Something he had never, ever wanted to do. "Ophelia, I—"

"I came upstairs to check on you. You had to go into a cell today. You saw a dead body. You were interrogated by cops. I was worried about you. But, you're okay. I'm okay. We'll sleep and train tomorrow." She swung away and headed for the stairs.

He had to stop her. And the only way he knew to do that... "The first time my dad hit me, I felt more shock than pain."

She froze.

"He said he was sorry. Apologized over and over. Hugged me so tight. Promised it wouldn't happen again. But it did. My dad got worse. So much worse. I-I didn't know he was sick. How could I know about the tumor?"

"It's why you wanted to become a doctor." Ophelia looked back at him. The light from his room spilled toward her.

Yes. He'd first wanted to study medicine as some way of atoning for the past. He'd thought that maybe he could stop someone else from living with the hell he'd experienced. "My mom was on the floor. Blood was everywhere." He hated that memory. Fucking despised it. "I was holding her when she pulled in her last breath. If you know nothing else about me, understand that I would *never,* ever physically hurt a woman. You have nothing to fear from me on that score." *And I'm sorry if I just hurt your feelings. I can be a bastard, but I do not want to be one with you.*

"I wasn't afraid of that." Again, her voice had gone soft. Gentle. "I know you'd never physically hurt me."

He didn't deserve gentleness. "I trust my sister. She's the only one in the world I trust completely."

"And here I am, asking you to trust me..."

"Even as you build a profile on me." His hands were still fisted. Deliberately, he forced himself to relax. He exhaled. "My sister ran upstairs to get the gun. My dad used to keep it for protection." *I always keep my gun unloaded, son. Locked away. Bullets separate. I have to be safe.* His dad's image flashed in his mind. An image from the precious time before Roger Lawson had turned into a stranger. *I couldn't stand it if something ever happened to you or your sister. You kids are my world.* Lane inhaled. Exhaled again. Hard. "I took the gun from her. Pushed Lark behind me. I was going to shoot him but—" He stopped.

"What happened?"

"My mom made a sound. A cry." Fuck it. Why hold anything back now? "My name. She said my name. I looked at her, and my dad drove into me. We slammed into the floor, and he hit me so hard. Over and over. He got up. I...couldn't." He'd tried but just hadn't been strong enough. "I knew he was going to kill me. I could see my own death coming. Then the gun fired."

"Lark fired the gun."

His head moved in a jerk that was a nod. But his eyes did not leave her. "If you tell anyone else this story, I'll deny it."

She inched closer to him.

"My sister isn't going to have her life ripped apart for something that happened years ago."

"The shooting back then was ruled self-defense. Even if the investigators learned the truth—"

"No one else hears the story." He'd clenched his back teeth and gritted out those words. With an effort, Lane loosened his jaw. "I told you because, if you're going to make a profile, it should at least be based on the real me." There. Done. "I said you wanted to stop the killers because something bad had happened in your past. Something that sent you to the FBI in the first place."

She tipped back her head.

"I think you and I are alike." Was that why he was so drawn to her? Because they shared a darkness deep inside? "I want to stop them, too, and all my past is...it's darkness." *Share with me, Ophelia. Let me in.* And he realized he'd just bared his twisted soul because he wanted a piece of her soul in return. A secret from Ophelia. Something for him alone. "Tell me."

Her lashes flickered. Such long, dark lashes. "I was sixteen."

His body turned to stone. Nothing in this world could have made him move in that instant. Not when Ophelia was opening herself to him.

"It was our first official date. Joseph and I had grown up together. Elementary school. Middle school. High school." A smile came and went on her trembling lips. "But my dad had a rule—he's always been big on rules—and I didn't get to date until I turned sixteen. So Joseph waited. And on my sixteenth birthday, he picked me up. He brought me sixteen red roses, and we went to a concert." She rocked forward onto the balls of her feet. Her toes pressed against the hardwood floor. "I had to be home by eleven. Curfew. So we left before everyone else. And we snuck through an alley to get back to the car. But there was a man in the alley. He just—just sprang out of the dark, and he had a knife."

Lane's hands flew up and curled around her shoulders. He had to touch her. A sudden, surging fear pierced him, even though she was talking about the past.

"Being in that alley with Royce? It sent me back there. Back to when I was sixteen, and my world changed. I tried to act like it didn't—I didn't want to show any fear to Royce. But everything was the same. Same scents. Same feel of hard bricks. See, Joseph pushed me away. He tried to shove me to safety. I hit the bricks. And he..." Her voice trailed off. This time, she didn't wipe away the tear that trickled down her cheek.

Since she didn't wipe it away, he did. With very careful fingertips.

She wet her lips. "When he picked me up from my house and gave me the flowers, Joseph told me that he loved me. He'd told me before. Joseph would talk about our future and the house we'd have and the places we'd visit one day. I know we were kids. Kids are supposed to be too young for love, aren't they? So...I didn't say the words back to him. I was waiting. I don't even know what I was waiting for. To grow up? Maybe? Who the hell knows? But I did love him. I felt it inside, and I knew it with utter certainty when he was dying in an alley, and I couldn't stop the blood."

He hauled her closer. Wrapped her in his arms. Why the hell had he started this? Why? *Because I wanted her to come to me? To share her darkness?* Screw this. He hated Ophelia's pain. And he'd just made her relive it all.

She wrapped her arms around his waist. For a moment, she just held on. So did he. He held on far too tightly.

But then she eased back. When she looked up at him, her lashes were wet. "And, yes, I joined the FBI because of what happened. The man who killed Joseph was never caught. A scared sixteen-year-old girl didn't run after him even though she wanted to. She wanted to pick up the knife he'd left behind, and she wanted to chase him. To drive it into his back. To hurt him as he'd just hurt her. But I didn't do that. I stayed with Joseph. I called for help. He didn't have long. Barely minutes. I tried to stop the blood, I tried to tell him how I felt about him, but he was...he wasn't really there." Her hands were back at her sides. "And I had my hands covered in his blood as he released his last breath."

Lane forced himself to let her go.

"Our pasts make us into the people we are. I wanted to stop the predators who hid in the shadows and ripped lives apart. I joined the FBI, only to find out that a killer was training me." Her gaze remained on him. "I get that trust is hard for you. It's hard for me, too. But I just took a big first step with you. Consider it the start of your precious lesson seven." Ophelia turned away from him. "Good night, Lane."

She disappeared down the stairs.

"Good night, Ophelia," he rasped.

He knew the night would be anything but good for him. It never was.

Now, though, he'd have a new nightmare to join the others that swirled in his head. A young, innocent Ophelia...crying in the alley as the boy she loved bled out in front of her.

CHAPTER ELEVEN

She heard the creak of the stairs.

It was a historic house. There were plenty of creaks and groans that came with the place, that was just part of the package. But she knew *that* creak in particular. A slightly hollow sound, one that tapered at the end like a moan. That was the creak that came from the seventh step on the staircase.

Her eyes opened. Her head turned on the pillow. She kept her phone on the table beside the bed. And her gun in the nightstand drawer. The phone was charging, and she angled it up to see the screen.

Two a.m.

She could let him go. Maybe that was what she should do. Let Lane head out on another of his night walks. Only this time, she wouldn't follow him. He could wander into the darkness. He'd come back, she knew he would.

But Ophelia could still hear the echo of pain in his voice when he told her about his mother's last breath. And maybe he'd been right. Maybe they were a great deal alike.

She could remember Joseph's last breath. That faint exhale haunted her.

Something bad happened to us both. Made us darker than we ever expected to be.

Ophelia tossed aside her covers. Before she could second or even third guess herself, she darted across the room, yanked open her bedroom door, and walked out into—

Well, into him. She collided with a big, powerful body. A body she knew intimately. Lane's hands flew up and locked around her upper arms even as her hands pressed against his hard abs.

"Lane!"

"I was...checking on you."

She yanked back her hands.

He didn't remove his. Well, they did ease down her arms. A careful caress. *Then* he let her go.

She could see him clearly because she'd left on the small lamp that rested on the decorative table near the stairs.

I always keep a few lights on. Some habits would never die.

"I was worried you might not be sleeping well," Lane said in his deep, rough voice. "Digging up the past might have led to nightmares." He drove a hand through his tousled hair. "And as we've already established, you and I don't exactly have good dreams on a regular day. Much less the clusterfuck that we recently experienced."

Something else they had in common. No good dreams for them. Too many nightmares. "I'm fine." But it warmed her that he'd been worried.

And this is why you aren't the big, bad beast, Lane. If you were the villain, you wouldn't give a damn how I feel.

"How'd you know I was coming to you?"

"I..." She stopped. "I didn't know you were coming to my bedroom." Ophelia pointed to the stairs. "Seventh one creaks. I heard it when you were coming down. And, like I said, I didn't know you were coming to my room. I thought you were going out on another walk."

His head tilted as he studied her. "And you were planning to stop me?"

She pulled in a deep breath. Slowly let it out. "I was coming to say that there are other ways to work off stress." Did she put that delicately enough? Hopefully. "You don't have to walk alone into the dark."

His face hardened. His jaw. His mouth. His eyes. "What other ways did you have in mind?"

Seriously? Was he going to make her say the words? So much for putting things delicately. "Lane, I want—"

His mouth took hers. Swooped down and claimed her lips and she didn't have to say the words. She didn't have to say anything else because he was kissing her with need and drugging passion. Just what she wanted. What her body craved.

Her body brushed against his. Her hands skated over him. Her fingers darted over the jagged scar that marked his side.

He jerked back. "*Ophelia.*"

"Lane." Her breath came too fast. Her hands were still on him. Still...going down. Heading for the top of the sweatpants he wore. Just those, nothing else. He'd been wearing those sweatpants when she spoke with him upstairs.

When all of their secrets had come tumbling out. Every last savage and bloody detail.

"I'm not going to fuck you to relieve stress." Anger hummed in Lane's words.

She swallowed. Nodded.

"And you're sure as hell not fucking me because you're stressed."

She needed to get her hands off him. Her gaze fell to her fingers. Right at the top of those sweats. So close to, ah...

His dick tented the sweatpants. He wanted her. No doubt, but he was calling a halt to things. Maybe he had just been coming to her room to check on her. Being a *good* guy. And she'd jumped the gun, and now she had no way to gracefully pull out of this situation.

His hand curled under her chin. Lane tipped back her head. Forced her to meet his stare, and there was no missing the almost feral lust that fired back at her. "Do you remember the first day we met?"

She had not expected a pop quiz at that moment, but, yes, yes, she did remember it.

"You had fucking *flown through a window* in order to cause a distraction. Memphis was still training my ass, he'd told me he had someone else around as backup, and when I saw you, there was still glass in your hair."

She didn't remember the glass being in her hair. She had, indeed, jumped through a window on that case, though. A necessary act to cause a distraction and save lives.

"I knew right then I'd never met anyone like you."

Was that good? Or bad? She supposed it could go either way.

His thumb rubbed over her lower lip. A sensual caress. "Do you have any idea how many times I've dreamed about you since that meeting?"

He could not be serious.

"Maybe fantasized is the right word. The reason I was so hungry for you last night? It's because when a fantasy comes to life, you tend to lose control."

Shock rocked her body. "You barely spoke to me before we became partners." On the instances when their paths had crossed, he'd been all tall, dark, and broody. And *silent*.

"I barely speak to anyone."

Oh, fair enough. That was a true statement, based on her observations. Her tongue swiped out. Licked the pad of his thumb.

He hissed out a breath. Because she liked that hiss, her mouth opened wider. She took his thumb inside. Sucked.

Saw his pupils flare and the darkness nearly swallow the green of his eyes.

Her tongue swirled over his thumb, then she let him go.

He growled.

Ophelia liked that sound even better than his hungry hiss. "Before I heard the creak of the stair,

I was in bed, and I was having my own fantasy about you." One confession deserved another.

A muscle flexed along his jaw.

"We weren't in a hotel room. We were in my bedroom. But we were doing our best to wreck the bed." Her hand drifted down to the tent that saluted her. She stroked his cock through the soft cotton. "I didn't get a chance to taste you last night. Don't you think it's important for us to have an equal partnership?"

His fingers flew out and curled around her wrist. "Sex between us is *not* about stress."

No, it wasn't. Her heart drummed too fast. "What is it about?" She'd really appreciate it if he could spell things out for her.

"It's about me needing you more than I have ever needed anyone else." His Adam's apple rose. Fell. "Truth be told, I lose control with you. That's probably dangerous." A stark pause. "For us both."

He could be so cute. "I'm not scared of you, Lane."

"You sure about that?"

She stroked him once more. Felt his cock jerk beneath her touch. "One hundred percent." She'd seen plenty in her life that was scary. Lane didn't frighten her. But... "I am a little afraid of the way I feel when I'm with you."

His head lowered toward her. "How do you feel?"

"Like I want to lose my own control." She pushed onto her toes, and her mouth met his. No, this wasn't about stress. Or adrenaline. This was about the firestorm of need that ignited when they touched. A lust that burned even hotter now because she knew the pleasure that waited.

When she kissed him, her whole body shuddered in anticipation of what was to come. They didn't need rules when it came to the physical side of their...partnership. What happened when they were alone? That was their business. Only theirs.

She caught his lower lip. Nibbled. Licked. Then let go. "Equal partnership," Ophelia said. Then she lowered to her knees.

"*Ophelia.*" His hands clamped around her shoulders. Holding her. Not stopping her.

Good. She pulled down the top of his sweats. His dick thrust toward her. One of her hands curled around the base. The other guided the broad head to her mouth. Her lips parted. She blew lightly over the head.

"*Fuck.*" His hold tightened.

She smiled and shoved his sweats all the way down. He kicked them to the side, and she took him in her mouth. Only a little at first. Just the tip. She swirled her tongue over the head. Tasted. Savored. Then she sucked. Pulled him in a little deeper. Licked. Her left hand pumped the base of his cock as she opened her mouth wider. His taste was rich and heady, and she could not—

She was on her feet.

No, in his arms. He'd moved lightning fast and scooped her up and he was carrying her into her bedroom. One of her arms flew around his neck as she held on. Then she realized... "I don't have condoms!"

He stopped. Held her right over the bed. His head turned to meet her wide-eyed stare.

So much lust.

His eyes blazed with it.

Ophelia swallowed. "Told you, it's been a year. I don't just keep boxes of condoms here."

A jerky nod. "I have some upstairs."

Oh, okay. Great. He could leave her there, go get them and—

And he was carrying her out of her bedroom. Up the stairs. The seventh one creaked beneath his foot.

He didn't even strain as he carried her up the staircase, and Ophelia had to admit that Lane's easy strength was definitely hot. His steps never faltered, and his hold didn't waver, not even when she leaned forward and licked his neck. A growl broke from him, but he didn't stop.

Then they were in his bedroom. The lamp on his bedside glowed. The balcony doors were thrown wide open to let in the night. In the distance, she could have sworn she heard the rumble of thunder.

A storm was coming.

He lowered her onto the bed.

Strip. She should do that. But he backed away, and she realized his dick had remained hard and at full saluting attention all the way up the stairs. Well, that act clearly deserved a reward, so she slid to the edge of the bed and put her mouth on him again.

"Ophelia. Baby, dammit, I'm trying not to come in your mouth."

She licked him. A slow swirl over the tip. Then let go. Her gaze rose to find his and her breath caught. *No more playing.*

His face had turned savage with need. A branding lust that marked her as his stare roved over her body. She caught the hem of her shirt and lifted it. Tossed it aside.

He grabbed for his bag and hauled out a condom.

She ditched her shorts and underwear.

His eyes *blazed* as he rolled on the condom.

Thunder rumbled again. She swore she could smell ozone hanging in the air. The scent of a storm. From the corner of her eye, she saw the flash of lightning.

They should shut the balcony doors.

He came back to the bed. Condom on. Lust stamped on his face. His hand reached out and parted her thighs. His fingers slid right to her core. Over her clit. Then into her.

"You are so wet."

She'd gotten turned on when she tasted him. Ophelia arched into his touch, but that touch was not enough. She wanted all of him. Driving deep and hard.

What if it's not as good the second time?

"It will be even better."

Her eyes widened. Had she voiced that question? She hadn't meant to say a word. Certainly not speak her worry out loud.

He turned off the lamp. For a moment, she almost protested but then realized...

There was something sensual about the dark. About not seeing him but just *feeling* him. The mattress dipped as he climbed onto the bed. Slid between her legs. His arms were braced on either side of her, and her own hands rose to hold his powerful shoulders. His cock lodged between her legs, pressing at the entrance to her body.

He kissed her. Drove his tongue into her mouth even as his dick sank into her body. He filled her completely. Her hips arched against him. Her legs locked around his hips.

Then he withdrew.

His mouth left hers to kiss a fiery path down her neck.

His hips bucked against her. In and out. He thrust hard. The bed rammed into the wall. Thunder rumbled.

She caught another streak of lightning. Without the lamp's glow, that streak was the only illumination as it seemed to light up the whole room for the briefest of moments.

"You feel fucking fantastic," he rasped.

She could say the same about him.

His hands went to her nipples. Tight, aching peaks that he plucked and teased, and his touch had spikes of arousal and pleasure shooting through her body. She gasped and moaned, and her nails sank into him as her own control shredded.

How could anything feel this good?

Basic. Primitive.

They were driving toward release. Bodies pounding. Hearts racing. Nothing else mattered.

Nothing—

He rolled with her. A sharp cry of surprise broke from her. His hands bit into her waist. He was beneath her. She rose above him. Her knees pushed into the mattress on either side of him.

A hard streak of lightning flashed and illuminated the whole room.

Rain erupted in a pounding plummet.

His hands lifted her up. Then pulled her right back down. Up and down.

She leaned forward. Lifted up. Felt his cock driving all the way inside as she came down.

His left hand moved to her clit. Stroked. Fast and hard. No easy caresses. Harder. Rougher.

Her head tipped back as the rain pounded and thunder rumbled, and a powerful orgasm ripped its way past all sane thought. It tore through her, and she didn't hold back a scream of his name. The night was savage, and in that moment, so was she. She held *nothing* back as the release sent her body shuddering and her inner muscles contracted greedily around him.

He tumbled her back on the bed. Caught her legs and lifted them over his shoulders. He sank into her—if possible—even deeper than before. Rapid-fire thrusts that she couldn't match. She grabbed the covers and fisted them in her hands as she just held on.

Another flash of lightning revealed his face.

A need that was ferocious. A hunger that wouldn't end.

Then darkness.

The pounding of his body rocked hers. Fierce, predatory growls broke from him. Gasps and moans whispered from her.

Lightning.

Primitive possession. He stared at her as if she belonged to him. His eyes blazed.

Darkness.

In and out, he drove into her. She was open and exposed fully to him. Every thrust stroked along her sensitive core.

Lightning.

She came again. An orgasm even more powerful than the first. It stole her breath, and she couldn't scream. She couldn't do anything but quake and arch and take the pleasure as it swept through every cell in her body.

Darkness.

He erupted inside of her. Bellowed her name as his hips kept shoving against her. His grip was almost bruising along her waist, but she didn't care.

Lightning.

He stared down at her. Sated but...

Still hungry.

Possession. She could see it on his face. See—

Darkness.

CHAPTER TWELVE

A bird was chirping.

Lane cracked open one eye.

The bird chirped again.

He opened the other eye and turned his head toward the balcony doors.

I shut the doors. At some point, anyway. A vague memory. Rain had blasted inside the room, and he'd hurried to close the balcony doors. A quick run to grab them. He'd been eager to get back into bed with—

His head turned in the other direction. Ophelia slept beside him. Her dark hair fanned over the pillow. Her full lips were slightly parted. Her eyes closed.

Beautiful.

She was resting on her side, with one of her hands stretched toward him.

She'd stayed with him for the rest of the night.

And he...*I didn't go out for a lonely walk. Didn't have to escape into the night.* Why escape? He'd had what he needed right beside him.

"Sorry about the bird," she murmured without opening her eyes. "Should have warned you about him. He does his wake-up call every morning around this time."

Her voice was husky and sensual and it seeped into his pores.

"If Charles is singing, then it means I'll have to get to work soon."

"Charles?"

Her eyes opened.

Sonofabitch. I could drown in those eyes.

"I named him," she admitted, a bit sheepishly. "And...I have a bird feeder outside. One of the reasons he comes each morning. He has to arrive early because he knows I let Velma out later."

He had no clue who Velma was. And he didn't ask in that instant because he was too busy staring into her eyes.

Ophelia bit her lower lip. "I should have gone back to my room."

No, you should have stayed exactly where you are.

Her lashes flickered. "Why are you looking at me like that?" Hesitant. Confused.

"How am I looking at you?" Like he wanted to eat her up? Guilty as charged.

But she didn't answer. Ophelia rolled from the bed. Stood quickly.

Naked. With the light spilling through the glass balcony doors, he could see her perfectly. Every gorgeous inch and— "What. The. Fuck?" He leapt out of bed and didn't care that he was naked, too. In a flash, he was at Ophelia's side. His hands slid over the long slash on the lower left side of her back. "Who did this?" Rage boiled. But his touch was feather light as he studied the scar. *Too dangerous.* Too close to her spine.

"I told you that a man came at me with a knife on my sixteenth birthday."

In the alley. And her boyfriend had been killed protecting her. The moment that had made Ophelia want to become a hunter.

"Joseph shoved me out of the way, but the man with the knife was too close. He sliced with his knife even as Joseph was trying to get me to safety." Her head craned as she looked over her shoulder. "I didn't even realize I'd been cut until the EMTs arrived. I thought all of the blood was from Joseph."

Sixteen. *She could have died in that alley.* And he suddenly wished he could find her sixteen-year-old boyfriend and tell the kid what a fucking hero he'd been that night.

But the dead were gone.

"It's okay. It was a long time ago."

His head lifted. His eyes met hers.

She sent him her big smile. "No pain anymore. I promise, I healed from it."

No, she hadn't. He'd heard the pain in her voice when she talked about the attack and the boy she'd loved and lost.

"Yours doesn't hurt either, does it? Not anymore," Ophelia added.

He didn't care about his scar.

His fingers trailed over the line on her back once more. Then his hand slid over her hip as he moved to stand in front of her and...*What the hell?* "Fuck, Ophelia!"

Another scar. One he hadn't seen or felt because it was about two inches away from her right hip. He frowned at that scar. Considered what could have caused it and knew it must have been... "Who the hell shot you?"

Her hand caught his. He hadn't even realized that he'd moved to stroke the old bullet wound. But her fingers stilled his touch. "Told you about that one already, too."

"I would have remembered you telling me you were *shot*." His gaze lifted to pin her. "Hard to forget a detail like that." And he tended to be detail oriented. Especially, he was discovering, where Ophelia was concerned.

"I told you that Sam broke into my house, and I was able to kill him before he could kill me."

Her silken fingers still rested against him. His fingers pressed to her scar. A bullet wound. "You neglected to mention he got off a shot." An important point to add.

"He was already falling because of my shot, so his aim was off." Her head tilted as she looked down at the scar a bullet had left on her. "Not a big deal. No pain at all now."

He caught her chin. Tilted her face up toward him even as his head dipped toward hers. His mouth stopped just an inch away from her lips. "You are a liar." And he'd thought she hadn't wanted lies.

Her head shook. "I'm not."

"Baby, you can't fool me." His mouth feathered over hers. "It still hurts on the inside. Still twists you up and gives you nightmares. You go back there, over and over again in your head, and you hate what he did. The pain echoes through you no matter what you do."

Her hand released his. "Now who is doing the profile?" A whisper against his mouth.

He wasn't doing a profile. Just saying what he felt when he thought of his own past. The scar from the shank the other prisoner had used on him—that wound didn't physically hurt. No phantom pains. But even though he wasn't locked up, Lane couldn't escape that cell. He slipped back into it nearly every time he closed his eyes.

Unless I'm dreaming about Ophelia. Fantasizing about her. Then he didn't go to hell. He went to heaven.

"What about this scar on you?" Her hand feathered to his right shoulder. "Looks like a slice from a knife to me."

Because it was. "My father."

Sadness flashed on her face.

"Doesn't hurt anymore," he told her. The words she'd given to him.

A shake of Ophelia's head. "Now who is the liar?" Her fingers fluttered over the old mark. "'It still hurts on the inside.'" Again, the words he'd just given to her. "'Still twists you up and gives you nightmares. You go back there, over and over again in your head, and you hate what he did. The pain echoes through you no matter what you do.'"

If you could have another half of your soul somewhere out in the world, he was pretty sure that Ophelia might be it for him.

Everything I feel, she does, too.

He backed away from her because...

His own thoughts had just terrified him.

She sent him a small smile. "Too much sharing for the day?" She looked at her bare wrist, as if checking a watch. "And it's not even 7 a.m. Probably should at least have had breakfast before we unearthed more painful memories, hmmm?"

How did she do that? Smile brightly when things felt like ash around him?

"I'm going to shower downstairs. I'll meet you in the kitchen for breakfast. You have never fully lived until you've tried my chocolate chip pancakes."

Lane found that he couldn't move.

Part of him actually felt like...

I hadn't fully lived until I met you. His second utterly insane thought of the morning. Could good sex truly drive a man to madness? But, total honesty, it hadn't just been good.

The sex had been phenomenal.

He'd fucked her at least three times during the night.

And if he hadn't thought she was sore, he would have gone for time number four.

Naked and with her hips rolling, she left him. His stare could not help but drop to her ass. What a fine, fine view it was.

The door clicked closed behind her.

He looked down at his saluting dick. "Cold shower," Lane decided. Very, very cold. And maybe that icy shower would help to bring his sanity back.

Because he wasn't the emotional type, and he sure as hell didn't believe in soulmate BS.

Ophelia was his partner. His trainer in all things killer related.

And she was also...

The best sex I've ever had.

And maybe...maybe the best *everything* he'd ever had?

Third fucking terrifying thought of the day.

***

Lane's boots thudded down the stairs. His hair was still wet, but he'd changed into fresh clothes, and he could smell the ever-so-tempting scent of fresh coffee in the air.

Ophelia had beaten him to the kitchen.

He reached the landing and—

Her front door opened.

Lane immediately tensed. Then he surged forward because no one was breaking into her house. Who the hell thought they could just walk right in her place?

The man in the doorway blinked. Tall, fit, with close-cropped black hair that had grayed at the temples and around his forehead. Dark sunglasses covered his eyes. And in his hands...a black cat.

The cat hissed at Lane.

Hold up. Who broke into a house while carrying a cat?

And...almost like he could hear Ophelia's sly voice in his head...*Cat burglar.*

"Who the hell are you?" the stranger barked.

Lane blocked the guy's path into the house. "I was just about to ask you the same thing," he snarled back.

The cat hissed again.

"Easy, Velma," the man muttered. "You only go for his eyes if I say so."

Velma? The name rang a bell. Ophelia had mentioned that name but she'd been naked so he hadn't followed up.

The stranger used one hand to rip off his sunglasses. Angry, pale blue eyes glittered at Lane. "I want to know what the *ever-loving hell* you are doing in my daughter's house at seven a.m. in the morning."

His...daughter's house.

Pale blue eyes.

Velma. The cat that scared Charles the bird.

Oh, hell.

Lane backed up. "I...I'm Ophelia's partner."

"Bullshit," the man called as he advanced like an angry bulldog. "Ophelia doesn't have partners. After that clusterfuck at the Bureau, she doesn't trust anyone enough to have a partner."

Where *was* Ophelia? Still in the kitchen? Because he could sure use her help right then. "I—"

"I know your face, son," her father snapped. "I'm not like the rest of the world who sees someone once or twice and forgets. *I don't forget shit.*" His blue eyes became chips of ice. "You were on TV. You were locked away for murder."

The cat hissed again. A much angrier hiss.

Ophelia's father put down the cat. Its tail immediately curled around the man's khaki pants. Lane wasn't sure if the guy had lowered the cat so that Velma could attack or if her father had just wanted his hands free.

So *he* could attack.

There was a hardness to her father's face. A sharp intelligence in his eyes. A battle-readiness to his body that told Lane the man was trouble.

Much like his daughter.

"Murder," her father said again.

Lane stiffened. "I was innocent."

"There are no innocents." Her father's gaze dropped to something behind Lane.

Lane turned his head to follow that gaze. What was her dad frowning at so hard?

Oh, shit.

"Son, those sweatpants on the floor look way too big to be my daughter's."

Fuck. He'd left the sweats down there last night after, after—*Screw it.* He peered back at her father. Squared his shoulders and got ready to take a hit. "You probably deserve to punch me."

Her father drew back his hand.

"Dad!" Ophelia's delighted voice. She rushed between them and grabbed her father in a tight hug as she bounced.

He patted her shoulder. And over that shoulder, her father glared at Lane.

I am fucked.

She stepped away from her father. Glanced toward Lane. Then back at her dad. "Dad, have you met my new partner, Lane?" she asked brightly. She flashed her killer smile.

That smile was not going to work on the man who appeared to eat granite—and not chocolate chip pancakes—for breakfast.

"Why the hell is he in your house at 7 a.m.?" her father thundered.

Her smile stretched a bit more. "Because he slept in the guest room upstairs?"

"And why are his sweats in your hallway?"

She craned. Looked over at the sweats. "Oh, simple. I stripped them off him last night." She gave a pat to her father's shoulder. "Breakfast is ready." And, humming, she headed for the kitchen.

Lane didn't move.

Neither did her father.

The cat hissed...and chased after Ophelia.

"You and I are going to have a problem," her father said very, very softly.

"Figured we were," Lane agreed.

CHAPTER THIRTEEN

The house seemed normal. Tidy yard. Flowers blooming. A slightly faded picket fence. Two swings on the porch. Could have been any house on any street, yet the sight of it made Ophelia tense.

Pain lived in that house. Heartbreak.

"Your father seemed...nice."

She killed the engine and kept her eyes on the house. They hadn't talked much during the drive. "He's not. Don't believe it for a second." She pocketed the keys. "He's former military intelligence and knows about a thousand ways to kill a man without leaving evidence behind."

"Wonderful."

"While you were walking my dad out, I texted a contact at the FBI." Now she sent him a quick glance. "Even though I clearly don't have mad love for the Bureau..." *Understatement.* "I had to tell him what I'd found on Thomas's body. If Shay wasn't going to take me seriously, I had to go above her." So she'd gone straight to the top. Or, at least close to the top. The FBI's Executive Assistant Director. Why waste time with flunkies? She'd wanted action so she'd gone to the man with power. Mostly because she was convinced this was going to go from bad to worse. Every instinct screamed that there would be another attack.

She even had an idea of who the next victim might be and thus... "I also texted Detective O'Brien." Shay hadn't replied to the text, though.

Shocking. *Nah. She hates me.*

Lane unhooked his seatbelt. "Pretty sure the detective said she didn't want to hear from you again. You know, when she was giving us the escort out of town."

"Right. I do recall that." She did. "But I thought she might want to keep an eye on the next victim."

His brows climbed. "You know the next victim?"

"I have a suspicion." Maybe she was wrong. *Only I don't feel wrong.* "If the first guy we got locked away wound up dead within hours, what do you think will happen to lucky perp number two?"

His jaw hardened.

"The killer picked Thomas because I brought him in." This she believed with certainty. "The cops thought it was *you* committing the crime."

"You think he was trying to set me up."

Her gaze darted back to the quiet house. Then to Lane. "I think he was watching you."

"What?"

"You. Us. The crime was committed when you went walking into the night, Lane. That is no coincidence. He knew your routine." Something that actually worried her quite a bit. *In order to know your routine, he would have needed to study you.* "He attacked Thomas when he thought you were alone. Or at least, that's what I suspect." *Had the killer been watching Lane's hotel?* Her fingers tapped along the steering wheel. "You and I took down Royce Nicholson. Royce didn't make the news, not like Thomas did, so maybe our perp didn't know about him right away. Or maybe he was just waiting, but my gut tells me that Royce could be next."

"If he's watching me—you—then how the hell do you know that one of us won't be next? How do you know that this guy won't come after us?" He leaned toward her.

She swallowed to ease the dryness in her mouth. "I don't know that. So, absolutely, that's a reason why you and I need to stay on our guard." Was there any other way to be? She felt as if she always lived her life on guard. "You watch my back, and I'll watch yours. Deal?"

His gaze narrowed. "Someone comes after you, he'll be dead."

She'd asked for a *deal.* Not the promise that someone would be *dead.* But she'd take what she could get. Ophelia huffed out a breath. One more thing needed to be said. "Sorry I didn't warn you about my dad."

His lips thinned.

"He, uh, cat sits for me when I'm out of town. Has a key to my house. I'd texted him to say that I'd be back, but I forgot how early he likes to take his walks." Her fingers tapped again. "My dad is very protective."

"You don't say."

"Everything that happened when I was sixteen? He blamed himself for it all."

"Why would he do that?"

"Because he let me go out. Because if I'd stayed at home both Joseph and I would have been safe. Because my dad picked the curfew. If it had been earlier or later, Joseph and I would be..." Her words trailed away. "Any reason you can think of, my dad used it and took the guilt. Let me be clear, it wasn't his fault." She'd never blamed her father. Never. "I've told him that, but I don't think he believes me. And he hasn't let it go." *Neither have I.* "He takes the job of protecting me very seriously. So if he said or did anything that upset you, I'm sorry." There. Done. "Now, about this house..."

"You don't need to apologize because your dad loves you." Lane shoved open his door but paused before exiting. "You should consider yourself lucky." He climbed out.

She hurried to follow suit. Ophelia slammed her door and met him in front of her Jeep.

"Even if I'm pretty sure your father plans to rearrange my face at the earliest opportunity," he added roughly. "You're still lucky."

"My father won't rearrange your face."

He quirked one brow. "Pretty sure he told me those were his plans when I was walking him out."

Her mouth opened. But she didn't know what to say. Then... "I'll talk to him. I can smooth this over." *Mental note. Make sure Dad knows that Lane's face is off-limits.* She liked Lane's face.

She liked...him.

"Figure your dad deserves a punch or two."
The back of Lane's hand skimmed lightly over her
cheek. "You're worth plenty of hits."

That was really sweet. But completely
unnecessary. "He is *not* hitting you. Look, I'll fix
this. I told you, he's protective. But he respects
me, and if I say you're my partner, then you're my
partner."

"This isn't about being your partner,
sweetness. It's about me fucking you."

"Lane—"

"Why are we here?" His gaze drifted to the
house. "And why did you get more and more tense
the closer we got?"

"It's Marjorie's house. Marjorie
Mayweather." The wind slid a lock of hair over
Ophelia's cheek. She brushed it away. "She hired
me to find out what happened to her daughter,
Patience."

He nodded. She saw understanding fill his
eyes.

"I want to tell her what happened." In person.
"And, seeing as how Memphis told me your victim
interaction was shit—"

He winced.

"I thought this could be another training
lesson." She crept closer to him. Even though
she'd already been plenty close. "I also didn't want
to come here alone. I was hoping to use you for
moral support." Wind blew the lock of hair back
over her cheek.

Before she could brush it away again, he did.
Lane tucked the hair behind her ear, and his hand
lingered against her cheek.

"Here's lesson eight for you." She was pretty sure they were on lesson eight. "Victim interaction is *always* shit. You hurt for them. You wish you could make things better. You get angry and sad, but you're supposed to keep a professional mask in place at all times. And if you're dealing with a grieving family, you'll want to grieve with them. Only you have to stop yourself from crying. You have to put on a brave front and tell them that you will do your best to give them justice. *Do your best.* You can never make a promise that you won't be able to keep." This was very, very important. Her own main rule. "Don't tell the families and the loved ones that you *will* find a killer or a perp. Don't make that promise because they will take it to heart. They'll count on it. On you. And if the years pass and you can't stop the perp, it doesn't just eat away at them. It eats away at you."

"Who did you give the wrong promise to?"

"Joseph's mom." A confession she'd never made to anyone but Lane. "After his funeral, I-I told her I'd find the man who killed Joseph. That he wouldn't get away with what he'd done." Her gaze returned to the house. But she didn't *see* the house. She saw the woman in the house.

Marjorie Mayweather. Waiting years and years for the police to come and tell her what had happened to her daughter. Waiting all that time for justice.

"I never caught Joseph's killer. Still don't know who he was." Her shoulders straightened. "When you talk to them, tell the families that you will do your best. Tell them that you will be there for them when they need you. Don't give false hope. I think that hurts the most of all." She walked away from him.

And missed his touch so much.

His footsteps padded behind her.

She swiped her hands over her cheeks, just to make sure no pesky tears had leaked out. She usually had better control of her emotions. But, being around Lane seemed to stir up so much for her.

No, the whole case was stirring up the past. *Forget-Me-Not.*

Ophelia climbed up the three steps that led to the porch. A wind chime sang softly as the wind blew through it, and Ophelia lifted her hand to rap against the door.

She could have called Majorie, but the woman deserved to hear the news face to face.

A few moments after she knocked, the door slowly swung open. Marjorie crept forward, her right hand holding tightly to her cane. "Ophelia." A wide smile curved her lips. "Sweet Ophelia."

Ophelia didn't feel very sweet. When Marjorie reached out to hug her, Ophelia immediately hugged her back. Marjorie smelled like baby powder and cinnamon. Her bones felt so fragile. Her soft dress brushed against Ophelia's skin.

"He confessed," Ophelia whispered in Marjorie's ear.

Marjorie trembled.

"He told me that he'd hurt Patience." She eased back. Made sure that Marjorie was steady on her feet. "The police arrested him."

Tears filled Marjorie's eyes. "I-I know."

She did? Marjorie didn't usually watch the news, and Ophelia didn't think the story had even made it to the local station in Savannah. "Something happened, Mrs. Marjorie."

Fear. It came and went on Marjorie's face.

"Thomas Bass is dead," Ophelia rushed to say. She didn't want Marjorie to ever fear him again. "He was killed in his cell."

Marjorie swayed. Ophelia held her shoulder. Made sure the older woman was okay.

"I got the flowers," Marjorie said. "They were on my porch first thing this morning. Didn't even hear the delivery driver."

Ice poured through Ophelia. She looked at Lane. Ophelia cleared her throat. "Mrs. Marjorie, this is Lane. He's my partner."

Marjorie sent him a weak smile. "You were right. He won't ever hurt anyone else."

"Ma'am." Lane dipped his head forward. "I don't think we've ever talked before but—"

"You called me." Her eyes blinked quickly. "Don't you remember? We talked last night. You told me that he'd been caught. I remember your name. You told me...told me you were Lane. Told me that you were sending me flowers. So kind of you. Thoughtful."

Lane's gaze cut to Ophelia. She could read his face so clearly.

I did not call her.

"Here. Come inside." Marjorie backed up a step. "I just baked some fresh bread. We can have some bread and talk and..." She cleared her throat. "I need to get my handkerchief for a moment. If you'll excuse me?"

"Of course," Ophelia murmured as she stepped into the house.

She watched Majorie make her way toward the kitchen. She could see the tears falling on Marjorie's cheeks, but Ophelia didn't comment on them.

The cane and Marjorie's footsteps stopped near the mantel in the den. She picked up a photo. A smiling Patience. Forever young and beautiful.

Marjorie's left hand gripped that photo until her knuckles whitened. Her right lifted the cane. A few moments later, she disappeared into the kitchen.

"I did not call her," Lane quietly stated as he followed Ophelia into the house.

"I believe you." Which just led to a big problem. A very big one. Because now they had someone pretending to be Lane.

Except, isn't that what the killer might have already been doing when he was caught on film? If the guy had known where all the other cameras were in the holding area, it stood to reason he'd also known about the ones that caught glimpses of him, too. So, in her mind, at least, those glimpses had been deliberate. He'd shown the cameras what he wanted the world to see.

An image that *could* have been Lane.

"Oh, fuck," Lane muttered.

Her head whipped toward him.

He wasn't looking at her. His gaze was on the coffee table. She followed his stare and realized he was glaring at the large vase full of blue flowers.

"Come into the kitchen." Marjorie's cane thudded softly as she appeared in the kitchen doorway. Her tears were gone. "I have the bread ready."

"Uh, Mrs. Mayweather?" Lane called. "Are these the flowers that you said I sent to you?"

A nod. "Arrived first thing. They're lovely. Just lovely..." She turned away.

Ophelia had spotted a small, white envelope nestled in those blue flowers. In a flash, she'd plucked out that envelope. *No florist name.* Nothing at all listed on the envelope. She opened the envelope. Pulled out the little card.

Carefully handwritten words were on the card. *Patience can be at peace.*

"Ophelia."

"What in the hell is this?" Her head whipped toward Lane. "What is he doing by sending this to her?"

"Forget-Me-Not."

"Yes, absolutely," she snapped. A low snap because she didn't want to alarm Marjorie. "I think the perp sent them, too. I don't like this. Not one bit."

"No." He shook his head and pointed to the flowers. "Those. They are Forget-Me-Nots."

Slowly now, as if the flowers were a snake that might strike her, Ophelia looked back at the vase. At the blue petals.

"My sister owns a florist shop. She *knows* her flowers. Because Lark knows them—because she's been obsessed with flowers since we were kids—I know them, too. Those are Forget-Me-Nots."

She could not take her gaze off the flowers.

"I think at this point," Lane continued in a voice gone grim, "it's safe to assume that you were absolutely right."

She reached down and touched one of the blue petals. "He wants me to know it's him. He wants me to know what he's doing." The petal broke beneath her fingers. "He will be killing again."

And we have to stop him.

***

"I need access to her phone records." Ophelia unlocked the door to her PI office. Second-story office in a converted warehouse. The first floor was a bar. One that was busy as hell at night, but quiet as a mouse during the day. That was why the place worked so well for her. She saw her clients during the day. And during the night, she was out hunting so she didn't care how loud Beau and his crew at LeBlanc's became.

The rental rate was cheap because of the bar and because the owner owed her. Plus, she got a beautiful view of the river. A view that she normally loved. But at that moment, her emotions were too tangled for her to appreciate it. She rushed through the small waiting area and hurried into her office to see—

She stopped.

Froze.

Went absolutely ice cold.

"Uh, Ophelia?" Lane said from behind her. His fingers brushed over her shoulder. "Something wrong?"

About a million things. But the current *thing* would be...

Ophelia stepped to the side so he could see what had snagged her attention. "I can assure you," her voice came out surprisingly steady, "those flowers should not be on my desk."

But there they were. A clear vase full of water and blue flowers. Flowers that she now knew to be Forget-Me-Nots.

"Sonofabitch," Lane snarled.

She could have echoed him. Would have, but she was already rushing across her office and snatching up the small, white envelope that lay nestled amidst the petals. No writing on the outside of the envelope, just like at Marjorie's. But when she opened up the envelope...

Ophelia swallowed. *You won't stop my work this time.* And she finally did echo Lane. "Sonofabitch."

CHAPTER FOURTEEN

"That's a threat, Ophelia." Fury flooded through Lane, but he thought he'd done a fairly decent job of keeping the emotion from his voice.

But when Ophelia slanted him a fast, searching glance, Lane realized that—maybe—he'd let the fury bleed through. Too damn bad. He was currently furious. Fucking fucker.

Someone had broken into Ophelia's office.

Someone he suspected had not only murdered Thomas Bass but also followed Ophelia all the way home. *I think he murdered Thomas because of Ophelia. I think everything the prick is doing is because of her.*

If that didn't spell obsession, Lane didn't know what the hell did.

"He's not saying he plans to kill me." She put the envelope and card down on the desk.

"He's saying you won't stop him. That means he'll do whatever it takes to ensure you don't get in his way." Tension knotted at the nape of his neck. "That's a threat, Ophelia," Lane repeated. "Just like breaking and entering is a threat. Just like stalking you back here is a threat. Everything he is doing is a threat."

She stared at the card. "Gonna get it dusted for prints. The vase, too." Her head lifted. "There was no sign of breaking and entering at my office door. The alarm wasn't triggered."

"Because he knew how to get past your security." *Problem.*

"And that tells us something about him already, doesn't it?"

It tells me he's dangerous as hell and knows how to get to you. What if the guy hadn't come to her office? What if he'd gone straight to her house?

I would have been there waiting. "Definitely staying with you," he swore. "From here on out. No hotel."

"Glad we cleared that up." Her hand hovered over the flowers. "Okay, Mr. Flower Expert. These things in season now? How hard are they to get?"

"They're in season, and, no, it's not hard to get them. You can pick them up from any florist or any grocery store at this time."

"Crap."

"Right. And if he followed you all the way here, then he could have picked up the flowers at any point." So narrowing down the location wasn't going to be easy. Lane could hear the echo of his heartbeat in his ears. "He's down here, Ophelia. He came *here.*"

She hummed. "That means we can catch him much easier."

"It means he came here for a reason." Lane was afraid he was looking at that reason. All five feet and six inches of her. And that gorgeous reason looked all cool and confident. Like a dead serial killer just sprang up and threatened her all the time. "Aren't you scared?"

She turned toward him. "Sam Hitchcock is dead. He scared me because he was trained to kill. To hunt. He was a mission-oriented killer. He thought he was delivering justice, and nothing was going to get in his way. Certainly not little old me." Her chin tipped up the smallest bit. "Whoever left the flowers is an unknown quantity. A copycat? Someone who might have worked with Sam? Someone who just put all the puzzle pieces together and now has his own mission? I don't know yet. And I—" An inhale. "I can't be scared. I can't afford fear right now."

Bullshit.

"There's a security camera downstairs," Ophelia said as she suddenly snapped her fingers together. "I don't have one up here because my clients need privacy. But Beau has one downstairs. Actually, he has two. One at the front and one at the back of his bar. I always figured I could use them in a pinch if anything went to hell up here."

Uh, went to hell?

"This is one of those hell situations. Leave the flowers. Touch as little as you can until we can get a crime tech guy in here. Come on." She grabbed his wrist and tugged him toward the door.

Lane dug in his heels. "I think you should be calling the cops."

"I'll call the Feds. Already texted them a heads-up last night, anyway. But before I reach out again, I want to see if we can recover video footage. Come on." She tugged harder.

He followed. But Lane damn well didn't like it. On their way out, Ophelia paused to look at the lock on the door. Lane couldn't see so much as a scratch on it. "Anyone else have a key to this place?" he asked her.

"Beau does."

Again with the Beau.

"He has a backup key to my place, and I have a backup key to his."

Lane's eyes narrowed at that bit of trivia, but he didn't speak again, not until they were downstairs and in front of the bar. *LeBlanc's.* Graceful, swirling letters etched on the glass near the entrance. He eyed the small security camera to the right of the door.

"There's usually a bouncer on duty at night, too," Ophelia explained as she leaned forward and peered through the glass. "Beau is the only one who ever shows up during the day. He *should* be here, anyway." She pounded on the glass. "Yes! I see movement inside. *Beau! Beau!*" She pounded again.

Lane had also caught sight of a shadowy form moving inside. He tensed right before the door swung open. A male—looked like he was close to Lane's age—filled the doorway. White t-shirt. Battered, holey jeans. Blond hair that dropped over his forehead. Probably around six-foot-two or three, and the guy's brown eyes immediately locked on Ophelia. And seemed to lighten.

"Ophelia." A faint drawl dipped in his voice. "Didn't know you'd be back in town so soon." A wide smile curved his lips. "You are looking extra gorgeous today. That red lipstick is always killer."

"Save the false flirtation, Beau. I need to see your video feeds."

Beau frowned. "False? That's hurtful. Wounds my heart." He touched his heart even as his gaze slid to Lane. His brown eyes immediately went hard. "New friend?"

"New partner," Lane corrected.

"Really? You took on a partner?" Beau swung his gaze back to Ophelia. "Thought you were always gonna fly solo. Your business, your rules. Isn't that what you told me once—or was it ten times?" He whistled. "What happened, Ophelia? Did you meet Mr. Tall, Dark, and Moody and you decided to go all in with a stranger? So disappointing. I had such hopes for us."

"You had zero hopes. What you have are flavors of the week. The day. The minute. You have never been seriously interested in me so don't pretend otherwise now." Her right foot tapped. "As fun as this chat is, I am operating under some extreme stress. The video, Beau." Her voice gentled as she added, "Please. This is important. I need to see video footage from yesterday and last night."

Any and all humor fled his face. "I'm sorry. I can't help you."

"Can't or won't?" Lane demanded. He did not like this guy. At all. The dislike had started the minute the man began flirting with Ophelia.

"Can't," Beau fired back. "Look, Ophelia, I would give you my right kidney if I could. You know that. I owe you more than I'll ever be able to repay. But I can't give you the footage."

"I will *pay* you!" Ophelia offered quickly. "This is extremely important."

"I would like to help, I really would. I swear. But the cameras weren't on last night. Or during the day yesterday. Or…" His hand raked over his face. "For the last week." Sheepish. "I meant to get them fixed, I promise, it was on the agenda, but I just didn't have time." Worry filled his eyes. "Why do you need the footage? What happened?"

"Oh, just a little matter of a breaking and entering."

"Shit," Beau said.

Yeah, shit indeed. Only it wasn't just a *little* matter of breaking and entering. Was that even a little thing? It was the matter of a killer targeting Ophelia.

But she was standing there and shrugging one shoulder.

Lane's hands fisted.

Beau leaned toward Ophelia. "The partner looks a little tightly wound." His voice was an exaggerated whisper. "Guess he didn't take kindly to the B&E?"

Lane cleared his throat. "Let me be clear." He didn't like the way the other man looked at Ophelia. Didn't like the familiarity in his tone or stare. Didn't like that the jerk had complimented Ophelia's lipstick. Didn't like the fact that the dick didn't have the camera footage they needed. Aw, hell, he just didn't like *Beau*. "I don't take kindly to anyone doing *anything* that will inconvenience, hurt, or even annoy Ophelia. If people piss her off or upset her in any way, consider me not taking that *kindly*."

"Settle down, slugger," Beau advised mockingly.

Lane surged toward him.

Ophelia put her hand on his chest. "Easy."

Fuck easy.

Beau smirked at him. Smirked.

"Beau doesn't get what is going on," Ophelia said quietly. "And I am okay."

Lane's gaze flew to her.

He found her staring straight at him.

"No one is hurting me. I am safe."

You're not. The killer broke into your office. He followed you to Savannah.

"I am safe," she repeated. "Because you have my back, don't you?"

"Yes," he gritted out. One hundred percent, he had her back.

"So we aren't going to attack Beau just because he's being a bit of a prick, are we? Though I certainly understand the temptation. But his prick exterior is just a mask. You know all about wearing masks." She gave him a quick pat.

A pat? Seriously?

Then she looked back at an avidly watching Beau. "You don't want him as an enemy," she assured Beau.

"He looks kinda familiar." Beau scratched his chin. "Am I supposed to be scared of the new partner?"

Lane sent him a cold smile. *Yes, be scared.*

Beau reached out and wrapped his hand around Ophelia's wrist.

Lane lost his smile.

"Ophelia, I want to help." Beau's tone was more serious. "You want me to talk to my people and see if anyone saw somebody nosing around your place?"

"Yes. I definitely want that. And see if any customers mention anything, either. I know you get repeats every night."

His fingers began to stroke her wrist.

"You can stop that," Lane told him.

Both Beau and Ophelia turned to stare at him.

Since Beau didn't stop, Lane helped the guy. He caught their hands and separated them.

"Ophelia..." Again with the exaggerated whisper from Beau. "I'm not sure about this new partner of yours."

"That's okay," she replied without any hesitation. "I'm sure of him."

"He seems real possessive for a partner."

Yeah, Lane was real possessive.

"Not normal circumstances right now," Ophelia told Beau. "We're both a bit stressed."

Beau eyed Lane. "You look stressed."

Lane bared his teeth in a tiger's smile. *I will show you stressed.*

"Ah, Beau?" Ophelia waved to get his attention once more. "I'm gonna need you to talk to your staff ASAP for me. Will you do that? ASAP?" she emphasized.

Beau nodded.

"Great." She pulled out her phone. "And, just so you know, things might get a tad busy upstairs for a while. Got to call an old associate to help out a bit. He'll get the ball rolling fast for me."

A frown pulled at Beau's lips. "Which associate would that be? Because, honestly, some of the people who visit you scare even me."

What was that supposed to mean?

"Oh, this will be the scariest one," she assured him without missing a beat. "I'm calling a Fed."

"Hell."

"I need a private place to talk with my contact." Her gaze flew around the bar. "Mind if I use your office, Beau?"

He motioned lazily with one hand. "Make yourself at home."

"Thanks." She headed behind the bar counter. Then tossed a quick glance over her shoulder. "You two be nice."

"When am I ever anything but nice?" Beau asked. "That's hurtful and insulting."

Ophelia kept her gaze on Lane.

He wasn't making any promises. Nice was the last thing he felt.

She headed for the office. But paused in the doorway. And right before she went inside...

Ophelia looked back once more—and she winked at him.

What. The. Hell?

***

"So...you screwing Ophelia?"

Lane had been seated at the bar, waiting for Ophelia to finish her call with the Fed. She'd already been in the office five minutes. How long was the chat gonna take? But, at Beau's question, his attention shifted to the jerk who seemed determined to annoy the hell out of him. "None of your business."

Beau hopped onto the barstool near him. "I'll take that as a yes."

"Take it any damn way you want." *It's a yes.*

"When you got all pissed about me holding her wrist, I figured you were either already sleeping with her or you wanted to sleep with her. I get it, I do. I *want* to sleep with her."

Lane growled.

Beau sent him a half-smile. "There it is again. Man, you need to watch yourself. You are giving away tells left and right."

He didn't care about watching himself. "*You* are the one that needs to be careful."

"Because if I flirt with your partner, you're gonna tear into me?"

Lane just stared at him.

Beau leaned closer. "By the time I was fifteen years old, I had been in more fights than I could count. I know how to protect myself, and I am never, ever scared of anyone tearing into me. See, I fight dirty. I fight hard."

"Fabulous for you." Was this talk going someplace?

Laughter erupted from Beau. "I swear, if you weren't such an up-front asshole, I might *almost* like you. But, you are an asshole. So I don't."

"The feeling is mutual." His gaze wanted to track back to Beau's office. Ophelia's wink had made him suspicious as hell. And *why* had she wanted to use Beau's office? They could have gone outside for her to make the call. Could have gone back up to her place.

Unless...

Was Ophelia searching Beau's office?

She'd only do that if she suspected her downstairs neighbor. And, honestly, after the story about the cameras being down and the fact that the guy had a key to Ophelia's place...*I suspect the jerk, too.*

"I haven't slept with her," Beau revealed.

Lane flattened his hand on the bar.

"Just thought that needed to be said. I tried, of course, because she is a gorgeous woman with the most incredible eyes I've ever seen and that red lipstick—paired with her dark hair—is helluva sexy. But, alas, she shot me down. So, if you're just *wanting* to sleep with her, you need to know that she will probably shoot you down, too."

"Thanks for the warning."

"You don't sound grateful."

I'm not.

"Uh, huh. But...if you *have* slept with her...will you be a pal and tell me how you did it?"

Lane rose from the barstool.

"Like, not the mechanics," Beau hastily amended. "Clearly, I get that. But what the hell worked? She usually freezes everyone out."

Lane stared at him.

"Does that glare mean you have *not* slept with her?"

"It means that what I do with Ophelia isn't your concern. Stop being worried about who she is or is not fucking. Because unless it is *you,* then it is none of your damn business."

Beau's eyes widened. "Holy shit."

Was he supposed to be keeping this guy distracted while Ophelia searched? His partner should have told him more. Not just *winked*.

"I know you," Beau added as his fingers snapped together. "You're the killer."

Not like it was the first time he'd heard those words. But they still rubbed him raw.

Funny thing about having your face splashed all over the news and social media. At first, tons of people had recognized him. There had been whispers and gossip wherever he went. But the more time that passed, the more people forgot.

Not his story. It was too wild not to remember. The man who'd gone to jail for multiple murders. The suspected serial killer who'd attacked women who looked just like his twin sister. The guy who broke out of a maximum-security facility and vanished.

Only to eventually be proven innocent.

Yeah, people remembered *that* story.

But they tended to forget his face. They knew Lane Lawson was tall and dark-haired. That was about it. Most people couldn't pick him out of a lineup.

Funny how minds worked. Over time, images just became blurry. Memphis had told him that would happen. He'd said it was one of the reasons why eyewitness testimony could be so unreliable. People forgot. Images shifted.

Happened to most people, sooner or later.

Apparently, it hadn't happened fully yet for Beau. Or he wasn't like most people.

Ophelia's father had recognized me, too. Two for two. Shit.

"He's not a killer." Ophelia's voice. A distinctly annoyed voice.

A glance over his shoulder showed her glowering as she stood just a few feet away. She advanced, her steps silent on the floor, and he wondered just how much she'd overheard.

"Lane was completely cleared of all charges," Ophelia added when she stopped right next to Lane. Her shoulder brushed against his. "And, Beau, seriously, you know that people who live in glass houses shouldn't throw stones."

"*You* cleared me," Beau exclaimed.

"Yep, I did. Little old me. Cleared you of the murder charge that could have sent your world crumbling down."

"And I'm letting you rent the office upstairs for a steal as a thank you!"

Lane glanced between them.

"Where is my key, Beau?" she asked, voice turning all sweet.

He'd learned that when Ophelia went sweet, trouble was coming. *What angle is she working now?*

"It's locked in my office safe," Beau replied. "Same place it always is."

"Gonna need you to show me the key."

"Are you serious?"

"Dead serious. There were no signs of a break-in upstairs. Seeing the key would make me feel a whole lot better."

What could have been pain flashed on Beau's face as he jumped from his bar stool. "You think I would break into your place?"

"I think I'd just like to know where my key is."

Muttering, he led the way back into his office. Lane started to follow—

"That didn't look like you two were being nice."

His head turned. He leaned down and his mouth brushed over her ear. "I don't remember ever saying that I am *nice*."

"True."

His lips grazed her ear.

She shivered, then hurried to tail Beau. Lane wasn't about to be left behind. When he entered the office, he saw Beau opening a safe that was hidden in a small closet. Ophelia crowded in as Beau flipped the combination.

I think she's memorizing the code.

The longer he was around her, the more Lane began to pick up on just what she was thinking and scheming.

The lock opened with a soft click. Stacks of money waited inside the safe. A gun. No, two guns. A cell phone. Some sealed envelopes and—

"See?" Beau pulled out the key. "And it hurts, Ophelia. Really hurts that you doubted me." Beau waved the key. "I keep it safe. I wouldn't sell you out."

"How many people know the combination to that safe?" Lane asked.

"Just me. No one else."

Um, no. Lane and Ophelia both knew, too.

"Happy now?" Beau tossed the key back into the safe.

"Not particularly," Ophelia announced with a sigh. "And I think it's probably only fair to warn you that a serial killer could be hunting here."

Beau cut a glance Lane's way. "A serial killer, huh? You don't say."

"*Not* him. But someone who might not...particularly understand your past."

"What the hell does that mean?"

"It means, my friend," and her voice gentled, "I would really appreciate it if you got out of town for a bit. I'd hate for you to get caught in the crossfire."

CHAPTER FIFTEEN

"He's not leaving town." Lane paced inside the lobby of her office.

Ophelia glanced at her watch, then back at him. "Nope."

"Why'd you warn him?"

"Because Beau actually is a decent guy." She considered Beau's past. "*Now,* he is. People change. And I'd truly hate for him to get caught in the middle of a fight that isn't his." Speaking of... "Same goes for you."

He stopped pacing. Spun toward her. "You are shitting me."

"Nope. I am not." Where were the crime scene guys? The Feds were supposed to be coming with them. She was staying out of her main office so she wouldn't contaminate anything. And, granted, this was clearly not an emergency, not like she was bleeding out on the floor, but she had places to go. Profiles to create.

Copycat killers to catch.

It has to be a copycat. Her conclusion. She'd gone over things in her head again and again. Sam was dead. Not like he could have crawled out of his grave. And Sam had worked alone. Duo killers were extremely rare, and when she'd been creating her profile before on the Forget-Me-Not perp, there had been no sign that he was working with anyone else.

Unless she'd missed something.

Did I miss something? Doubt teased at her mind.

Lane stalked toward her.

She kept reclining on the couch, but Ophelia did tip back her head to stare up at him. When he was mad, he was extra hot. She almost told him that very thing.

"You're trying to kick me out?" Lane demanded as a muscle flexed along his hard jaw.

"No. I'm trying to give you the option to leave." Something else that she'd concluded had to be done. "When you signed on to be my partner, you didn't know what would be waiting. I didn't know."

"I'm not leaving you on your own, Ophelia."

"Ah. There it is again." A shake of her head. "How could you have thought even for a second that you were the bad guy? All you want to do is protect."

His hands slapped down onto the cushions behind her head as he leaned over her. Got really close. Close enough for her to pull in that delectable, masculine scent of his. "I don't think *protective* is the word I'd use to describe me right now."

Her hands rose to his chest. "No? Then what word would you use?"

"Beau wants to fuck you."

Hello, change in topic. "Beau wants to fuck anything that moves." Full disclosure.

"He wants *you*."

"I'm not interested in Beau that way. We're..." She thought about it. Despite the way Beau could push her buttons earlier, they were... "Friends."

"You searched your *friend's* office."

"Guilty. So good of you to notice. Memphis was right. You've got great instincts." His chest was rock hard beneath her touch. Just how often did he work out?

"Why?"

"Because I can be suspicious, even of my friends. He had the key, he had access, and he had magically unavailable video cameras. I wanted to do some digging." Her head tilted back a bit more. "But you knew that already, didn't you? You realized what I was doing—or what I wanted to do—the minute I said I needed to use his office. And you kept him busy for me. I could not ask for a better partner." Truth.

"I barely kept from punching him."

"I did ask you to be nice."

"Why didn't you fuck him?"

There was a whole lot of tension in those words. And, honestly, those words had just pissed her off. "Because I don't want to fuck everyone I meet."

He shook his head. Kept caging her in. "Why did you fuck *me?*"

Ah. Her right hand rose from his chest. Drifted up to touch his cheek. "Because I want you. I like the way you make me feel even when all I'm doing is touching you this way." She looked at her hand against his cheek. "I have never felt more aware of someone than I am of you. And when we touch, I feel it through my entire body." But she put both hands in her lap. Straightened on the couch.

He backed away.

"And I thought all of that was something worth exploring." Her stomach twisted. "Don't you?"

If possible, his jaw hardened even more.

She heard footsteps outside. Ophelia rose. "Saved by the bell," she murmured. "Or..." She went to the door. Opened it and peered outside. "The local FBI agents who are coming to take our statements."

***

He'd gotten bail. Fucking hell, yes, he'd gotten bail.

Royce Nicholson kicked his condo door shut. He smelled like shit. Piss and shit, and he'd just had the worst time of his life. Interrogated. Searched. Locked in that cell. Trapped.

But he'd gotten bail. He'd gotten out.

He would not be going back.

Oh, but that bitch who'd tricked him would pay. The bitch with the black hair and the devil eyes. And that hulking bastard who'd been with her? *Pay.* He would destroy them both.

But first, he was getting in the shower. He was washing off the piss and shit.

I won't go to prison. I won't. He could run. He had money. He could disappear into the night and never be seen again.

Maybe head down to Mexico. Hell, yes. Drink some margaritas on a beach and live out the rest of his days with a new identity.

Or...

He could go after the bitch who'd tried to ruin his life.

***

"Your office is clear." FBI Special Agent Pierce Wayne inclined his head toward Ophelia. "Got our crime techs to bag and tag all the evidence we collected. If we turn up anything useful, we'll tell you."

His partner, Special Agent Tameka Bryant, cleared her throat. "I've been dying to know all day..." First her stare raked Ophelia, then it measured Lane. There was plenty of recognition in her dark eyes when she looked at him.

Right. Of course, she knows who I am. He was sure both Feds did. They'd been eyeing him with suspicion ever since their arrival.

"Why are you getting such special treatment?" Tameka finished as her stare returned to Ophelia. "Not like Feds are sent out to every breaking and entering in the city."

Pierce grunted. "Especially when the perp *leaves* something and doesn't take it."

Ophelia tapped her right foot. They were in the parking lot, standing in front of her Jeep. She didn't respond as the moments stretched by, and

Lane wondered if she was trying to decide what she wanted to tell the agents.

"You must know the Executive Assistant Director pretty well," Tameka finally ventured. "Because Ballard called our field office personally and told us to make certain that we give you every bit of assistance possible."

Lane knew the name. Executive Assistant Director Colby Ballard had certainly thought that Lane was guilty as hell once upon a time. The man pulled strings left and right at the Bureau, but, until this moment, Lane hadn't realized that Ophelia was tight with the guy.

In general, most of the people Lane knew viewed Ballard as being a straight-up dick.

Was Ophelia actually friends with him?

"I appreciate the Executive Assistant Director's cooperation," Ophelia finally replied in a smooth-as-silk tone. "I've done some contract work for the Bureau over the years, and Ballard has appreciated my efforts. He knows that I don't cry wolf." A tight smile. "Quite the opposite, in fact. So why I can see that a bouquet of flowers in my office hardly seems FBI worthy, Ballard trusts me. He trusts my instincts. He knows how important this case is, or you wouldn't be here."

"Want to enlighten us?" Pierce pushed with a cough. "Because I'd love to know why some blue flowers sent the EAD into panic mode."

"I've never seen Ballard panic," Ophelia replied.

"Well, he called, told us to get our asses to this address and to give you every bit of assistance that you requested. And if we couldn't arrive within twenty minutes, he threatened to demote us." Pierce scratched his cheek. "I consider that his panic mode."

"Or his pissed mode," Tameka tagged on. "Maybe something about this case is pissing off the boss?"

Ophelia glanced over at Lane. "I have to confess, I am pissed, too."

So was he. More than pissed. *Is the killer in this town? Is he watching Ophelia?*

"The best way you can help me," Ophelia focused her attention back on the agents, "is by letting me know if your techs turn up anything useful with the vase of flowers or with the note." She dug her keys out of her bag. "Lane, we need to go. Got a case waiting tonight." Her head dipped toward the agents. "Thank you. I appreciate your assistance." After giving her thanks, she turned from the agents and headed for the driver's side of the Jeep.

"Speaking of the note..." Pierce's voice followed her. "Just what 'work' is it that the perp doesn't want you to stop?"

She opened her door but spared the agent a quick glance. "Oh, you know. The usual. Murder." Ophelia hopped in the Jeep. "Thanks again for your help. Give my regards to Ballard, would you?"

Lane had already climbed into the passenger seat. Ophelia reversed a few moments later, and they zipped down the road. A glance over his shoulder showed Lane that the FBI agents were watching them leave. "So..." It seemed as good of a time as any to ask. "Want to tell me why you didn't tell the two Feds that you think a serial killer left those flowers for you?"

"I told Ballard. Also told one or two others at the Bureau that I trusted. People who knew what went down years ago."

His stare slid to hers. Got caught by her profile. "So you trust Ballard. You're...friends." Yeah, some disgust rolled out at the end. Lane couldn't help it.

"I get that you have some bad blood with him."

It was one hell of a lot more than just some bad blood. "The man wanted me to die, Ophelia. The only way he wanted me leaving a cell was in a body bag."

She braked at a light. Her head angled toward him. "I'm sorry."

His brows shot up. Her apology seemed damn sincere. Come to think of it, she usually seemed pretty sincere when she talked to him. But he could easily tell when she was baiting or working her sarcastic charm on others.

"I'm sorry that you were locked away, Lane. I'm sorry that you had to fight so hard every single day just to survive." Her hand reached out and curled around his. "And I am sorry that Ballard and so many FBI agents were wrong about you."

"They said I was a monster." Flat. Bitter. "They profiled me, and they said I was twisted and disturbed. A predator who would never stop. They thought I got off on torture and pain. That's what the world believed about me."

Her hold tightened on the hand he'd just fisted. "I don't believe that about you."

He stared down at their hands. Hers was so much smaller than his. So delicate.

Breakable.

"Ballard knows he was wrong about you. *I* know he was wrong. Not like it was the first time he was wrong, either. He missed Sam. Hell, if you want the full truth..." An exhale. "Sam's case was personal for the Executive Assistant Director. They were tight. Best friends, in fact. Partners, until Ballard got promoted. He worked side by side with Sam for years, and Ballard never saw the man for what he was. So when I called the Feds to tell them about my suspicions—that someone using the Forget-Me-Not signature had killed again, I went straight to Ballard. He wants the past kept under wraps as much as possible. That's why I didn't tell Pierce and Tameka everything. I won't tell them about Sam, not unless it becomes absolutely necessary. I'm waiting to see what they turn up first."

"Because you're protecting the FBI."

"No."

"Yes."

"Lane."

"Ophelia."

Someone honked behind them. She let him go. Drove forward. "I'm waiting to see what in the hell is happening here. That's what I'm doing."

Looks like protecting the FBI to me. "Do you really have another case that you had to work? Or were you just looking to ditch the Feds?"

"I have a case. And you're gonna need a tux."

What?

"I had the job scheduled before everything exploded on us. I told the client I would be there for her tonight, and I'm not going to let her down."

Just when he thought she wouldn't surprise him again. "You *agreed* to another case tonight, even though you were hunting down Thomas Bass just days ago?"

"I knew I would be back. I gave my word to Isabelle." A quick glance his way. "My word matters. I told Isabelle I would be there for her tonight, so I will be. The Feds will check for evidence. Ballard has someone digging through all available intel to see if there are any hits that point to vics who fit the killer's signature—"

"You mean he's using FBI resources to check and see if any MEs or cops reported string tied around the fingers of dead bodies."

A nod. "Dead bodies who belonged to vics who might fit the killer's profile."

There it was again. "I fucking hate that word."

"The FBI has resources I need. They can discover more than I can on my own."

Yeah, but what she wasn't getting... "You aren't on your own, Ophelia." Not any longer. "You have me."

She braked. A little harder than necessary at the red light. Her head swiveled toward him, and he so wished that he could read all of the emotions suddenly flashing in her eyes.

"That's what a partner is for, right?" Lane continued carefully. "To make sure that you have backup. You have me. Count on me. Not some prick Fed. Me. *I will make sure you aren't alone ever again.*"

She licked her lower lip. "I'm...I'm supposed to just work with you for a month."

Fuck that. Nope. Not the time to say those words. "What's the job tonight?"

"Isabelle Delgado has a dangerous ex. She's got an engagement party tonight, and she's terrified the ex will show up and either hurt her or her groom." The words tumbled out quickly, as if Ophelia was nervous.

She hadn't been nervous with the Feds. She seemed nervous *now.*

Because of what he'd just said to her?

"She wants extra security in the crowd. That's where we will come in. We just need to blend. Pretend to be a couple. Keep our eye out for the ex who could be a major problem."

Pretend to be a couple. "I think I can handle that."

"I figured you could." Her hands tightened on the wheel.

"Why you?" Lane asked her.

She accelerated. "Why me—what?"

"Why did this Isabelle decide you needed to be the one to keep an extra eye out for the ex?"

"Because I'm the one who broke them up in the first place."

He had not expected that. *Fine, this woman will always surprise me.* "You're gonna need to elaborate." His phone vibrated. He pulled out the device. Read the text from Memphis.

WTF? Thomas Bass is dead? You good?

Good wasn't the right word.

"Isabelle's grandfather left her a substantial amount of money. She came to my office about a year ago. She had been dating a man named Gerald Baldwin. He'd burst into her life. Swept her off her feet. Three weeks after their first date, he proposed. He swore he loved her. Wanted to do nothing but make her happy."

"But she had doubts." Or else this Isabelle wouldn't have gone to a PI.

"She wanted to be told that he was perfect. That she could follow her heart and marry him. That she'd live happily ever after."

"You believe in that?" Lane asked. "That anyone gets a happily ever after?" Then he wished he could take the words back. Right then. Right there.

"For a long time, I believed my happily ever after bled out in an alley when I was sixteen years old."

You good?

He read the text from Memphis again. No, no, he was not good. *Will text later.* His fast reply.

"But, yes, actually, I do think that people can get happy endings," Ophelia revealed in a considering tone. "I think we have to make them ourselves. I wanted to be able to tell Isabelle that she was wrong to doubt Gerald, but when I started digging..." Her voice trailed off.

Lane knew how this story would end. "Let me guess. He was a fortune hunter."

"Gerald Baldwin didn't exist at all. There was no paper trail on him. No job history. Everything he'd told her was a lie. Then he found out that I was looking into his life."

Text right now. The vibrating response came from Memphis.

"Gerald—or at least the man calling himself Gerald—followed me home one night."

He dropped the phone. It clattered on the floorboard. "The sonofabitch did not."

"He did." A pause. "That is the second time that an unwanted man has tried to get into my home and hurt me. Because of my first encounter—with Sam—I had a top-of-the-line security system at my house. No one was going to get into my home without me being instantly alerted."

"What happened?" He wanted to rip Gerald Baldwin apart.

"He set off the alarms when he tried to break in. As the alarms started blaring, he broke and ran. I chased him—

"Of course, you did," he muttered.

"I did. I'm not sixteen any longer. I don't sit in an alley and bleed while people die. I give chase."

His heart seemed to squeeze in his chest. And he admired the hell out of her, even though he was absolutely terrified *for* her.

And when was the last time he'd been terrified? When he thought his sister's life was in danger?

Two different women. Two women he would die to protect.

And that realization cut to the bone.

"I chased after Gerald, but he had a motorcycle waiting down the street."

"Do not tell me he got away."

"He got away."

He'd just said for her not to tell him those words. "Dammit."

"And he's been in the wind since then."

Sonofabitch.

"I suspect he moved on to another target. He knew Isabelle wasn't going to marry him. The con he was running with her just wasn't going to work. But the thing with guys like him—guys who were never real in the first place—is that they can change their identities far too easily. New name. New hair. New eye color. Change their style, their walk, everything. So if you don't know what to look for, you can meet them again and have zero clue of who you are actually talking to."

"And that's why Isabelle wants you at her engagement party."

A nod. "She's worried he'll appear. If anything could draw him out, it would be the engagement party. I agreed to come and search the crowd." She turned the vehicle to the left. "Isabelle simply wants to be happy. *I* want to help give her that happy ending." Her attention was on the road ahead of her. "The promise I made to Isabelle is the whole reason I left Atlanta."

"Uh, you mean when you were *escorted* out of town?" He'd thought the escort had something to do with her leaving.

"I had to take care of Isabelle." Another determined nod. "After we finish tonight, I plan to go back to Atlanta. I think the key is there."

"Looks to me like the sonofabitch we're after is *here*," Lane argued. Or, at least the flowers were. Flowers that Lane suspected had been personally delivered.

Ophelia had called around to some florists while they waited for the Feds to finish at her office. No one had taken credit for the Forget-Me-Nots.

"I want to see more of Thomas Bass's life," Ophelia said. "You were hunting Thomas. I was hunting him. I suspected, at first, that our perp killed Thomas because we brought him in, but what if...what if the perp was hunting Thomas, too? There could be clues we need in his life." Her delicate jaw set. "I want to search Thomas's home."

"The cops already did that. The place is a crime scene." And that meant they didn't just get to waltz inside and search the home at will.

"The jewelry and photos of his vics were too easy to find. They were just right inside the nightstand."

"Maybe because the prick liked to relive his crimes easily." Wasn't that the whole point in keeping souvenirs for killers?

"Or maybe someone wanted to make sure they were found easily. I just—I need to go back. I have to be sure. And maybe Benny has discovered something useful on the body."

A rough laugh. "Sweetness, your buddy Benny isn't going to tell you a damn thing." But he liked her optimism.

He pretty much liked everything about her.

"Don't be too sure. I'm usually pretty good at getting people to cooperate."

"Because I'm starting to think everyone owes you."

A shrug of one shoulder.

"You told Benny his debt was paid," Lane reminded her. He was highly curious about Benny's debt. And about Beau's.

"True, I did. So maybe Benny will help out of the goodness of his heart."

"Don't count on it," he groused. Lane bent and picked up his phone. His fingers typed out a quick text. *Need help from the Ice Breakers. Will call when Ophelia isn't around.*

Three dots appeared in response to his text, and he knew that Memphis was replying.

"You have to stop thinking everyone is full of darkness, Lane. There are some good people in the world. A lot of them, in fact."

His phone vibrated with the incoming text. *Why are you keeping secrets from Ophelia?* Memphis wanted to know.

That was simple. He actually did think there were good people in the world. Ophelia was one of those people. And he would do whatever it took to keep her safe. *Because I need to protect her.* His response to Memphis.

Ophelia was one of the good people in the world. In *his* world. And he wasn't about to let anything happen to her.

No one hurts Ophelia. Not on his watch.

***

Lane shut the door of his guest room. He pulled out his phone and dialed Memphis as he paced toward the balcony. The French doors were closed, but he could easily see down to her garden. A bright explosion of colorful flowers greeted him.

Damn if the sight didn't make him want to smile.

The phone rang in his ear.

His breath slowly exhaled.

Ophelia was still downstairs, so he had a little time. They'd made a pitstop on the way to her house. His new tux waited on the bed.

The phone rang a second time.

"What the hell is happening?" Memphis blasted before the phone could reach the third ring. "I barely leave you alone at all, and now I'm hearing about a dead body? Already? Ophelia was supposed to *train* you. Not link you to another murder."

"Relax. I'm not linked to it." Not anymore, anyway. "She's my alibi."

"You needed an alibi?"

Yes, okay, he needed to get the other man to focus. "You ever heard of the Forget-Me-Not killer?"

A sharp inhale.

"I'll take that as a yes," Lane stated.

"He's a myth." A stilted response. "Someone you use to scare the predators. The boogeyman for the monsters. He's not real."

You don't need to cover, Memphis. I know the truth. "According to Ophelia, he is. Real and very dead."

"If he's dead, then why are we talking about him right now?"

Lane turned away from the garden and let his gaze sweep toward the closed bedroom door. Why the hell did he feel guilty for talking to Memphis about this? "Thomas Bass had a string tied around the ring finger on his right hand."

"So?"

"So, again, according to Ophelia, that was the Forget-Me-Not killer's signature."

"Fuck."

"Indeed. And the fact that Forget-Me-Not flowers were left in her office today? Well, you can see where I might be feeling a little on edge."

"They were left where?"

"Inside her locked office. Oh, and some were delivered to one of her clients. Granted, I am the new Ice Breaker. I don't have all the crime-solving and criminal-hunting experience that you possess, but, to me, those are some seriously waving red flags."

"I'm coming to you." Immediate. "I can give you backup. Whatever you need. I am on my way."

"No. We're leaving first thing in the morning." Because Ophelia was determined. "We have a job tonight, but we'll head out early on a return trip to Atlanta. We want to talk to the ME who worked on Thomas. We also want to search the guy's house."

"Uh, can't help but notice that I sure am hearing a whole lot of 'we' talk."

Lane straightened his spine. "We're partners."

"For a man who sure as hell seemed resistant to the idea of working with Ophelia, you seem to have jumped in with both feet."

"She threw me in the deep end," he retorted. "I had to learn how to swim."

"*Lane.*" That was worry. No missing it.

Just as there was no missing the creak he'd just heard on the stairs. Stair number seven. "Samuel Hitchcock," he said as his voice lowered even more.

"Who? Can you speak up?"

No, he couldn't. "Samuel Hitchcock. A dead FBI agent. Send me anything and everything the Ice Breakers can find on him, will you?"

"You mean, send it to you and your partner."

No, that wasn't what he'd said. "Send it to me, and I'll share it with Ophelia. Look, I have to go. Just know that I have her back. She has mine."

"And...the two of you are hunting a killer."

"Better than him hunting us." *Though I'm worried that is exactly what he's doing.*

"Why do you want Samuel Hitchcock's file?"

Ophelia had to be at the top of the stairs. He didn't have more time to waste.

"You know..." Memphis continued carefully. "I am actually familiar with the name. Ophelia and I go way back. Agent Hitchcock was obsessed with her. He broke into her house. He tried to kill her."

"But she killed him instead. Yeah, I know. I heard that story." Was Memphis testing him? If the guy was as close with Ophelia as he claimed, Memphis would know the truth. Even on a bad day, Memphis was a bloodhound. No way he hadn't dug into Ophelia's life. "I'm interested in a different story about him."

"You know." Surprise. "She told you?"

"I know. I'm her partner, after all. Lesson seven. There are no secrets between partners."

"Holy shit." Now it was surprise. It was amazement. "She is giving you numbered lessons? And you're quoting them to me? What is happening in my life right now?"

"For the record, I actually came up with lesson seven. But she liked it, too. Now, to get back on track. I want to see the files on Samuel. The ones that I know the FBI has, but that Executive Assistant Ballard would never in a million years turn over to me."

"Because you don't have clearance."

"Because the man hates me."

"Fair enough."

"Listen..." Lane didn't want any more BS. "You don't need to hold back with me. Don't play games. I know the Forget-Me-Not killer isn't a myth. I know what he was doing, and I know Ophelia stopped him."

"Sorry." Gruff. "Didn't want to share her secrets out of turn."

Time was up. He pictured Ophelia with her head pressed to the door and hearing every word he spoke. "Are you going to help or not?"

"I'll see what I can do. Just don't go getting your ass killed, got me? Pretty sure your sister would never forgive me if you did some stupid shit like that. Your sister or her husband. And I kind of like them both." Memphis hung up.

Lane tossed the phone onto the bed. It landed next to his new tux. He hurried to the bedroom door. Grabbed the knob and twisted. Had Ophelia heard any part of that conversation? "I can explain—" he began.

Ophelia wasn't there.

But he heard a hiss. Lane glanced down. Ophelia's black cat sat in front of his door. Her yellow eyes gazed straight up at him.

He'd never had cats growing up. Not before the nightmare with his father. And definitely not like he could haul a pet from foster house to foster house with him after his father had been buried.

Lane didn't know what you were supposed to do with a cat.

And Ophelia's cat clearly hated him.

But Lane found himself crouching in front of the cat. He stared into those yellow eyes. "Are you going to claw me to pieces if I try to pet you?"

Her tail swished.

"That had better be a no." Taking his life into his own hands, he reached out and gave the cat a little pet.

She stretched beneath his touch. No clawing. No hissing.

So he scratched her behind the ears.

Her body vibrated with a purr.

"Animals are really good judges of character." Ophelia's considering voice.

He looked up. She was climbing up the last few stairs. He had *not* heard the seventh stair creak. And he was pretty sure that had been deliberate. She'd made sure to approach without making a sound.

"At least, that's what I've been told." Ophelia stopped on the landing. "Velma clearly is warming up to you."

Are you warming up to me, too? He gave the cat one more scratch, then rose to his feet. Velma walked forward and rubbed her head against his leg. Her tail curled around him.

"She's claiming you." Faint surprise filled Ophelia's voice.

What would it take for me to claim you? Lane was wise enough not to voice those words.

"Huh." Ophelia eyed her cat with a bit of chagrin. "Well...there's that." Her stare rose to meet his once more. "By the way, you don't have to call Memphis in order to get information on my past and on Sam."

Shit. She had heard.

"There is another way for you to access his files. A much faster way."

He sawed a hand over his jaw. The stubble there pricked his palm. "What way might that be?" He didn't deny calling Memphis. What would be the point?

"I left my study open downstairs. Even have my secret passage open for you, too."

"You have a secret passage?"

"You're sounding judgy."

Guilty.

"The file I have on Sam is down there. You can read the profile I created. All the crimes I connected to him. And you can also see the full report that I submitted to the FBI." A nod. "The report that they have since classified. I'm not sure that even Memphis would be able to get access for you. Despite his considerable connections."

"Why are you sharing this with me?"

"Because we're partners. That's what we do, right? No secrets. Lesson seven." She turned away. "We'll be leaving at six p.m. I'm sure you'll look extra sharp in the tux." She started down the stairs.

"Ophelia." He hurried after her.

She paused. Her hand trailed down the banister.

"Are you still making a profile on me?" That had been what Memphis wanted, after all. And maybe...maybe Lane wanted to see what she truly thought of him.

She looked over her shoulder. "No."

Her answer had him taking a step back. "Why not?"

"Because I don't profile friends."

Friends. An F word that he hadn't expected to hear from her. "Is that what we are?"

"Yes. Turns out, my cat isn't the only one who likes you."

"We're...friends." The word tasted wrong. Wasn't strong enough. Didn't define them. "Friends don't usually fuck."

"Put it all out there, don't you?" Ophelia continued her path down the stairs. "We do." She stopped. Seventh stair. It creaked. "Unless you don't want to be friends with me?"

And there was something almost sad about her words. Vulnerable.

"I would very much like to be friends with you." A low response from him.

She glanced back and sent him a wide smile.

Then she was gone.

He stared after her. Considered the possibilities that waited.

But we won't just be friends, Ophelia. We will be so much more.

No, he could never, ever just be friends with her.

CHAPTER SIXTEEN

"You look dashing." He did. Or, more accurately, Lane looked dead sexy.

They were dancing at the engagement party, he wore a tux that fit him like it had been made just for his body, and Ophelia was pretty sure that most of the women in that ballroom were imagining what Lane's body would look like *without* the tux.

Luckily, she didn't have to imagine.

His hands tightened on her waist. "You look beautiful." His head lowered. His lips came to rest near her ear. "The sexiest woman I've ever seen."

Her breath caught. Mostly because he'd just given a sensual lick to the tip of her ear. "You, ah, like the red?' Sure, black was her favorite color, but she'd switched things up. Gone a bold red. A dress with spaghetti straps that hugged her curves and ended mid-thigh. A dress that screamed...

Come and get me.

She wanted to attract attention—Gerald's attention. If he was there, she wanted him to see her. To come after her.

And to leave Isabelle the hell alone. The woman was happy. Beaming as she stood with her groom, August Wade. They were the picture of a loving couple.

And her jerk ex wasn't going to ruin that for them.

The band played a slow, romantic tune, and as Lane swept her around the dance floor, Ophelia made sure to study everyone in the room. Right after arriving, she'd given orders to the security staff. They already had received pictures of Gerald, but, as she'd told Lane, men like Gerald were extremely good at reinventing themselves. The staff knew that if they saw anything suspicious, they were to alert her, immediately.

"So, ah, how did your afternoon reading go?" Ophelia asked, hoping she sounded casual as she eased her head back and peeked up at Lane.

"You didn't tell me you tried to save him."

Her steps stumbled. But he kept moving, gliding her effortlessly. "Where did you learn to dance?" she asked. "You are really light on your feet."

"It wasn't in the foster homes. Most of the people there hated me."

Her heart squeezed. "Not all of them, surely."

"They hated me," he said again. "They thought I was a ticking time bomb. They wanted me gone." A twisted curve of his lips. "Different families tried to keep Lark. They wanted to make a home for her."

"But no one wanted to make a home for you?" A careful whisper. Her heart wasn't squeezing. It was breaking. For him.

"Quite the opposite." A mocking laugh. "They wanted me *out* of their homes."

Damn them. "You can stay in my home anytime. Always." Crap. She should backtrack with that. But...Too late.

He smiled at her. "I'm already in your home, Ophelia."

Yes, he was.

"I've also been in *you*," he pointed out in a wickedly sensual tone.

Immediately her gaze whipped around. What if someone had heard those words?

"And I can't wait to be again. At the earliest opportunity."

The party was almost over. They'd gotten through the night without any incidents. Just a little longer, and the engaged couple would be leaving. Isabelle had given Ophelia a complete timeline earlier so she could better keep watch. About thirty more minutes, and Ophelia could depart with Lane. Then about thirty more minutes for the drive and then they'd be home. *Hello, earliest opportunity.* Until then, she had a job to keep doing.

"You tried to save Samuel after you shot him. Why?"

He'd certainly jumped right back to that topic. "Lesson three," she reminded him.

"Dead men can't give families closure."

Warmth slid through her. It was really rather adorable to her the way he remembered her lessons. "But it was more than that," she confessed because there was no need to hold back. Not with him. "I had never killed anyone before." She hoped to never kill again. "And even though I knew what he was, even though I knew he came there to kill me, I still kept seeing him as the guy who was training me. The guy who brought in coffee and doughnuts and laughed when he talked about his niece and nephew." That was the thing... "Even killers have families. They have lives. They don't just exist in some evil void." Her stare returned to him. "They have people who love them." Her hands gripped his shoulders, and her fingers pressed into the fabric of his tux. "I'd had dinner with Sam's wife the week before Sam tried to kill me." The woman had... "She came to my office at the FBI after his funeral," Ophelia whispered. "She was crying and, ah, she'd been told the truth. But she didn't believe it. And she was so angry. She slapped me, and I just—I told her I was sorry. Because I was sorry that she was in so much pain."

"Ophelia..."

She shook her head. Went back to scanning the crowd. "I need to go and check in with Isabelle." She stopped dancing. "Could you do another sweep through the kitchen area? All of the catering staff members were vetted, and I know it seems like overkill to keep checking back there, but I'd feel better if you did one final search in that room."

"On it."

She sent him a grateful smile and slipped from his arms. It was easy to navigate through the crowd and get to Isabelle's side. The woman was absolutely glowing. Ophelia hurried closer.

Her phone vibrated. An elegant, evening clutch dangled from her left hand. The delicate chain looped around her wrist, so her hand had been free. The phone vibrated again, and Ophelia plucked out her phone from the clutch. She frowned at the screen. She'd set the device to vibrate instead of ring, and the call was from a number she'd programmed in just days before.

Detective Shay O'Brien.

She took the call. "Hello?" Ophelia put a hand to her other ear so she could hear the detective.

"He's missing."

The band started playing a louder, faster tune.

"I can't quite hear you," Ophelia told her. "Say it again?"

"*He is missing.* Thought you needed to know."

"Who's missing?"

"Royce Nicholson."

***

Lane had nearly reached the kitchen doors when his phone pulsed in his tux pocket. Pausing for just a moment, he fished out the phone and swiped his finger over the screen. A text had just come through for him.

You're like me.

He didn't recognize the number. Had no freaking idea what the text sender meant, and he was—

Don't tell Ophelia. A second text.

His body snapped to attention. Instantly, he spun and looked across the ballroom. His stare landed on Ophelia. She was talking on her phone as she stood just steps away from Isabelle.

Another text. *I'm watching you.*

His stare whipped around the room. He saw couples dancing. People talking. The white-uniformed catering staff handing out food and drinks. No one seemed to be looking his way.

Lane's phone vibrated again.

Gerald is here.

How the fuck did the text sender know about Gerald? Lane fired out a response. *Who are you?*

He saw the dancing dots on the screen. Then...

Pictures of Ophelia. Ophelia jogging. Ophelia on her phone. Ophelia having dinner.

And his mysterious sender fired him one more text along with the pics. *He took these of Ophelia. Gerald isn't here for Isabelle. He's here to kill Ophelia.*

The fuck that was happening.

He's out back. Hiding in the rear of a catering truck. Another message.

Lane's heartbeat thundered faster.

Are you going to stop him... The text popped on his screen. *Or am I?*

Lane's head snapped up. He looked to the spot where he'd last seen Ophelia, only she wasn't there. His gaze swept the crowd. Once, twice. Nowhere did he see a beautiful woman in a red dress. He rushed through the dancers, looking to the left and right. No Ophelia.

His phone vibrated again.

Lane looked down.

You had your chance. Guess it's my turn.

***

"How can he be missing? You had him locked up!" Ophelia had ducked into the lobby so she could hear the detective better because surely, she'd been mistaken. Shay had not just told her that Royce was missing.

"Bail," Shay informed her flatly. "Guy comes from money, and he had plenty to throw around. He got out, and I put a cop on him because—look, I *was* taking what you said seriously, all right? I also wanted to make sure Royce didn't get anywhere near his vics again, so I assigned a uniform to watch him. But the perp vanished. Pulled a straight up Houdini. Went in his condo, and when he hadn't been seen in hours—hell, when his lawyer couldn't get Royce to answer his door—we did a welfare check. He was *gone*. His place was trashed, like he tore it apart looking for something, and he was in the wind." A pause. "But you need to know that his computer was still open and on. The last search was on the screen—a search for you. He had your PI office address on the screen."

"Fantastic." *Come for me, you bastard.* "Just make sure that Sylvia Stuart is protected, would you?" After Royce's arrest, Sylvia and her new boyfriend Derek had gone to the station. Sylvia had given her statement to the cops. She'd wanted Royce locked away.

And now he's out hunting.

"I'm on it," Shay assured her. "But you need to watch your ass, Ophelia."

It was sweet that the detective cared. "And here I thought you didn't like me."

"I don't, but...but, *dammit*, I remember another one."

"Another what?"

"Another string."

Ophelia's blood iced. "Excuse me?"

"I didn't think a damn thing about it. It was so small. And it wasn't a murder. There was no big investigation. It was an overdose."

"When. Where." She edged back toward the double doors that led to the ballroom. Her gaze swept over the crowd. One of the security guards caught her eye and nodded.

The happy couple kept dancing.

"About two months ago. And the location where the body was discovered? It was—hell, it was behind Pyro."

Pyro. The name was certainly familiar to Ophelia. Royce had hunted at Pyro. She'd brought him down in the alley behind Pyro.

"Drug overdose," Shay repeated. "Fentanyl. Do you know how many of those we see? I would have forgotten him. I know that's shit to say, but it's true. There are so many ODs..." A sigh. "He had this string wrapped around his finger, and I thought...poor sonofabitch. Whatever you wanted to remember so badly, you never will." Another sigh. *"You never will."*

"Are you *sure* it was an overdose?"

"Yeah, Benedict ran the labs. There was no sign of foul play. Just your standard OD in a back alley. That crap is like a broken record some days."

"Did *he* have a record?"

"What?"

"The dead man in the alley. Did he have a record?"

"Well, yeah."

"For what?"

"He was a drug dealer. Got busted three times near a school last year. Petty larceny. Vehicle theft. But drugs were his main game. Not real surprising that they were what took him out."

"You wouldn't be telling me this story if you still believed the man overdosed." Everyone was smiling as they watched Isabelle and August. The security staff members were positioned exactly as they should be.

She didn't see Lane. Was he still in the kitchen?

"I *do* think he overdosed," Shay protested. "Got the tox screens to prove it."

"But you also think that maybe he had help with that OD?"

"I think he had a string on his finger." Rushed. "I think that I felt like you needed to know. Miles Dodge. That was his name. And now I've got a hundred other cases to work. Just be on the lookout for Royce, would you? Keep your eyes open and your guard up. All of the breadcrumbs are saying he is coming your way."

"Thanks for the warning." She had a case to work, too. "And watch yourself, Detective." Ophelia hung up and slid the phone back into her small clutch.

Breadcrumbs, my ass. Royce hadn't left breadcrumbs. He'd left a giant neon sign pointing right at her. And maybe...*That's the problem.*

The dance ended. The crowd cheered for the couple. Ophelia stepped toward them.

Her phone vibrated.

She looked down. A text had just come through from Lane. *Gerald is here.*

Hell.

The happy couple was hurrying out—coming right toward the lobby. She knew they were supposed to take pictures and do more toasting, but it was time to *go.*

He's out back. Catering truck. On my way to get him. Another text from Lane.

Lane wasn't going to be on his way alone. *Wait for me.* Her immediate reply. There was a whole reason they were partners, dammit.

But...

Lane fired a response. *You protect Isabelle. I'll get him.*

How about they did both? She'd protect Isabelle and get backup for Lane. She grabbed the nearest security guard. "Go out back," she ordered him. "Got a report that Gerald is here. My partner needs help."

The guard's brow furrowed. He did not spring into action.

"Out back," she snapped at him. "*Now.*"

He rushed away. Finally, springing into semi-action. Ophelia pushed past the photographer who'd just snapped another pic of Isabelle and August. The man barked at her for ruining his shot, but Ophelia didn't stop until she was beside Isabelle. She caught her client's hand. "Time to go."

"But we don't leave for twenty more minutes!"

Ophelia shook her head. "You need to leave now, Isabelle."

Isabelle's dark eyes widened. "We need to leave." She pulled from Ophelia and grabbed her fiancé's arm. "August, let's go. Please."

***

There were four catering trucks out behind the venue. A few members of the catering staff— all wearing their signature white uniforms— rushed past him as they took in more supplies for the party. Tension held Lane in a tight grip. Hell, yes, this felt like a trap.

He pulled his gun from under his tux.

Lane wasn't exactly unprepared. He'd been packing all night. And Lane was a damn fine shot. His heart thudded fast as he crept toward the catering trucks. The nearest one had a back door that was partially open. He swung it open fully—

And he saw two of the catering staff making out. The woman had the man pinned against the far wall of the truck and their mouths were locked tightly together. But at the sound of the door swinging open—the hard grate of metal—they broke apart.

Not Gerald.

"Is that a gun?" the woman squeaked.

"Staff security." Lane was working with Ophelia, so, yeah, he counted as security. Lane turned away from the couple. Headed for the next truck. He could hear a hum coming from the vehicle. He passed the side, saw the big catering logo on the truck, and approached the rear door. The door was shut, but it pulled open easily with a tug.

When it opened, he caught sight of a massive chest freezer in the back. No kissing couple this time. But...

The freezer was open. Partially. He could see fabric hanging out the side.

Fuck me. Lane climbed into the back of the truck. There was some illumination back there, running from an overhead light in the back.

Is that a tablecloth hanging out of the freezer? The black fabric looked like the heavy cloths that had covered all the tables inside. He edged closer. His right hand still gripped the gun, and his left lifted up the top of the freezer.

It wasn't a tablecloth. It was part of a shirt. A shirt still being worn by the poor bastard in the freezer. A bastard with blood all over his chest. "Fuck—"

The back door to the truck slammed closed. Lane heard the wrench of the lock.

And his phone vibrated.

Had to be Ophelia texting again. He grabbed for the phone.

The text wasn't from Ophelia.

You missed your chance.

Lane looked back at the man in the freezer. Blood was everywhere. Covering his chest. Splashed onto the packaged bags of food beneath him.

And his skin was ashen. The man wasn't breathing. His chest wasn't rising, and when Lane touched him, the guy was ice cold.

Lane's phone vibrated again.

So I took my turn...

***

The *please* was all it took from Isabelle. August spirited her away. The crowd followed, tossing well wishes and clapping in the couple's wake. Ophelia stayed with the couple until August tucked Isabelle into the waiting limo. Moments later, Isabelle and August left with a flash of the limo's taillights.

Safe and sound.

Ophelia whirled back and stared up at the ornate building. Plenty of people were lingering. Plenty would still dance the night away and enjoy the open bar. But her client was safe. The job was done.

Gerald is here. Those words kept repeating through her mind.

She yanked out her phone and called Lane even as she hurried toward the back of the building. Her high heels clicked with every step.

The phone rang and rang, but Lane didn't pick up.

She kicked off her shoes and flat-out ran for him. Fear blasted through her. More fear than she could remember feeling in a very long time. Lane shouldn't have gone out back without her. They were partners. That meant something.

Her grip nearly broke the phone when his voicemail picked up.

She reached the back of the building and barely felt the rough concrete digging into her feet. Four catering trucks waited. The guard she'd grabbed earlier was climbing out of the back of the truck closest to her.

"Nobody in this one!" he yelled.

She raced past him to the second truck. She jerked on the door.

Locked.

"I'll check the next one," the security guard said as he jogged toward her.

There was a big handle attached to the rear of the truck in front of her. She could hear humming coming from inside. She knew some of the trucks had refrigeration systems because her aunt owned a catering business. Those systems were standard in an operation of this size.

Ophelia grabbed the big handle and wrenched it to the side. She hauled open the door. The guard was still close and he could—

"Ohmygod!" A stunned exclamation from the guard. He'd staggered to a stop close by.

Ophelia stared into the interior of the truck. Lane crouched over a man—and the small overhead light in the back of the truck revealed that the man who sprawled there was covered in blood. Deep slash wounds crisscrossed over his chest. His blood had soaked his shirt, and the blood was all over Lane's arms and hands.

"He killed him," the guard gasped.

"Lane is *saving* him," Ophelia snapped back. "Get that crap straight. And go call an ambulance, now! Get help!" She shoved the guard into motion when he remained frozen before she jumped into the back of the catering truck.

The guard shouted, "*Help! We need help!*"

Ophelia scrambled to Lane and sank to her knees beside him. One look at the bloody man, and she'd known it was Gerald. Different hair. Thinner. But Gerald.

So many knife wounds to his chest.

Lane's head turned toward her.

"Tell me what to do," she urged him. Yet even as she said those words, her gaze fell to Gerald's right hand.

And she saw the string tied around his ring finger.

CHAPTER SEVENTEEN

A bloody mess. That was what remained in the back of the catering truck. The knife was there—one of the knives that belonged to the catering company. Blood stained Lane's new tux, and Ophelia hated the grim set of his jaw.

"How did you know?" Lane asked quietly. His hands were fists at his sides.

"You texted me." The cops were still swarming. People at the party were gaping at the scene. This engagement celebration would not be forgotten anytime soon. "I got Isabelle to safety and ran to you as fast as I could." She glared at him. "Wait for your partner. That is lesson nine. You *don't* leave your partner."

"He was here."

"Yes, well..." *You still have Gerald's blood on you to prove it.* "We could have gone after him together." *And you could have been killed going off on your own. You could have been the one in the back of a catering truck with stab wounds all over you.* Unable to hold back—because she knew exactly what did happen when you held back—Ophelia surged forward and wrapped her arms around Lane. She held him tightly.

"Uh, Ophelia?"

"I haven't been that scared in a long time."

"Baby, I have blood all over me."

Right. "So do I." Because she'd helped him to *save* Gerald Baldwin. The man had still been breathing—barely, but he had been alive—when the ambulance rushed him away. "When the cops are done with us, we're going home and taking the longest shower in the world."

"Ophelia."

Her head tipped back.

"How did you know I hadn't been the one to attack him?" He shook his head. "As soon as you opened the door, *how did you know?*"

Oh, that was easy. "I didn't know."

Lane's brow furrowed. "But—but you said—"

"You were saving him." Ophelia remembered exactly what she'd said. "You think I was going to let that green guard scream to the world that my partner had just tried to murder someone?"

His brow smoothed as a mask settled over Lane's face. "So you weren't certain I didn't try."

Her mouth hitched into a half-smile. "I'm certain of you. If you were going to kill someone, you wouldn't hack them in the chest at least..." She thought of the wounds she'd seen. "Seven times."

"What would I have done?" His green gaze seemed extra intense.

"Probably stabbed him in the heart. One and done. Or sliced his throat open. You told me once that you knew how to give yourself an injury that would look like hell but wouldn't kill you." Her smile had vanished. "With that knowledge, I have to believe the reverse is true, too. I think you could kill easily, swiftly, and not have to carve up a man's chest to do it."

"I don't know if that should make me feel better or worse."

She glanced to the right. "The cops are closing in on us. Want to clue me in on what went down?"

"I found him that way." Low. "He was in the chest freezer against the wall in the truck. Thought he was dead at first, then I felt a weak pulse. I was trying to save his ass."

"I think you *did* save his ass."

"That was Gerald Baldwin."

She nodded.

"I received texts from the SOB who tried to kill him," he added. "I was told Gerald was here."

Chills skated down her spine. "Show me."

Lane handed her the phone. But even as she scrolled through the texts and a heavy knot of lead filled her stomach, *another* text appeared for him.

From the same number.

The phone vibrated in her hand.

You disappointed me.

The lead grew heavier.

And another text appeared...

You're just as bad as they are.

"What the hell?" Ophelia breathed.

The phone vibrated once more.

So you'll get the same end they do.

"I think I made an enemy," Lane said as he read the texts.

She shook her head. "Lane..."

"FBI!" A voice blasted. A vaguely familiar voice. She looked up to see FBI Special Agent

Tameka Bryant and her partner Pierce Wayne pushing through the crowd. Tameka's dark eyes zoomed in on Ophelia. The Feds hurried forward.

"One damn day," Pierce groused when they closed in. "And you two are already covered in blood? What in the hell happened here tonight?"

Ophelia spared a glance for the nearby catering truck. Her heart raced too fast, and her grip on the phone had turned sweaty. "Attempted murder."

"That's a whole lot of blood on the tux, my man," Pierce told Lane.

"I am aware." Lane's flat response.

"Lane saved the vic's life." But Ophelia knew that hadn't been what the perp sending the texts wanted. The man had *wanted* for Lane to finish off Gerald. Finish him off—or, hell, just stand there and let Gerald die.

But Lane hadn't.

And now the killer seemed to be turning his fury onto Lane.

She pushed the phone toward the Feds. "Really gonna need you to find out who sent these texts, ASAP." The Feds should be able to do it.

"Why?" Pierce asked.

But Tameka was already scanning through the texts. "Damn," she said.

"Because Gerald Baldwin's attacker is the one who sent the messages," Lane told him. "And it seems like he might be planning to come for me next." He shrugged.

Shrugged?

"So you can stop him," Lane continued in his emotionless voice. A voice that perfectly matched his expressionless face. "Or I can."

***

"No." Ophelia slammed the front door shut. "This isn't happening." She dropped her clutch on the nearby table and tossed her high heels beside the door.

Lane quirked a brow and stared at her. His tux had been taken as evidence—mostly because it had been so blood stained. He'd been interviewed by the cops and the Feds, and it was close to two a.m.

He and Ophelia should probably have been exhausted.

Instead, she seemed to burn with energy.

He wore sweats and a t-shirt that the Feds had given him. Borrowed sneakers because the Feds had taken Lane's shoes, too. Getting stripped by the Feds had not been on his bingo card for the night.

As far as finding a nearly dead man in a freezer? Not on the card, either.

"I'm the one who taunts killers." She bent down to pick up Velma. The cat had immediately rushed out of the dark to rub against Ophelia. Ophelia stroked her cat, and Velma slid her head against Ophelia's cheek. "You don't get to throw out challenges to them. That is my job." She spun to fully glare at him. "*Mine.*"

He just stared at her. Her words were barely registering because she just seemed so gorgeous to him. In fact, he'd pretty much missed everything she'd said, except for the last bit.

Mine.

Lane nodded.

"Good." She rubbed her fingers over Velma's back. "Glad we got that settled." With gentle care, she put her cat back on the floor. "I'll challenge the killer. You won't." Ophelia pivoted sharply and began striding to her room.

He caught her arm and whirled her right back toward him.

"Lane—"

"Mine," he growled a second before his mouth crashed onto hers. Because that was the part of her speech that mattered. And he knew it with utter, bone-jarring, soul-breaking certainty.

Mine.

Ophelia was his.

His friend.

His lover.

His partner.

His everything.

Her lips parted beneath his. Her tongue met his. Her body molded to his as she gave a desperate, greedy moan and clutched tightly to him.

This was what he wanted. Ophelia sinking into him. Ophelia as close as she could get to him. His sanity and his safety. All in one beautiful package.

He feasted and he took and he knew that he would never, ever be able to get enough of her. Not in one lifetime. Too impossible.

His hands went to the straps of her dress. She eased back, just a little, and he shoved the straps off her shoulders. The dress fell. A soft slither of sound.

He let her mouth go and looked down.

Strapless bra. A scrap of lace for panties.

Sexy as hell. And... "Mine," he said again. Swore it.

Her breath shuddered out. "Why do I feel like that might be the only word you heard me say?"

He unhooked her strapless bra. Loved the feel of her silky skin as his fingers slid behind her back. The bra fell to join the dress.

"Lane, I meant what I told you."

His fingers went to her nipples. Tight, beautiful nipples. He caressed them. Teased them.

"Lane."

His hands dropped to her waist. He lifted her up. Held her easily as he took one nipple into his mouth.

"That's hot. The way you're so strong. The way you're...oh, God, that feels good." Her words ended in a moan. "But we...we need to—"

"Fuck." He let her nipple go long enough to say the one word. Because that was what he needed. To be as deep in her as he could go.

"I was going to say talk and, ah, *shower!*" Her voice rose to a fever pitch when he lightly bit her nipple. *"Lane."*

He carried her down the hallway. They'd shower. They'd fuck. Then it would be time for *his* lessons.

Lesson one. *No killer ever goes after Ophelia.* No more of the shit where perps were following her home.

Her legs wrapped around him. "I was scared." A soft confession.

Her bedroom door was open. He took her past the bed. Past the dresser. Into the bathroom. When they crossed the threshold, her hand flew out to turn on the bathroom light. The flash of illumination didn't even make him pause. Carefully, he eased her down until her feet touched the plush rug near the shower. Her hands clung to his arms. "Why were you scared?" Lane asked. His voice was rough. Ragged at the edges.

Only fair because he felt ragged around the edges, too.

"You didn't answer me when I called." Her long lashes lifted. "I had sent a guard back to help you, but the guy was green as hell. I was so afraid that something would happen to you before I could get there." Her nails dug into him. "I haven't been that scared since I was sixteen years old."

Those words...

"Not even when Sam pointed a gun at me, and I was pretty sure I couldn't get off my shot before he fired at me."

His hands slid down her body. Hugged her waist. "I was okay."

"He wanted to push you over the edge. He wanted you to kill Gerald."

"Everyone thinks I'm a monster..."

"I *know* you're not." Her right hand flew up. Pressed to his stubble-covered jaw. "I know exactly what—and who—you are. There is nothing evil about you."

"Everyone but you," he finished roughly. His mouth took hers again. A deep, drugging kiss, and he knew that it was true. He also knew that the only opinion that mattered to him?

Ophelia's. And not because Memphis had wanted her damn profile. But because Lane needed her so much.

He swallowed her moan and wanted to absolutely devour her. And he would. But first...

He let her go. Stripped. Yanked open the shower door, turned on the water, and hauled them both beneath the spray. Ophelia laughed because she still had on her panties. Her hands went to shove them down, and he tried to help.

They ripped the panties. Shredded them.

She laughed again. Such a beautiful, free sound. Perfect for Ophelia.

They kissed beneath the warm spray. He stroked the soap over her body. Every perfect inch. Dipped his soapy fingers between her legs. Made sure to rub her so well.

"Lane!" Her hand slammed into the tiled shower wall for support.

He thought her knees might have almost buckled. He loved the way she held nothing back with him. Only fair because from the first night in the hotel, he hadn't been able to hold anything back with her. He'd wanted her too much. Still did.

She paid him back for the sensual cleaning by stroking soap over him. Teasing his nipples. Pumping his dick until he thought he'd go out of his mind. He barely managed to yank off the water. Lane picked her up, and screw it, he put her over his shoulder and carried her to the bed.

She laughed again. Music to his heart.

Soaking wet, they crashed onto the bed. He crawled on top of her. Her legs parted. His eager dick shoved against her. "Condom," he gritted out.

"I borrowed a few from you earlier. You'd left them out in the guest room, and I took the liberty of putting some in my nightstand. Hope you don't mind..." Breathless.

Mind? He kissed her harder to show how much he did not mind her taking the condoms. Then he leaned over and nearly broke the bedside drawer as he took a condom from the nightstand. But before he could put it on, Ophelia stole it from him. She opened the pack. Positioned the condom, then slowly rolled it over his dick.

Torture.

"Baby..."

Her head lifted. She smiled at him.

That was the moment his control shattered.

He tumbled her back onto the bed. Shoved her thighs apart and sank into her as deep as he could go. She moaned and he growled and he knew... *"Mine."* His thrusts were savage, so wild, and she met him with eager arches of her hips.

He should hold back. Take his time.

But she was tight and hot and nothing had ever felt as good in his life as Ophelia did. His hand snaked between them. He didn't just stroke her clit. He owned it. He knew what she liked.

What she wanted. What it would take to make her detonate beneath him.

He drove into her and pushed her straight into her first climax. A quick scream broke from Ophelia.

Gentle. Gentle. A mantra in his head, but his body wouldn't listen. He thrust into her faster and harder, and her climax made her slick and so fucking hot beneath him. He pounded into her even as her legs clamped greedily around him.

His mouth went to her throat. He licked. Sucked the skin. Bit.

She heaved beneath him, and her nails raked down his back. She had to come again. Once more before he could let go.

He caught her nipples with his fingers. Pulled the taut peaks. Plucked. Pinched.

"Lane!"

She was coming again. The telltale clench of her inner muscles sent him straight into the hottest, longest release of his life. Pleasure poured through every cell in his body. His world narrowed down to one focal point.

Ophelia.

Mine.

***

"Royce Nicholson has disappeared."

He'd been sprawled in bed, with Ophelia cradled against him, and feeling pretty close to heaven. At her words, hell came calling.

His head turned toward her.

"Detective O'Brien called me when I was in the ballroom tonight. She wanted to let me know that he'd disappeared."

He waited. There was more. Lane was sure of it.

"He had my PI office address pulled up on the computer at his place."

Sonofabitch.

"And, uh, Shay—Detective O'Brien—remembered that she came across a vic a few months back with a string tied around his ring finger."

His body tensed. "She just remembered it?" Talk about convenient.

"His death was ruled a drug overdose. No foul play suspected. She saw the string and it stuck out in her mind because of the discovery with Bass."

"Forget-Me-Not," he muttered.

"The OD vic was found behind Pyro."

"Fuck."

"Agreed. Too much of a coincidence for me, too." Her gaze held his. Light drifted into the room from the open bathroom doorway. "I want to find out the exact date of the guy's death. I want to see the results of his tox report for myself."

"Is the detective gonna hand that over to you?"

"Maybe. If not, we'll still get them. I can have EAD Ballard apply pressure to her boss. I can also just go directly to Benny."

Lane wasn't so sure that old Benny was going to help with anything. Before he could tell her that, he heard the loud peal of a doorbell echoing through the house.

Lane had been tense before. Now his body went into battle-ready mode. No way was Ophelia expecting guests at this hour. And with her track record of having perps show up at her home looking to hurt her... "That shit is over," Lane swore. He jumped from the bed. Raced into the bathroom and grabbed his borrowed sweats.

When he came back, Ophelia had hauled on a robe. She'd also taken a gun from her nightstand. Before she could head for the bedroom door, Lane stepped into her path. "I've been agreeable."

"Excuse me?"

"I've pretty much went with the flow where you are concerned. Even when I was pissed as hell or thought that the plan was shit."

She tried to step around him.

He did not let her.

"New lessons, sweetheart."

"Uh, Lane, someone is at my door. And it's nearly three a.m. Don't you think we need to investigate?"

"You have killers knocking at your door."

Her head tilted. "They don't usually knock or ring the doorbell. Too polite for them."

Oh, was she trying to be funny? Not working this time. "You risk yourself too damn much. Like you don't have anything to lose, and it doesn't matter what happens to you." He reached for her hands. Took the gun from her. "It matters. A whole hell of a lot to me. So how about when someone tries to hurt you, we say that they have to go through me in order to do it?"

The doorbell rang again.

"I like that you're protective," she assured him. "It's sexy. Truly, but I've got a ton of experience in the PI world—"

"Fuck your experience."

"Lane!"

"To hurt you, people will need to go through me." Simple fact of life. The sooner she accepted it, the better.

"It's that naturally protective streak of yours again." She licked her lower lip. "You're always trying to protect everyone."

He shook his head. "Not everyone. Just you."

"Why did you help Gerald Baldwin?"

The doorbell pealed again. Without answering her question, he whirled and stormed down the hallway, keeping her gun gripped in his hand.

"Lane!"

He didn't stop.

She grabbed him in the foyer. Spun him toward her. "Wait, dammit! Let me check the app to see who is outside." Then she picked up the small evening clutch she'd dropped earlier on the entrance table. She pulled out her phone and swiped her fingers over the screen. A frown crinkled her brow. "Why are they here?"

He peered down at the screen. The Feds. On her doorstep. At nearly three a.m.

He didn't let go of his weapon. While Ophelia disengaged the alarm near the door, he held tight to it, and when they finally swung open the front door—

"Wow!" Pierce Wayne threw up his hands. "You always greet visitors with a gun?"

He didn't have the gun up or aimed at the Fed. "You always pay visits in the middle of the night?" Lane threw right back.

Ophelia eased to Lane's side. "Why are you here?"

"Had a break in the case. Wanted to tell you personally."

"Phone calls work better," Lane assured the agents. "They work just fine."

Tameka cleared her throat. "It's a phone that gave us the break. Or, rather, the texts that were sent to your phone." Her gaze darted between Lane and Ophelia. And noted their dress. Or undress.

Whatever. Lane didn't care that he was half-dressed. He didn't like it, though, when Pierce's gaze dipped down Ophelia's body. He moved a little to partially block the agent's view. "What did you discover?"

"We traced the texts," Tameka told him. "Found the man who sent them. Considering all the pressure Ballard has been applying on us, thought you'd want to know. Thus, the personal visit."

Lane waited.

Tameka grimaced. "I'm sorry, Ophelia."

Why was she apologizing?

"I believe you're friends with the suspect."

Lane glanced down at Ophelia.

"The texts came from a phone that we traced back to Beau LeBlanc."

Ophelia shook her head. "That can't be right."

"I assure you," Tameka said, voice sympathetic but certain, "our intel is correct. And when we located Mr. LeBlanc a short while ago, he was in the process of entering your PI office."

"*What?*" Shock broke in Ophelia's voice.

"He's at the local station right now."

"I want to talk with him!" Ophelia said quickly. "Now!"

But Pierce shook his head. "With a murder charge pending, I really think the rest of the investigation is best left to actual FBI agents and police officers."

Lane's stomach clenched. "Gerald Baldwin didn't survive."

"Died on the operating room table," Tameka confirmed.

CHAPTER EIGHTEEN

"I need to see my client," Ophelia announced.

Lane slanted her a quick glance. He was vaguely curious to see if this would actually work. It was a little past eight a.m., they were at the Savannah PD, and Ophelia was hell-bent on getting an audience with Beau LeBlanc.

Meanwhile, Lane was hell-bent on having a one-on-one chat with the bastard. Unlike Ophelia, he wasn't convinced the man was being framed. He just thought the guy was a dick.

"Your client?" Tameka's brows rose. "Since when?"

"Since always. Beau and I have a long-standing arrangement. In return for getting a discount on my office rental space, I provide him with legal services."

Lane was pretty sure that she'd worked a PI case for Beau in return for the discount, but he wasn't about to correct Ophelia. After the Feds had left their doorstep, Ophelia had been stunned.

She'd also been convinced there was a mistake.

"You're his victim, Ophelia," Tameka corrected. She crossed her arms over her chest, and the move pulled her suit coat tight over her holster. "You don't get to be both victim and lawyer."

"Why not?" Ophelia asked.

"She likes to multitask," Lane added.

Tameka cut him a disgruntled stare. "She didn't mention this multitasking last night when I was on her doorstep."

True. He waited for Ophelia to tackle that one.

"I was sleepy," she said with a sigh of regret. "And so stunned. But I am ready to help my client today."

Ophelia-speak for she'd figured out a way to get an audience with Beau.

Tameka's stare hardened. "How fortunate."

Lane shrugged. "She's not going away. Trust me. I have personal experience in a situation like this with her. Allow Ophelia to talk to her client."

"If you don't," Ophelia informed the agent sweetly, "I'll contact Executive Assistant Director Ballard and make sure that he's, ah, how did you and your partner describe him before? Pissed, I believe? I will make sure he is plenty pissed with you. I am pretty sure there was talk—from you and your partner, not from me, of course—about some threat of demotion if you didn't fully assist me?" She tapped her chin thoughtfully. "I believe I recall something to that effect."

"You think you can control the EAD?" Tameka's doubt was apparent.

"I think he wants me happy."

Lane thought what she meant was that Ballard wanted her quiet. And Lane suspected that if she contacted Ballard, she'd be practically blackmailing him into allowing her to see Beau.

"Five minutes. That's all I need."

Ophelia and her five-minute requests. She'd asked for the same amount of time from Detective Shay O'Brien not too long ago. Shay had given in. Would Tameka?

"Fine." Tameka's nostrils flared. "Five minutes. That's all you get. And I watch everything, though, because I don't buy that you are actually his lawyer. He hasn't even *asked* for a lawyer yet." She whirled away.

Ophelia sent her beaming smile to Lane.

He shook his head.

***

They weren't taken into interrogation. They were guided straight back to lockup. Tameka led the way, with Ophelia in the middle of the line and Lane at the end.

There were a handful of people in the cells. A few were slumped on their narrow beds. Some cells were dead empty. And then there was the cell with Beau...

As soon as he caught sight of their group. Beau jumped toward the bars and grabbed them tightly with his fists. "Ophelia!"

She stopped in front of him.

"It wasn't me!" His knuckles whitened around the bars. "I swear, I did not attack anyone last night!"

Lane moved closer to the bars, something he had not thought he'd ever willingly do. "You sent those texts to me."

"The cops accused me of that shit last night—and my answer now is the same as what I gave them." He fired a fuming glare at Tameka. "No." A hard, negative shake of Beau's blond head. His frantic gaze flew back to Ophelia. "The phone was mine, yes, dammit, a backup I have, but it should have been locked in my safe! Somebody took it out! Somebody is setting me up!"

"Oh, please." Tameka rolled her eyes. "Was it *somebody* else in Ophelia's office, too? Or was that you doing some B&E when the cops rolled in?"

"I thought I heard someone up there," Beau rushed to say. "I was looking out for you, Ophelia. I went up to investigate, and that's when the cops showed up. I wouldn't hurt you. I didn't do this! I swear, it is not me."

Tameka propped one shoulder against a nearby cement column. "Still singing that tune."

But Lane stared hard at the man he'd initially hated. The faint lines around Beau's mouth were deeper, and an air of desperation clung to him.

"I can't do this again," Beau said to Ophelia. "You know I wouldn't ever want to go back in a cell. *Someone is setting me up.* You have to believe me."

"Yeah, they don't," Tameka answered. She waved to Ophelia. "Are you done now?"

But Ophelia wasn't looking at Tameka. She'd turned her head and was staring at Lane.

He swallowed. He didn't like this scene. Once upon a time, he'd been the one begging people to believe in his innocence. No one had. "We're not done," Lane heard himself reply. "We're just getting started."

"What the hell does that mean?" Tameka asked as she threw both her hands into the air. "I do not need some dramatic BS from you two. I told you—five minutes. You aren't getting started. Your time has been ticking since we started walking through the station."

But Ophelia took Lane's hand. "Lane means we have more work to do." Her gaze flickered to Beau. "I cleared you once. I can do it again."

"We can," Lane corrected.

"You are really not such an asshole," Beau rasped as his head tipped toward Lane. "Thank you. I won't forget this. Ever."

The man shouldn't thank him for a damn thing yet. Not while he was still behind bars.

Tameka led them out of lockup. Back through the station. And when they were right in front of the entrance doors, she shook her head and gave a disappointed sigh. "Thought you two would be more savvy. Don't you know when you're being played? That man is pulling on your heartstrings." She pointed to Lane. "And using your past against you." Another shake of her head. This time, a clearly disgusted shake. "You can't let them get to you. Everyone has a sob story, and the guilty are often the ones who sing their innocence the loudest." With that, she pivoted on her heel and went to meet her partner.

Pierce had just stepped out of one of the back offices.

Lane pushed open the door for Ophelia. They walked outside without another word. Dark clouds hid the sun. And the scent of coming rain blew on the wind. Ophelia strode away from the station, and he followed her.

When they were in front of her Jeep, she paused. "When he was a kid, Beau bounced from foster home to foster home."

Lane didn't speak. But he knew exactly what it was like to be pushed from place to place. Never belonging. Never finally safe or settled anywhere you went. Never trusting the people who greeted you at the door.

"No one ever wanted to keep him. He was viewed as one of the problem kids. He was angry. Always in trouble. Social workers said he had attachment issues." Her gaze slid his way. "Sound like anyone you know?"

He didn't reply.

"When he was sixteen, Beau got involved with a gang in New Orleans. Guy could wire a car in five seconds flat. And he loved the fancy rides. He was busted a few times. In and out of juvie. Looked like jail would be his future, but then one day, Beau did something special. Something dangerous and deadly."

Lane waited.

"He was boosting a car, and he smelled smoke. Rounded the corner and realized a house was going up in flames. He could hear someone screaming from the second story. So he rushed inside. Went straight into the fire." She bit her lip.

"He rarely takes off his shirt, but when he does, you can still see the scars on his right shoulder. The fire left a mark on him."

Damn.

"A fourteen-year-old girl was home alone. She would have died that night, if Beau hadn't fought the fire for her. The girl called him her hero. She visited him in the hospital every day he was there. She thought he was the most amazing person in the world." A slow exhale. "Sometimes, all it takes is for one person to believe in you, and that belief can change everything. When he got out of the hospital, Beau was done with the gang life. Done with stealing and theft. He wanted to be someone different."

Okay, he'd seriously underestimated the guy.

"Beau stuck to the straight and narrow for years. And then, just when he thought his past was dead and buried, he was linked to a murder. A patron at his bar had gotten too rough with one of Beau's waitresses. Beau fought with him. Threats were made. The next day, that patron was found beaten to death. Wanna guess who was the chief suspect?"

"Beau," Lane supplied. He didn't need to guess.

"Beau told me he was innocent. Hired me to prove it. I did."

"And now you're going to prove his innocence again."

"We are," she corrected as she pressed up on the balls of her feet. "Isn't that what you said inside?"

It was exactly what he'd said. "We're kind of a package deal now."

Her smile tilted her lips and lit her eyes. "Glad you noticed."

Hard to miss. *Where you go, I follow, baby.*

"Where do you think we should start, partner?" Ophelia asked him.

They both knew where they were going. He could see it in her eyes. "Thomas Bass." She'd been right before. Bass's life might provide them with the clues they needed to find the killer.

"You don't mind a little breaking and entering?" She nibbled on her lower lip. "I'm worried I may be a bad influence on you."

He wasn't even a little concerned. "Considering he's dead, I don't think Thomas will complain." Not that he gave a shit what Thomas would have done. But someone he *was* worried about? Royce Nicholson. The bastard was still out there. Another enemy he couldn't forget. So he would be sticking to Ophelia like a shadow. He hadn't been bullshitting her before. No one would hurt her.

She was too important.

***

They went back home for supplies. Their bags. Guns. A taser. Lane was heading down the stairs with his bag slung over his shoulder when the front door swung open.

Dammit, not again. He surged forward—

And drew up short at the landing when he saw Ophelia's father filling the doorway.

Wonderful. But, Ophelia *had* mentioned she'd get her sitter for Velma. The man glaring at him was the sitter in question.

Her father's gaze swept over him. Noted the bag slung over his shoulder. The bulge of a holster on Lane's hip. Her father nodded. "You're going hunting with my daughter."

How much had Ophelia told the older man? "Yes." Seemed like a safe enough answer.

Then he remembered...*shit. Ophelia's dress.* They'd dropped it in the hallway last night. But when he did a fast and frantic glance toward her bedroom, the dress was gone.

"Son, there something bothering you?" Her father's voice was surprisingly polite. Was that the calm before the storm?

But, since the man had asked the question, Lane would give him an answer. Lane swallowed and admitted, "Quite a few things."

"What might those things be?"

"Ophelia and I are chasing a killer. Some asshole we handed over to the cops in Atlanta has vanished, but not before finding your daughter's business address on his home computer. So I'm pretty sure that means the jerk thinks he's going to hurt her." Lane lifted his chin. "Not going to happen. I'll just hurt him first."

"Heard you tried to *save* a man last night." Her father's head tilted as he seemed to take Lane's measure again. "Didn't work out though."

No, it hadn't.

"A criminal. A jerk who tried to break into my Ophelia's home. A guy who wanted to cause trouble for her and her client. Yet you tried to save him."

"It was an impulse." A split-second decision. There'd been so much blood. The feel of that weak pulse beneath Lane's touch had spurred him into action before he even thought about what he was doing.

Her father advanced.

Velma rushed from the den. She headed straight for Lane. Her head butted against his leg even as her tail curled around his jeans. Automatically, he reached down and gave her a little pat behind her ear.

"How about that." No question. Just a general statement from Ophelia's dad.

Lane lifted a brow. "How about what?" *Is this the time you try to rearrange my face? Because Ophelia and I already have a lot on the schedule.*

"Velma doesn't like most people."

Velma headed for Ophelia's father. Locked her tail around his leg. He lifted her up. Cradled her carefully.

Well, it looked like her dad wasn't in the face-rearranging mood.

"You'd let me take a swing at you, wouldn't you?" her father asked.

Lane shrugged. "Ophelia is worth some hits."

"And you've had plenty of hits in your life, haven't you, son?"

"I'm not your son." And Lane had a flash of his own father. The rage in his eyes. And...the way it had been before all the rage came. The way his dad used to cheer for him at football games. The way they'd play catch in the backyard. The way—

"I know." Softer. Sadder. There was a flash of sympathy in the eyes so like Ophelia's. "My daughter tells me a lot."

Lane stiffened.

"Like...she tells me you're a good man. Said you would let me take a swing at you and you wouldn't hit back."

He didn't reply. What was the point.

"Doesn't necessarily sound *good* though," her dad continued. "More like a dumbass move to let some guy just hit you."

"You're not some guy. You're her father. Ophelia loves you." Lane rolled one shoulder. Where the hell was Ophelia? "I don't hurt what she loves."

"Why is that, exactly?"

Simple. "Because I won't make Ophelia unhappy."

"Why?"

"Because—" Lane stopped.

The door to the study opened. Ophelia stepped out and frowned at them. Then her gaze hardened. "Dad, you are not grilling him again, are you? We talked about this." She marched to her father. Poked him in the chest with her index finger. "Lane is important. He's my partner. He's here to stay."

To stay. Those words rolled through him. They'd signed on for a month. That had been the deal. But suddenly...

I want to stay. He knew it with certainty. He'd found a place where he actually felt like he belonged. Not drifting from door to door. Ophelia's home had been open to him from the beginning. No hesitation. She'd drawn him into her home.

And it felt like—crazy as it seemed—*their* home. He'd even thought of it that way when he'd been going down the stairs.

"Just having a chat with the man," her father murmured. "You jump to so many conclusions."

"Wonder where I get that from?" She backed up to stand at Lane's side. "You ready?"

Lane nodded.

"When you come back," her father said, "bring your partner over for dinner. Your mother has been wanting to meet him."

Ophelia's lips parted. "I-I will." A small stutter. Very un-Ophelia.

Her father fired a warning glance at Lane. "You keep her safe."

They should just be clear. "I would die before I let anyone hurt Ophelia."

"Then we understand each other." Her father turned and, still carrying the cat, he walked out.

The door clicked closed behind him.

"No." Ophelia's voice. Her angry voice. "No, that bullshit can just stop right here and right now, you understand me?" She grabbed his arm.

He gazed into her eyes and saw her fury staring back at him.

"You will never, *ever* do that for me, do you understand?"

"Ophelia—"

"I already had someone die for me. I live with that guilt every single day of my life. I will not do it again. Sure as hell not with you." Her eyes glittered with tears. "So take it back. Right. This. Second."

"Uh, Ophelia—"

"Take it *back!* I get that some people toss that expression around to sound big and bad and dramatic, but not you. You say what you mean. And you are not—not ever—going to trade your life for mine. I won't have it. I won't do it again. Not with a stranger, and certainly not with someone I—" She stopped. Her eyes widened. And when they widened, a lone tear trickled down her cheek. "Shit." She let him go. Jumped back as if an electric shock had jolted through her.

"Ophelia?" Worry filled her name. But he wasn't taking anything back. Sure as shit not something that he'd meant. Did she seriously think he wouldn't take a bullet for her? He would. Ophelia's safety meant everything to him.

"I told myself I'd always say what I felt. In this life, you don't know if you'll get a chance again. You have to say what you feel. I lost my chance before." Her hands fisted. "How is this happening? *Why?*" Her eyes squeezed closed.

"Ophelia, I'm not planning on dying."

"No one plans it. It just happens." Her eyes flew open. "We are not friends."

He sucked in a breath. They...were. He viewed her as one of the few friends he had. Dammit, probably his best friend even though Memphis had clearly been vying for the job. And the sudden rejection sent a pang through him. "You're not going to make me mad so that I'll stop wanting to protect you. You can say whatever you want to hurt me, Ophelia, but I will still protect—"

"I love you."

His mouth hung open.

"We are not *just* friends. And I haven't felt this way about anyone since..." She shook her head. Her hair flew over her shoulders. "I knew it was coming. I could feel it. I wanted you too much. I believed in you too soon. I hurt for your past. And I wanted you to have such a better future. It happened too fast. We were too fast, but it's there, and it is absolutely terrifying me."

Lane knew he should speak. But knowing it and doing it were two different things.

"I swore I would never make the same mistake again. I wouldn't hold back. I tell people *not* to hold back." She puffed out her cheeks and exhaled. "This is a shit time to tell you."

Ophelia loved him? "Why?"

"It's a shit time because we're going after a killer. Because I have to get on the road. Because the next twenty-four hours could be dangerous as hell. And because you are looking at me like I have gone absolutely mad."

That wasn't how he meant to look at her.

She sent him a smile. Sweet and sad at the same time. "I'm not asking anything of you, Lane." Gentle. "I just want you to know how I feel."

He shook his head.

Ophelia crept toward him.

"No," he said.

"Yes." She touched his arm, and he flinched. "Lane."

He'd been staring just over her head, but at the tender whisper, his gaze flew to hers.

"You are worth loving."

He had to swallow. His stupid throat had gotten clogged.

She rose onto her toes. Pulled him toward her. And feathered a kiss over his cheek.

You are worth loving.

"Now how about we go catch us a killer, hmm?" Ophelia murmured.

CHAPTER NINETEEN

She'd scared the hell out of him.

Made the man practically catatonic. Sure, he'd replied when she'd spoken to him during the drive. Mostly one-word responses. His eyes burned with too much intensity. His body was held far too stiffly. And Lane looked at her...

As if she'd wrecked his world.

Could she have picked a better time for the big reveal? Absolutely. She'd probably picked the worst time in the world. But the truth had just slammed into her. He'd made that infuriating vow to die for her—not happening, by the way—and the truth had just been there.

But maybe it had been lurking beneath the surface for a while. A realization she'd been afraid to see because love could hurt you. It could rip you into a thousand pieces and leave you scattered on the ground.

Or crying in an alley as you lose everything that matters.

So, no, she didn't regret telling Lane the truth.

And she truly wasn't expecting anything in return.

She wanted to hit Thomas's place at night. In her experience, a good B&E was always easier under the cover of darkness. So when they got to town, she had a bit of time to kill.

Ophelia headed for the medical examiner's office. Hopefully, Benny would be in a cooperating mood, and he wouldn't toss her ass out.

They parked in the lot. She glanced over at Lane. Found his brooding stare already on her.

Ophelia winked at him.

His brow furrowed. "You were...joking."

Oh, that was three words. Not just one. Progress. "Nope." Whoops. She'd gone to one word. Lane was rubbing off on her.

He shook his head. He seemed to do that a lot. "You don't love me."

She unhooked her seatbelt and leaned over the seat. Her lips pressed softly to his. "I love you, Lane Lawson."

"You're...profiling me."

Ophelia laughed. "Stop being adorable. We have a killer to catch." She eased back.

His hand flew up and curled under her chin. "Don't play with me." Ragged.

He made her ache. "I can be patient."

His fingers stroked her.

"I *can* be just your friend." Was that true? It would hurt her. Wreck her on the inside, but when you loved someone, you had to do what was best for them. "I can be your partner. Things do not have to change." She forced her tone to stay light. "I didn't get to tell Joseph how I felt. I swore I would never hold back if I was lucky enough to love again." And she recognized the feeling because she had been fortunate enough to love before, even though she'd been so young. But Lane...

Lane's life had been hard. Filled with pain and uncertainty. Could he love? Yes. She believed he loved his sister. And with time...

If Ophelia was patient enough...

He might be able to love me.

Or he might not. So she could just be his friend. His partner. His—

"Everything," Lane rasped. He leaned forward and kissed her. But this kiss was different for them. For him. Tender and soft. So gentle that she wanted to sink into him. A kiss that held so much promise.

He took her breath. Gave her his.

And when he pulled back, she stared at him, dazed. "Lane?"

"You are mine, Ophelia. I told you that already."

But there was a difference between a feverish *mine* in the heat of the moment and—and—

"My world. My everything. My Ophelia."

Her heart raced faster. Lane was telling her that he loved her. In the parking lot of the medical examiner's office. "My timing was bad." She had to lick her lips and taste him again. She also had to pull in a deep, fortifying breath. "But yours is worse." Couldn't he have spilled this news during the drive? Had he needed to wait until they were close to the dead bodies?

Lane smiled at her.

A real, honest-to-God smile that lit his eyes and made him so handsome and sexy that she could have turned into a puddle right then. "There it is," she realized. The Lane she'd been looking for. The man who hid behind the darkness.

Her Lane.

"Couldn't wait to meet you," she said. Then she kissed him again. Slow. Careful. Deep.

"Baby." A growl. "I am going to break a bed with you later."

Oh, such a fun promise.

"But if you don't stop right now, we will be fucking in the parking lot."

She laughed. "I love it when you talk dirty." But Ophelia pulled away from him. Her laughter died as she glanced toward the building that waited. Fear wanted to bubble and seethe inside of her. When you had something important to lose, you did fear more.

But she wasn't going to lose Lane. He wasn't going to lose her.

They were going to find the killer. They were going to win.

First, though, time to see a man about some bodies.

***

"No." Benny tried to shut his office door on her foot. "No, you are not coming in here. You are not supposed to be anywhere near me!" He glared down at her booted foot. "Would you move that thing?"

Lane reached around Ophelia and shoved open the door.

Benny barreled back with a yelp. Then, "Oh, for God's sake! You brought the muscle with you again." He glowered at Lane. "Still the new partner? She hasn't run you off yet?"

"She never will," Lane vowed.

Ophelia sent him a quick smile, then entered Benny's office. Paperwork was scattered everywhere, and an ancient coffee machine drip-drip-dripped in the corner. "Benny, we need your help."

"No." A definite shake of his head. "Detective O'Brien was furious that I'd let you see Thomas Bass's body!"

"Benny, we discovered a serial killer's signature. You helped us to do that." She headed for his desk. A fat manilla file spilled open on the desk's surface.

Benny grabbed the file before she could peek at it. He slammed the file closed.

"Detective O'Brien spoke with me just yesterday," Ophelia added.

Lane had taken up a spot near the door. Legs braced apart. Eyes intense.

Sexy.

She cleared her throat. "She wanted me to know that Royce Nicholson had gone missing."

Benny's Adam's apple bobbed. "Heard about that," he confessed. He licked his lips. "One of the new uniforms who came in with a body drop-off not too long ago told me. Said...said your address was on Royce's computer." He flinched. "Aren't you scared?"

"She doesn't need to be scared," Lane said before Ophelia could respond. "She has me."

Benny blinked. Twice. "What are you going to do?"

"Whatever needs doing."

Benny's lips parted.

"Benny." Ophelia drew his attention back to her. "I want to ask you about a case you worked a few months ago."

"I am not supposed to talk to you." His hands drove into the pockets of his white lab coat.

She smiled at him. "O'Brien knows about this case. She's the one who told me about the vic. A fentanyl overdose."

Anger came and went in his brown eyes. "Do you know how many of those I see each week? Lives get snuffed out and no one cares."

"You care, Benny. You've always cared about the victims." Ophelia knew this with certainty. "You've hated their deaths. You always fight for the victims. That's why you have this job. You want to give justice to the dead."

One hand rose from his pocket and jerked through his hair. "You're manipulating me."

"No, I'm just saying what I see."

For a moment, he yanked harder at his hair and... "Name," he bit out.

"Miles Dodge. He was found behind Pyro."

Benny's eyes widened. "I-I do remember him." But he still went to his computer and started typing fast.

Ophelia sidled up beside him.

"Definite overdose." Benny pulled up the report on the screen. "Do *not* tell anyone I am doing this."

She leaned down to better view the screen. "Absolutely. And if you need my services again, I'll take your case free of charge." She almost hugged Benny. Instead, Ophelia scanned the intel. She whistled when she realized just how much fentanyl had been in the man's system. "You never had a chance, you bastard."

Lane's phone buzzed.

Her head swung toward him.

It buzzed again. Lane pulled it out. "Memphis." A twist of his lips. "He texted on the drive up. The man is on his way. He wants to help us."

Right. Not like she'd turn away any backup in the form of Memphis Camden.

"I'll take it in the hall." Putting his phone to his ear, Lane left the room.

Benny frowned after him, and as soon as the sound of Lane's footsteps vanished, he hurried toward the door. He peeked out, then shut it quickly. "What are you doing?" he demanded as he whipped around to confront her.

She sat in his chair. Let her fingers fly over the keyboard. "Why isn't the string mentioned?"

"What string?"

"The one that Shay O'Brien remembers seeing around Dodge's finger."

His steps rushed back to her. "You're looking at a tox report. You won't see any info on—"

"I *was* looking at a tox screen. Now I'm looking at the full report you created before you released the body, and there is no notation of a string on his finger."

"I don't remember a string." He seemed disgruntled. Offended.

She peered up at him.

"*Why are you still working with that man?*"

Why was he harping on Lane? But she'd answer him since Benny was playing semi-nicely with her. "Because Lane is a fabulous partner, and I'd trust him with my life." She glanced back at the screen. "He's not a killer. I don't care what gossip you read. He's a good man and—"

Something jabbed into her neck. Hard and fast, and at first, she had a dazed moment when Ophelia thought a freaking bee had just stung her.

Her hand flew up to slap at her neck. And her fingers closed around a syringe. "Benny..."

"He may be good, Ophelia. But *you* aren't."

She tried to shove back the chair and stand. She reached for her gun, and then remembered it was in the Jeep. Civilians weren't allowed to bring guns into this building and she...

The chair rolled from beneath her, and Ophelia's legs just gave way as she slumped to the floor.

***

Lane threw open the door and stepped outside. He'd intended to talk with Memphis in the hallway, but the reception had been shit, so he'd headed out back. "You hear me now?"

"Yes." Memphis's voice came through loud and clear. "Where the hell are you? Thought you'd be in the city by now."

"We are. We're at the ME's office." Ophelia had worked her magic again. Actually gotten Benedict to cooperate. "Ophelia is checking on another vic who fits the killer's profile."

"I heard there was an arrest in Savannah."

Lane's brows climbed in surprise. When he and Memphis had texted on the way to Atlanta, Lane hadn't mentioned a single thing about Beau. "We think he's innocent."

"More 'we' talk, huh?"

"Yes." Just that. Because they were a team. From here on out, he and Ophelia would be working together. "The plan is to get intel from the ME, wait until dark and then..." His voice trailed off because a uniformed officer had just come out the back of the building. Not like he could just announce their B&E plans to a cop.

"Then what?" Memphis demanded. "You think this is the time to leave me in suspense?"

Lane paced away from the building and the uniform. "We're planning to take another look at Thomas's house." Like he really wanted to go back into that pit of hell. But he'd do it.

"I'll meet you there. Text me when you're on the move."

Well, damn. It was good to have friends who didn't balk at bending the law in order to catch a killer. "Did I ever apologize?" Lane suddenly asked him.

"For being a dick? Man, you do that on the daily."

Lane smiled. Hell. His second real one of the day. Rusty, but it felt good. He felt good. Like a chain had finally been cut loose that held him back. *Or a cell door finally swung open, and I got to walk out.* "I meant apologize for the freezer situation."

"You are apologizing for locking me in the walk-in freezer that time? Seriously?" Amazement coated the words. "Are you drunk?"

"Nah. But I am in love."

"*What?*"

"You've been good to me. Thank you. I appreciate it." Total sincerity.

Silence. "You know I have your back."

Yes. He had friends now. Memphis. Ophelia— *so much more than a friend.* He had a life. Hell, he even had a creepy-looking home that had just felt right the minute he stepped inside. The same way Ophelia had somehow felt *right* for him. "Thanks, man."

"You know it." Memphis cleared his throat. "And I do have more data on Samuel Hitchcock to give you. Being the stellar friend and crime solver that I am, I dug for you. Am still digging, in fact, but I thought there were a few things you needed to know."

Now who was playing the suspense game?

"The man had no kids. Did have some nieces and nephews. A few godchildren, too. They're scattered, and I'm still working on all of them. His wife—Sam's death hit her brutally hard. She started drinking. Went into a deep depression, and I'm sorry to say it, but she took her life about six months ago."

Damn. Did Ophelia know?

"Before the wife died, she confided to a therapist that she'd recently found an old journal belonging to her husband."

"How did you learn what she told a therapist?" That shit was supposed to be confidential.

"I have my ways," was all Memphis said. "The therapist noted that she was extremely distraught about the discovery. Two days later, the wife was dead. She'd slit her wrists and bled out in the bedroom that she used to share with Sam."

Lane pinched the bridge of his nose. "That journal could have been an account of Sam's kills."

"And the wife finally realized the husband she was grieving for so hard was a murderer. Tough to live with news like that."

No wonder Memphis had wanted to give him this info now. "What happened to the journal?"

"Most of her belongings were sold or donated to charity. There has been no other mention of a journal. But I *have* just started my search. Give the Ice Breakers time. We're good, but we aren't miracle workers." A horn sounded in the background. "Text me when you're heading to Bass's house."

"Will do. And thanks—really." He hung up. Exhaled.

And turned back toward the morgue.

***

Ophelia's eyes fluttered opened. Her legs dragged across the floor. And—

"You'll drift in and out. I didn't give you much of the drug. Not like I knew you'd bust into my office, and I'd have to act. Had to use what was available." Benny's voice. Sounding annoyed as he *dragged* her ass across the lab floor. His hands were under her arms, and her body felt like an absolute dead weight.

Dead being the scary word. She opened her mouth to cry out for help, but her tongue felt thick and heavy and all she managed was a moan.

Then his hands released her. Her upper body slammed into the floor. Her head hit with a sickening thud.

Her eyes closed.

There was a hard click. A creak. A screech.

She forced her eyes open just as Benny picked her up—and then he put her on a table.

His head lowered over hers. "He did what you couldn't."

Once more, she tried to speak. Couldn't.

"You spent your whole life looking for Joseph's killer, didn't you? The boy hero who died when you were sixteen. Only you couldn't ever find the man who ended Joseph's life. But *he* found him."

Who? What was—

"Sam. Sam found him. Remember the kill that freaking led you to the Forget-Me-Not cases? The jerk in the gutter who was dead, but had that string tied around his finger? You were tracking him because you thought he was related to a string of robberies that had resulted in three deaths. Oh, Ophelia, there were so many more. That guy you found? He'd been killing for years. He killed *your* Joseph. Yes, I know all about him." His hand stroked over her cheek. "I know all of your secrets."

She was on an exam table? No, *no*. When her gaze darted down, she realized that she was on one of those long, metal slabs that slid out from the body storage cabinets.

And she...

Was that a black body bag beneath her?

She tried to move, but her arms were limp at her sides.

"Sam killed the man who ruined your life. And how did you thank him? You started hunting *him*. Your trainer. You killed *him*."

This wasn't making sense. How did Benny even know Sam?

"Sam mentored a whole lot of people over the years. Did all kinds of outreach and motivational speaking. He loved justice. Loved the law."

Loved killing. Her fingers fluttered. Touched the hard edge of the body bag. A stupid flutter was all she could manage. What had he given her? What kind of damn drug?

"I was one of those people. Sat in some of his criminal justice lectures in college and got hooked. The man inspired me. Pushed me to help others."

This isn't helping. A dazed thought.

"I used to have dinner at his house. Felt like I was part of his family."

She'd had dinner at Sam's house, too. He'd been so good at making everyone feel welcome. And good at hiding who he really was.

Benny is just like him.

"His wife gave me his journal."

What journal?

"Then she went home and slit her wrists. Did you know that, Ophelia?" And he walked away.

She tried to heave her body. To roll off the stupid slab, but her muscles wouldn't obey her.

He returned. Something cold and sharp pressed to her wrist.

"This is a scalpel," he told her. "I could cut your wrist with it, just like Pamela cut hers."

And the sharp edge bit into her wrist. She tried to jerk free. Her hand barely twitched.

The scalpel pressed deeper. She felt it draw blood.

Lane!

"Not that Pamela used a scalpel. She just grabbed a knife from her kitchen. Don't worry, I think my scalpel is probably sharper than the blade she used. But...that would be too messy." The scalpel lifted. He smiled down at her as her eyes opened and closed again. Opened...

"I don't like messy kills," Benny confessed. "Discovered that with Gerald. I was experimenting. The knife didn't work for me, but I rather enjoyed putting the pillow over Thomas's face."

Her eyes sagged closed.

"With the drugs I've used on the other victims, I didn't feel them die. I felt Thomas. I...liked it."

Because you're a freak. Her eyes fluttered open. Her breath sawed out.

"Gerald was coming to kill you. And your client. Do you know that? I stopped him. I did your job for you."

She hadn't planned to kill Gerald. Her eyes fell closed once again.

"So messy. Don't get me wrong, I slice the dead all the time here in my lab. But it's different when the blood is still pumping. It sprays at you. Gets everywhere. No, I won't be cutting on you. You're just going to disappear," Benny told her. "You'll be a mystery that even your Ice Breaker friends won't solve. Your case will get colder and colder, and eventually, no one will remember you."

He reached down and began to haul up the zipper for the body bag. She knew—because there was no mistaking that sound. She couldn't even get her foot to kick out at him.

"The drug will wear off soon, but you'll be locked inside by then. You'll pass out again in a while. Not like there is a ton of air in there. I'll just wait. You'll go into the dark, and that's where you'll stay."

In there. No, no, no!

She managed a small shake of her head.

"Killers get punished, Ophelia. You killed Sam."

And he'd just confessed to killing both Thomas and Gerald. Didn't he get that? Or in his twisted mind, did he just see those murders as him carrying out justice?

"Because of what you did to Sam, now you get punished."

Her breath heaved. She forced her eyes open—she could at least do that.

Light. His face. His cold smile.

And he zipped the body bag up so that he covered her face. Her head. Her whole body.

Darkness.

No, there was a thin stream of light. At the top of the bag. The zipper hadn't closed all the way. There was a little gap that she could just see when her head tipped back the tiniest of inches.

Precious light.

The slab beneath her screeched as he shoved it forward. Her body lurched on that slab.

Click. Thud.

The door to the body storage cabinet closed. She knew that sound. The thud—that had been the handle sliding into place.

She felt her lips begin to quiver.

Darkness.

Death...

Lane. Lane!

CHAPTER TWENTY

"Where in the hell is Ophelia?" Lane demanded.

Benedict jumped and whirled around. He'd been staring at one of the body storage cabinets on the wall to the right when Lane burst into the exam lab.

Lane had gone to Benedict's office first, but no one had been there. So he'd headed straight for the lab, thinking that maybe they were looking at Thomas's body again. But while Benedict was there, Ophelia wasn't.

And tension knotted Lane's shoulders.

Benedict put a hand to his chest as he sucked in a deep breath. "You startled me."

Lane stalked forward. "Where the hell is she?"

Benedict grimaced. "Didn't she tell you?"

If she'd told him, would he be searching for her? Lane glared.

"She received a text." Benedict waved in the air—a rolling, vague gesture with his hand. "From Detective O'Brien. Shay got a report that Royce Nicholson was seen at the Pyro club. Ophelia went rushing out." His brows shot low. "I was sure your paths would cross."

"I was out back." He hadn't seen her.

A shrug. "She must have gone out the front. You just missed her." He made a shooing motion toward the door. "Now, if you'll excuse me, I have work to do. I've got a John Doe waiting for me who is not just going to identify himself." A sniff. "I have to get busy. I can't afford to piss off any other detectives."

Lane didn't move. "She would have texted me."

"O'Brien? Why would she text you?"

"*Ophelia.*"

"Oh, well, maybe she's waiting outside for you?" A helpless shrug. "I have no idea. Go look and see. Like I keep repeating, I have work to do." He gripped a scalpel in his hand and padded across the room to drop the instrument back on a waiting surgical tray.

Lane spun away and marched for the door. His hand flew out and slammed into it as he shoved it open. A few moments later, he was in the parking lot. Her red Jeep waited in its spot.

No Ophelia.

He yanked out his phone to call her—

His phone dinged and buzzed with her text.

O'Brien contacted me. Going to Pyro.

How the hell was she going to Pyro when her vehicle was right there?

Another buzz. *Getting ride with a uniform. Don't need your help.*

What? *Bullshit,* he typed back. *Lesson nine.*

She couldn't go forgetting her own lessons. And lesson nine clearly stated that you did not leave your damn partner.

The phone vibrated again. *We are done. Partnership is over.*

What. The. Fuck?

Then he slowly exhaled. He turned around and he stalked back toward the building he'd just exited. He shoved the phone into his pocket. He didn't have a gun on him because it was locked in the glove box of Ophelia's Jeep.

She had the key to the Jeep.

He entered the hallway. Was far too aware of the antiseptic scents and the bright lights from overhead. He didn't go to Benedict's office. Lane went directly back to the lab. His hand slapped into the door as he heaved it open.

Benedict had been whistling. He whirled at Lane's approach and stared with wide eyes.

"Where is she?" Lane asked. But he already knew. Oh, fuck, he knew.

His gaze slid toward the body storage cabinets. Benedict had been in front of those cold storage drawers when Lane arrived the first time. And the bastard had been gripping a scalpel.

Lane looked down at the floor near the wall of body storage cabinets. A drop of blood had fallen from the scalpel. Why the hell hadn't that drop registered sooner?

"Are you still looking for Ophelia?" Benedict asked him.

Lane's head turned—slowly, like a snake sizing up prey—as he focused on Benedict.

"Told you already, she's gone. She rushed out. Had a case to solve." An exhale. "I'm sure she'll contact you."

Lane pulled out his phone and held it in the air even as he advanced on Benedict. "She already did contact me."

Benedict's eyes narrowed as he tried to read the screen. "What does that—oh, oh, I'm sorry. She's ending the partnership?"

He kept advancing.

"That's too bad," Benedict told him sympathetically, "but I'm sure you can find another—"

Lane swung the phone and the fist that gripped the phone—and drove both into Benedict's face. Benedict yelled as he stumbled back, and he hit the nearby surgical tray. Instruments went flying across the floor. So did Benedict.

"What the hell?" Benedict's eyes had doubled in size as he rolled to look up at Lane. "Are you insane?" His hand lifted to his bleeding lip. He swiped the blood away, but made no effort to rise to his feet.

"If you've hurt her, you're dead." A cold, hard truth.

"You're crazy, you're—"

"She said it. Right in front of me. She said it all, and I didn't put the pieces together. Dammit, *she* didn't put them together because she trusted you. Her profile on you was right the fuck there."

"There is no profile." Benedict slowly staggered to his feet. He also gripped a scalpel in his fist. The one that had freaking *blood* on it. "You've gone off the deep end. No wonder Ophelia left you."

"She said you always cared about the victims. That you hated their deaths. That you wanted to give justice for the dead." He spared a glance around the lab. "What happened? You get tired of seeing the vics all the time and decide to deliver your own justice for them?"

"You don't know what you're talking about!"

He spun away from Benedict and rushed toward the body storage cabinets. Every instinct he had screamed that Ophelia was locked in one of those freaking things. He was getting her out.

"Stop!"

He didn't.

He grabbed for the cabinet door Benedict had been standing in front of moments before. When Lane had first rushed into the lab. His fingers curled around the heavy handle to open it.

Footsteps rushed behind him.

Lane spun around just as Benedict brought the scalpel slicing down at him.

***

Darkness.

Her eyes were open. Ophelia was pretty sure of that. But it was pitch black around her. Not a light anywhere.

I always leave on at least one light. That way, she could see her enemies coming. Her father had given her that lesson long ago. You didn't have to wake in the dark. Didn't have to waste time as your eyes adjusted. You could go straight into attack mode.

Only her eyes couldn't adjust because the blackness around her was so complete.

But she could wiggle her fingers. And...

"Help," Ophelia gasped. She'd finally managed to speak. Or croak. She wet her lips and tried again. "Help!" Her fingers slowly lifted. They touched thick, heavy fabric.

The body bag that she'd been zipped inside.

"Help!" she cried out again. And her weak fingers began to claw at the bag.

***

The scalpel sliced across Lane's cheek. He didn't even feel the pain. He took that slice, and his hand drove into Benedict's ribs. As brutally hard as he could. Lane thought he felt a crunch beneath his fist.

Benedict howled. He also scuttled back. His fingers remained clenched around the scalpel.

"You're not running for help," Lane noted grimly.

Blood dripped from Benedict's lips.

"You could have run. If you were innocent, you would have run when I turned my back on you. I wasn't a threat to you with my back turned. Instead, you rushed at me with your scalpel." He felt the blood slide down his face. "You have my Ophelia in one of those fucking cold storage drawers." The drawers for the dead.

Benedict smiled.

You sick sonofabitch.

"You don't need her," Benedict told him.

The fuck I don't. He needed her more than he needed anything in the world.

"We can be a team. I knew it from the first moment I heard your story. I've been watching you for a long time. Studying you." Benedict's fingers rotated the scalpel in his grip. "You must hate the monsters out there just as much as I do. You were innocent, and the guilty walked."

Yeah, that had pretty much just been a confession from the ME.

"Sam gave a talk on duo killers once. God, I used to love his lectures. Would catch as many as I could when I was an undergrad."

"Samuel Hitchcock," Lane supplied. And there it was. The fucking connection.

Benedict nodded eagerly. "He was brilliant."

Or insane. "You *knew* what he was doing? All those years?" Oh, hell, who cared? What mattered right then—*Ophelia is locked in a body storage drawer.* Lane could not leave her inside for another second. He spun around and yanked on the handle even as Benedict yelled behind him.

Lane got the door open. He saw a body bag inside. One that was moving. "Ophelia!"

"Get away from her!" The scalpel drove into Lane's back. Just below his shoulder.

Lane grabbed the shelf and hauled the slab from the drawer.

The scalpel drove into him again.

He caught the top of the body bag's zipper. Hauled it down.

Saw Ophelia's terrified face as she drew in a deep gasp of air.

The scalpel slashed him—

Lane whirled around and tackled Benedict. They slammed into the floor with a bone-jarring thud. And that scalpel? Lane wrenched it out of Benedict's hand.

And he put it right against Benedict's jugular. "I will kill you."

Benedict smiled his bloody smile. "You won't," he denied. "Because I'm not evil. I haven't done anything wrong. Every life I took—it was the guilty being punished. I learned that from Sam. The guilty pay."

"You were working with him?"

"Didn't know what he was doing back then, but I would have. Gladly." He didn't even seem to notice the scalpel. "His wife mailed me his journal. Included a note and said I'd know what to do with it. And I did. I knew *exactly* what to do. Ophelia killed him. So I started hunting her."

"You *hired* her. She helped you."

"I set up the case so I could get close to her. I knew if she saw me as a victim first, it would be harder for her to ever see me as a killer."

All along, the bastard had planned to eliminate Ophelia. "You set up Beau LeBlanc."

"He needs to die, too. He's as guilty as they come."

Lane shook his head.

"There have been so many that I hunted. Drug dealers like Miles Dodge. I took them out and no one cared. They came to my table after they died. I made sure no one asked questions. The guilty were punished."

"Lane?" Ophelia's voice. Far weaker than normal.

Very slowly, he lifted the scalpel off Benedict's neck. Lane rose to his feet.

Ophelia climbed from the slab. Her knees buckled, and she would have slammed into the floor, but he caught her with his left arm and held tight.

"Newsflash,"   Ophelia   whispered. "Benedict...killer."

"Yeah, sweetheart. I got that."

Benedict rubbed his hand over his throat. He smeared the blood that Lane had left behind when he cut the bastard with the scalpel. "We can hunt together," Benedict offered. He pushed to his feet. "I would have been partners with Sam. If he'd just *told* me the truth."

"Sam... killed an innocent woman," Ophelia gasped out. "You...freak. He isn't...hero."

Benedict stared at her with rage gleaming in his eyes. "You have to die for what you did to him."

Not happening.

"But after Ophelia's dead, we can work together." Benedict nodded and angled his head toward Lane. "Told you, Sam talked about duo killers. Rare, but powerful. That's what we are." He grabbed a syringe from the table to his left. "We're rare, but—" He lunged forward with the syringe, going for Ophelia.

Lane stepped into his path. Benedict's arm was up high, and Lane aimed low. He sliced right through skin and muscle, and he jerked the scalpel to the left and the right. Once upon a time, he'd been able to cut with perfect symmetry in med school.

He didn't give a damn about symmetry. He was going for maximum damage and immediate impact. And Benedict had been the one to pick the scalpel with a long, curving blade. Perfect for deep incisions.

So Lane went deep.

Blood drenched Benedict's white lab coat. His body began to shake.

"I already have a partner," Lane said as he yanked out the scalpel.

Benedict sagged to his knees.

The lab doors flew open. "I heard screams," Detective Shay O'Brien called out. "What is— *Drop the weapon, now!*"

Lane let the scalpel clatter to the floor.

"Hands up!" She raced forward.

Lane lifted his blood-stained hands.

"No!" A choked gasp from Ophelia as she stumbled in front of him. Her steps were unsteady, and he wanted to pick up that scalpel and absolutely fillet Benedict. Instead, his bloody hands wrapped around Ophelia's waist to steady her. "Lane...saved me," Ophelia cried.

"Oh, sure." Shay glanced at the hands around Ophelia. "Looks like a real hero."

Benedict let out a choked cry. "Help..."

"Should have carved out his heart," Lane said. No, it would have been faster to just slice open Benedict's jugular.

"Get away from him!" Shay shouted. "Back up, now!"

Lane pulled Ophelia with him, and he tucked her behind his body. She damn well was not being some human shield for him.

"Shit." Shay kicked the scalpel across the room and crouched beside Benedict. "It's going to be okay."

"Don't do that," Lane advised her. "Don't get closer—"

Her head wrenched toward them. "I'm trying to save a good man!"

"He's not good," Ophelia rasped. "He locked me in cold...body storage."

"What?" Shay's eyes widened.

Benedict grabbed for the gun in her hand. He yanked it toward him.

Should have gone for the jugular.

A bullet blasted, and Lane whirled instinctively. He wrapped his body around Ophelia.

"Don't...do this!" Ophelia punched at him. A half-strength punch because something was still wrong with his Ophelia.

Another bullet thundered.

The bullets hadn't hit him or her, but he'd heard a weird, metallic bang when the second one lodged in one of the body storage cabinets. Lane looked back over his shoulder.

Benedict and Shay were still struggling over the gun.

"*You're* not...good," Benedict gasped at the detective. "You...let them go...over and over..."

Hell, seemed like he wanted to kill the cop, too.

Benedict heaved back with the gun gripped in his hands.

Time to go for the jugular. Lane dove for the scalpel that Shay had kicked aside.

"Benedict, don't!" Shay pleaded. She scuttled back. "I'm your friend! I'm a cop!"

Lane didn't think it mattered. To Benedict, all that mattered was the guilt he thought Shay carried.

Benedict had full possession of her weapon. Blood soaked him. He was totally focused on Shay right then as he huddled on the floor with the detective's gun.

Mistake, asshole.

Lane grabbed the scalpel. He leapt toward Benedict.

But, still on the floor, body heaving, Benedict turned toward him. Still grinning with the wild smile on his face. Scalpel versus gun was the worst choice ever, but Lane was out of options and time.

He was—

Ophelia slammed the surgical instrument tray into the side of Benedict's head. It hit with a clang. Then she hit him again. A third time.

On the fourth hit, Ophelia's legs gave way, and she sprawled on the floor. But she'd done the job.

The gun fell from Benedict's fingers as blood streamed from his head. Then he fell back, too.

Shay leapt to grab the gun that had just dropped from Benedict's fingers.

And Lane—Lane brought the scalpel down over the bastard's throat.

"Lane?" Ophelia's voice. Soft.

He looked at her.

"I...love you."

It would only take seconds to slice the jugular. Just seconds.

"I've got him." Shay was shaken but determined. "You can back away now."

He didn't want to back away. He wanted to end Benedict. The bastard had put Ophelia in a body bag.

"I love you," Ophelia said once more.

Shay was calling for backup. More blood poured from Benedict. His skin had gone waxy. His breathing ragged. "You're dead," Lane promised him.

Blood trickled from Benedict's nose and mouth.

He lifted the scalpel from Benedict's throat. With it clutched in his hand, Lane went to Ophelia as she staggered back to her feet.

"He...drugged me," she mumbled. "So I...bashed his head in." Her long lashes fluttered. "You...with me?"

"Always."

The doors flew open. Footsteps thundered into the room. The gunshots—and maybe all the yelling, too—had attracted attention. He looked over. Uniformed cops were swarming. Two other people in white lab coats crouched next to Benedict. They were trying to stop the blood flow.

Good luck with that.

He finally let the scalpel fall, and he scooped Ophelia into his arms.

Her head pressed against his shoulder. "Just for the record." Her words still slurred a little and that worried the hell out of him. "You're the best partner...I've ever had."

He swallowed. His head dipped, and he pressed a kiss to her temple. "I'm going to be the only partner, from here on out." He carried her toward the doors. Shouldered through them.

"My dad likes you."

They were in the hallway. More people were running by them. His bloody hands held Ophelia so carefully. He wanted to get her out of there. *Hospital.* That was where she needed to be. "I think you might be delirious."

"My cat does, too."

Her body was seemingly boneless in his arms.

"But you know who loves you the most?" she asked with a sigh.

He looked down at her.

"I do," Ophelia whispered.

His hold tightened on her.

"Thanks for pulling me out of the dark," Ophelia told him. "I didn't like it in there."

He had to swallow again. Twice. Then he finally managed to say... "Same." Another kiss to her temple as he thought about what his life had been like. Before Ophelia. "*Same.*"

EPILOGUE

The doorbell rang. A loud peal that echoed through the house.

"Son, can you get that?" Ophelia's father called out from the kitchen. "Almost done in here!"

Lane hopped off the last stair and hurried for the door. But right before he could open it, Velma sprang into his path. He picked her up automatically, and her head rubbed lovingly beneath his chin. Lane swung the front door open.

Memphis Camden stood grinning at him. With a bottle of champagne clutched in his hand. "I am here to celebrate."

Lane smiled at him. The smile didn't feel so rusty any longer. Over the last few weeks, he'd smiled more and more. His body had healed from the injuries. He had a few new scars. Ophelia claimed the line on his face just made him look sexier and more dangerous.

Benedict hadn't survived. Too much blood loss. Too many internal injuries.

Too fucking bad.

But the cops and Feds had uncovered the web of his kills. Benedict *had* gotten Sam Hitchcock's old journal. No one knew exactly what Sam's wife had wanted Benedict to do with the journal. Ophelia swore the woman had probably wanted it turned over to the authorities. That she had *not* intended for Benedict to pick up where Sam had left off.

But Ophelia often looked for the good in people. Wasn't that the reason she'd stared right at Benny, had the profile spot-on about him wanting justice for the dead, being mission oriented, but she'd *missed* that her friend was a killer?

Or hell, maybe after Sam, she just hadn't wanted to think that someone close to her could be so evil.

As far as the motivations of Sam's widow...Lane wasn't sure what she'd wanted done with the evidence of her husband's guilt. What he *did* know...Benedict had begun his kills after her suicide. Fentanyl had been his weapon of choice because no one hunted a murderer when a drug overdose was suspected. A smart way to dispatch the guilty.

Miles Dodge had been one of his victims.

So had Royce Nicholson. The "John Doe" that Benedict had casually mentioned to Lane? The one who needed identifying? That body had been hauled out of another cold storage locker. The John Doe had been Royce Nicholson. Dead of an overdose.

There had been seven other victims. All documented because Benedict had added their deaths to the old journal he'd been given.

He'd started tying the strings on their fingers as homage to Sam.

And he'd framed Beau LeBlanc. The bastard had included Gerald Baldwin in his kill list. The Feds figured Benedict had driven to Savannah— he'd been off work ever since Ophelia and Lane had left Atlanta. Benedict had only returned to work that morning.

Since Benedict had visited Ophelia at her office before, he'd become familiar with Beau. Beau even remembered the guy coming to his bar a few times. And a waiter had confessed that *he* gave Benedict the combination to Beau's safe, in exchange for a grand.

Benedict had framed Beau.

And he tried to frame me, too. Benedict had been following Lane. *He really thought we were the same. That I would help him hunt.* Fuck that.

Benedict's phone had been filled with surveillance pics of Lane. Older pics going back for weeks. And more recent images of Lane with Ophelia.

Apparently, the ME hadn't liked it when Lane and Ophelia teamed up. So he'd killed Bass and played a game at framing Lane. Benedict's masterplan had been to continue Sam's punishment kills.

Ophelia thought he'd tied the string around Bass's finger as a way of telling them that the hunt was on. It hadn't just been a signature. It had been a taunt in Thomas Bass's case.

But you're the one in the ground, Benedict. You lost.

Lane and Ophelia were still standing.

"I'm assuming I will be the best man at the wedding?" Memphis demanded as he wiggled the champagne bottle. "Seeing as how *I* am the one who teamed up you and Ophelia?"

"I—"

"Is that...a cat?" A soft female voice asked in surprise. "Lane, are you holding a cat?"

Memphis stepped to the side. A grin tugged at his lips. "I didn't come alone."

Lane stared at his twin sister. Lark stood a few feet back, with her hands twisted in front of her. Of course, her husband, Oliver Foxx, was right at her side. Once upon a time, Lane had absolutely hated Oliver. The man *had* been instrumental in getting Lane locked up for murders he hadn't committed but...

Oliver had also worked desperately to free him, and Lane knew, beyond the shadow of any doubt, that Oliver would live and die for Lark.

Just like I would live and die for my Ophelia.

But this was the first time that Lark would officially meet Ophelia. The two most important women in his life, finally coming together.

Velma purred.

"Son!" Ophelia's father called out. "Dinner is nearly ready! Five minutes!"

Lark flinched. In that moment, as he stared into her eyes, he could see their past. Dark. Bloody. Painful.

Lane exhaled slowly and gave Velma another pat.

The past was over. "My sister is here," Lane called back. "Can't wait for you to meet her."

There was an excited yell from the kitchen. Ophelia's yell, he knew. She'd talked with Lark on the phone, but meeting in person would always be different. Lane figured he had about twenty seconds, maybe thirty, before Ophelia exploded on the porch.

"This is Velma," he told his twin. "And she's a really good judge of character."

Lark's hand extended toward the black cat. "I always wanted a cat."

"I'll get you a dozen of them," Oliver instantly promised her.

Lark laughed. Her green gaze lightened and the shadows vanished from her eyes. Yes, Lane knew that Oliver loved Lark. His sister was happy. As for Lane—

Ophelia exploded on the porch just as he'd expected. She zoomed to his side. Gave Lane a big hug, then immediately focused on Lark. Ophelia stuck out her hand. "I know we chatted already but...I'm Ophelia. Your brother's partner."

Lark took her hand. Stared at her with open curiosity.

"She's also my fiancée," Lane added. "As of last night."

He'd waited until the case of the Forget-Me-Not copycat was officially closed. Waited until he could get down on one knee and present Ophelia with the biggest ring he could find.

A ring that currently glinted on the ring finger of her left hand.

"I love him," Ophelia announced simply.

Lark's lower lip trembled. Then she was pulling Ophelia in for a tight hug. "I adore your house," he heard Lark tell Ophelia.

Oliver offered his congratulations.

Memphis asked for champagne glasses.

Velma darted back inside the house with an excited meow.

They all eventually spilled inside—they went in the house that was home for Lane—and Ophelia's parents came out of the kitchen to meet them all. Ophelia's parents...and even Beau. Because, yeah, Lane had become fast friends with the cagey bastard. Easy to do, when you had so much in common with someone.

And Lane was even currently helping Beau with a very special case. A case that would wait for another day.

Right then, everyone was laughing and talking and...celebrating. The engagement. The future.

Lane had let the past go.

After all, it was too hard to carry the past when you were holding tight to the future.

Lane took Ophelia into his arms and kissed her.

THE END

A NOTE FROM THE AUTHOR

Thank you very much for reading LOCKED IN ICE. I appreciate you taking the time to enter the Ice Breaker world. I hope you enjoyed the mystery—and the romance. I have loved writing the Ice Breaker books (I'm a cold case and true crime addict). After his first appearance in BURIED UNDER ICE, I couldn't wait to give Lane his own story...so my fingers were flying fast when I wrote LOCKED IN ICE. I definitely think Lane deserved a happy ending, don't you?

If you'd like to stay updated on my releases and sales, please join my newsletter list.

https://cynthiaeden.com/newsletter/

Again, thank you for reading LOCKED IN ICE.

Best,
Cynthia Eden
cynthiaeden.com

ABOUT THE AUTHOR

Cynthia Eden is a *New York Times, USA Today, Digital Book World*, and *IndieReader* bestselling author of romantic suspense and paranormal romance. She's a prolific author who lives along the Alabama Gulf Coast. In her free time, you'll find her reading romances, watching horror movies, or hunting for adventures. She's a chocolate addict and a major *Supernatural* fan.

For More Information

- *cynthiaeden.com*
- *facebook.com/cynthiaedenfanpage*

HER OTHER WORKS

Ice Breaker Cold Case Romance

- Frozen In Ice (Book 1)
- Falling For The Ice Queen (Book 2)
- Ice Cold Saint (Book 3)
- Touched By Ice (Book 4)
- Trapped In Ice (Book 5)
- Forged From Ice (Book 6)
- Buried Under Ice (Book 7)
- Ice Cold Kiss (Book 8)
- Locked In Ice (Book 9)

Wilde Ways

- Protecting Piper (Book 1)
- Guarding Gwen (Book 2)
- Before Ben (Book 3)
- The Heart You Break (Book 4)
- Fighting For Her (Book 5)
- Ghost Of A Chance (Book 6)
- Crossing The Line (Book 7)
- Counting On Cole (Book 8)
- Chase After Me (Book 9)
- Say I Do (Book 10)
- Roman Will Fall (Book 11)
- The One Who Got Away (Book 12)
- Pretend You Want Me (Book 13)

- Cross My Heart (Book 14)
- The Bodyguard Next Door (Book 15)
- Ex Marks The Perfect Spot (Book 16)
- The Thief Who Loved Me (Book 17)

Wilde Ways: Gone Rogue

- How To Protect A Princess (Book 1)
- How To Heal A Heartbreak (Book 2)
- How To Con A Crime Boss (Book 3)

Trouble For Hire

- No Escape From War (Book 1)
- Don't Play With Odin (Book 2)
- Jinx, You're It (Book 3)
- Remember Ramsey (Book 4)

Death and Moonlight Mystery

- Step Into My Web (Book 1)
- Save Me From The Dark (Book 2)

Phoenix Fury

- Hot Enough To Burn (Book 1)
- Slow Burn (Book 2)
- Burn It Down (Book 3)

Dark Sins

- Don't Trust A Killer (Book 1)
- Don't Love A Liar (Book 2)

Lazarus Rising

- Never Let Go (Book One)
- Keep Me Close (Book Two)
- Stay With Me (Book Three)
- Run To Me (Book Four)
- Lie Close To Me (Book Five)

- Hold On Tight (Book Six)

Bad Things

- The Devil In Disguise (Book 1)
- On The Prowl (Book 2)
- Undead Or Alive (Book 3)
- Broken Angel (Book 4)
- Heart Of Stone (Book 5)
- Tempted By Fate (Book 6)
- Wicked And Wild (Book 7)
- Saint Or Sinner (Book 8)

Bite Series

- Forbidden Bite (Bite Book 1)
- Mating Bite (Bite Book 2)

Blood and Moonlight Series

- Bite The Dust (Book 1)
- Better Off Undead (Book 2)
- Bitter Blood (Book 3)

Mine Series

- Mine To Take (Book 1)
- Mine To Keep (Book 2)
- Mine To Hold (Book 3)
- Mine To Crave (Book 4)
- Mine To Have (Book 5)
- Mine To Protect (Book 6)

Dark Obsession Series

- Watch Me (Book 1)
- Want Me (Book 2)
- Need Me (Book 3)
- Beware Of Me (Book 4)

- Only For Me (Books 1 to 4)

Purgatory Series

- The Wolf Within (Book 1)
- Marked By The Vampire (Book 2)
- Charming The Beast (Book 3)
- Deal with the Devil (Book 4)
- The Beasts Inside (Books 1 to 4)

Bound Series

- Bound By Blood (Book 1)
- Bound In Darkness (Book 2)
- Bound In Sin (Book 3)
- Bound By The Night (Book 4)
- Bound in Death (Book 5)
- Forever Bound (Books 1 to 4)

Stand-Alone Romantic Suspense

- Waiting For Christmas
- Monster Without Mercy
- Kiss Me This Christmas
- It's A Wonderful Werewolf
- Never Cry Werewolf
- Immortal Danger
- Deck The Halls
- Come Back To Me
- Put A Spell On Me
- Never Gonna Happen
- One Hot Holiday
- Slay All Day
- Midnight Bite
- Secret Admirer
- Christmas With A Spy
- Femme Fatale

- Until Death
- Sinful Secrets
- First Taste of Darkness
- A Vampire's Christmas Carol

Made in United States
North Haven, CT
04 July 2024

54388585R00178